Also by Tony Flower:
That Bloody Book
The Girl Downstairs
The Resurrection of Skinny Ted and the Brothel Creepers

www.tonyflower.co.uk

Contents

THE BLACK SWAN
DETE TIVE AGENCY

By Tony Flower

We were able to purchase this book thanks to the support of the Wendover Community Library Trust and friends' group.

068939539

1. The Interrogation

The bland bleached décor in the interrogation room was similar to that of his therapist's but, unlike Philip, this interrogator didn't seem interested in the creation of a supportive atmosphere. A bulky, balding man of middle years with eyebrows like sleeping caterpillars, the detective browsed the notes before him, deep in thought. Suddenly, the left caterpillar awoke and arched itself inquisitively.

'So, can you tell us about your relationship with Ms Forrester?'

'There wasn't one,' said Steve. 'I asked her out twice. The first time took her by surprise, so I asked again a few days later, in case she'd had second thoughts. Once she'd said no the second time I gave up. I am a realist; I look in the mirror every morning when I'm shaving. I am fully aware that someone so beautiful is hardly likely to be interested in the likes of me; but I'm also a dreamer and, occasionally, I dare to dream again.'

Undeniably things had changed since he was younger, but he still didn't think there was a law against asking someone out. Nevertheless, he found himself under investigation and under suspicion. Steve hoped his answer came across as steady and reasonable, but that old fear and distrust of authority still ate away at his confidence. The reflex twitch in his cheek and sweaty palms wiped on his jeans must have screamed guilty, before he'd even uttered a word.

'We have made some enquiries, sir, and we have been told that you were infatuated.'

'Hmm, I may have expressed my admiration to a few trusted friends; at least I thought they were trusted. Look, I'm a sad, lonely geezer looking for love; there's nothing more to it than that. I'm used to rejection and I'd do no-one any harm. Anyway, this happened months ago; I've moved on since then.'

A younger, brusque detective joined in, with a derisory air of arrogance. – 'So, if, as you say, there was no relationship, can you tell us how we came to find your DNA in her room?'

'No, I can't. Where exactly did you find it?'

A plastic bag containing the *Home* CD by Terry Hall is placed on the table before him.

'Ah, yes, that's mine. I lent it to her after we had a conversation in the pub about the Specials. I asked if she'd heard any of Terry Hall's solo stuff and said how you wouldn't know it was the same person. It's a great album; you should give it a listen.'

'Thank you, sir, I may well do' said the older of the good cop/bad cop double-act. 'I'm a big fan of the Specials. Now, here's the bit where you'll need to help us solve this mystery. The jacket with which we believe Ms Forrester was suffocated – that has your DNA all over it too.'

So far Steve had been as calm as could be expected in a police interview room. He assumed that they were systematically cross-examining all the known customers of the Black Swan and that he was simply next on the list. He knew that they'd all been subjected to a routine DNA test and had thought no more about it. With this astounding revelation, the cross-examination had taken a much more serious turn.

The disquiet must have shown on his face, for good cop continued – 'How can you explain that, sir?'

'I can't.'

'And do you have an alibi for the night in question?'

'I left the pub at around eleven, I think. I walked home, watched a bit of telly then went to bed.'

'And can anyone corroborate that?'

'My friends would have seen me leave, but after that, no. I live alone.'

'You have failed to mention that you went out again at one-thirty,' said bad cop. 'We have a witness statement from one of your neighbours.'

'What?'

'Can you tell us why you left the house at one-thirty and where you went?'

Steve could sense the panic erupting within; a cold sweat and a feeling of nausea – he'd forgotten his nocturnal stroll and had to accept that things looked bad. He took a gulp of water from the plastic cup before him and attempted an answer. He immediately knew that it sounded less than convincing.

'I-I often have trouble sleeping. My therapist recommended that, instead of lying awake with my problems, I should get up and go downstairs, maybe go for a walk. That night was the first time I'd

2

tried it. Only went round the block and it didn't work – still couldn't get to sleep when I got back.'

Good cop looked sceptical. – 'Can I ask why you are seeing a therapist, sir?'

'No, you can't, it's personal.'

'We also have a recent record of another incident involving yourself. Would you like to elaborate on that?'

'Not really. What relevance does it have to this investigation?'

Steve thought of someone who was there on that evening of the 'incident'. She would have been obliged to submit a report of the events and he didn't blame her for placing her fears on record. All the hopeless feelings of that night flashed through his mind. He thought he'd turned the corner, rekindled the hope of his youth; but here he was, under suspicion of murder. It could be described as a setback.

The fact that the officers before him were aware of his previous indiscretion didn't do much for his argument that he was a rational and reasonable citizen, incapable of murder. That, coupled with the unexplained DNA evidence and lack of alibi placed him, understandably in the eyes of the police, as a prime suspect.

Despite his desperate protestations of innocence, he was invited to spend some time as their guest whilst investigations continued and it was suggested that he might wish to obtain some legal representation. As they escorted him to the cell, a distraught Steve reflected upon how the hell it had come to this…

2. Steve

Steve had trod this path many times; the uneven, potholed one that meandered gently up and away from town, on its way to the outskirts. It was so familiar that his well-worn shoes could have made their way without him. Steve wasn't dressed to impress – a blue and black check brushed-cotton shirt and a pair of worn and faded Levi's, built for comfort rather than style.

The evening air was cool on his face, as the promise of a pleasant spring day turned to the certainty of another lonely night. He squinted some way up the track as a small unidentifiable rodent crossed and left a puff of dust in its wake, before scurrying into the undergrowth. Steve raked his fingers through his unkempt mop; he needed a haircut, but hadn't seen the point lately.

At the bend he rubbed his annoyingly itchy, watery eye and turned to take in the view. From here he could look back at a hotchpotch of familiar structures, the random by-product of generations of unsympathetic town-planning. None of it matched; from the stunning 13th century church that still stood proud against the horizon, its narthex nestled amidst timeworn cobbled streets; through the ugly grey monstrosity that housed the Council; to the recently refurbished, bland and uninspiring shopping centre, complete with obligatory multi-storey car park. So many memories flooded his thoughts, all linked to that expansive mess of brick, concrete and steel below, punctuated by the occasional flash of greenery.

Over to the right sprawled a suburban mass of houses that seemed to stretch further away with each year that passed. He could still just about pick out the home in which he was born, nearly forty-five years ago now. Once, it had stood on the edge of town, bordered by a never-ending landscape of verdant fields, his carefree playground as a child. Now his childhood home was swallowed by a conglomeration of uniform developments that threatened to consume the surrounding villages; the trees they used to climb, the camps they used to build in the bushes, the open spaces where they used to run – all lost to the ravages of progress. The view was so familiar, yet somehow, this evening, he felt detached from it, away with the fairies.

He recalled coming up here as a kid with his mates, back in the days where the only instruction was – 'Be home before it gets dark.' Their parents had no idea what they got up to, unless things got out of hand. Like the time they'd coerced the diminutive Peter Groves to walk along the ledge on the old railway bridge just as the train sped by beneath. In retrospect it was bloody stupid and they'd watched terrified as Peter wobbled and teetered on the brink, before he'd steadied himself and grabbed Steve's outstretched arm. Steve reflected upon the foolishness of youth; on how those careless decisions made with little thought for consequences might have ended so tragically.

He lifted his collar, as the breeze grew stronger and the low sun dipped behind a wispy, mottled cloud formation. Surround-sound birdsong filled his head; a refrain that might have brought some peace to his troubled soul if he could have deciphered its missive – that tomorrow would be a better day, full of hope and potential. But the message was muffled by the constant background hum of the traffic on the bypass, and the drone of an overhead jet on its descent into the nearby airport. There were few places left on this Earth of complete tranquillity.

Steve wondered if his absence was felt at the Black Swan. Probably not; he'd missed a few quiz nights in recent months, but he'd usually let Trev know if he couldn't make it. He was sure they'd be fine without him and his intermittent contributions. Still, the promise of a couple of pints and the customary good-natured banter almost made him turn back.

With a sigh he stood and took another look at his home town, a place that had brought him many things – security, employment, friendship, entertainment; but the one thing it had never brought him, was love. And it was love that he craved above all else.

Tears welled as the words of that old Beatles song echoed through his mind – "I don't care what they say, I won't stay in a world without love…"

Steve had trod this path many times, the uneven, potholed one that meandered gently up and away from town, on its way to the outskirts; but never before for this purpose.

3. The Quiz Team

'Steve's a bit late, isn't he?' said Sarah. 'We're going to need him for the music round.'

'I've texted a few times, but he's not answering,' said Trevor. 'And it's not the first time he's not shown up, is it? He can be a moody bugger; and prefers to be on his own when the black dog comes a-calling.'

'He's not been himself lately,' said Sarah, 'noticed last week he was pretty quiet. I'm a bit worried about him.'

'Well, there's nothing we can do about it now,' said Trevor, 'it'll be starting soon. We can check up on him tomorrow.'

Their quiz team was a loose alliance of friends and acquaintances – five of them when everyone showed up.

Trevor, in his late 40s, was an old football teammate of Steve's. A former goalkeeper of some repute, he now wore thick black-rimmed glasses; evidence of the reason he'd given up the beautiful game. They'd all thought his reactions were diminishing, whereas in reality his eyesight was failing and he couldn't see the damn ball until it was right in front of him. Trevor was well aware how sad was the sight of a despondent keeper picking yet another ball from the back of the net, while his teammates looked on despairingly. He rarely talked about it, but he was scarred by those last few years of letting the team down. It was only local Sunday league, division two, but they all took it fairly seriously. Now, the glasses, beneath a substantial shiny dome, conjured the appearance of a mad professor on a day off and there was no hint of his former agility.

Trevor ran an award-winning micro-brewery that supplied fine ale and related products to some of the local pubs, along with the regular customers to his brewery shop. A magician of the brew, an alchemist of subtle skill, he regularly sampled his own wares in the interests of quality control, both in the community and at home.

Longsuffering Sarah had put up with Trevor for eleven years, their marriage built on love and tolerance. Trevor often joked that the first attraction was that Sarah is about the right height upon which to rest his pint, which, if said in earshot, invariably resulted in a painful kick to his shins. Sarah undertook all the administration and accounts for the business, along with freelance work for other local enterprises. With a raucous laugh, beaming smile and huge heart, her personality was much bigger than her diminutive stature.

Karen and Alan joined them, looking a little flustered. – 'It was him again,' said Karen. 'I was there on time to pick him up, but you know how long he takes to get ready – told him it's a bloody pub quiz, not a fashion show, but he has to attend to every last detail of his image.'

'Hey, you can't look this good without a bit of effort,' protested Alan. He and Karen were forever winding each other up with good-natured repartee. 'Have you seen Karen's latest tattoo?' he asked.

'No, let's have a look,' said Sarah.

Karen rolled up her sleeve to reveal a delicate sprig of heather, a tasteful addition to the array of flora and fauna that adorned the rest of her arm.

'Very nice,' said Sarah, 'I'm surprised you don't get one done, Alan.'

'Don't need to, love, I'm already a work of art. How are we all on this fine evening?'

'All the better for seeing you two,' laughed Trevor, as he handed Alan a twenty-pound note, 'here, get you and Karen a drink. I've just got ours and I'm not queueing again.'

'Steve not here again?' said Karen.

'No, and he's not answering his phone,' said Trevor. 'It's becoming a bit of a habit. How was he at work?'

'His usual self,' said Alan. 'You ask if he's OK and he always says, "fine".'

'That's what we all say, isn't it,' said Karen, 'regardless of how we're really feeling.'

Steve had worked with Karen and Alan for some years. He'd once told Trevor that the staff-room would be pretty boring without them, and Steve's big-wheel of emotion might be permanently stuck at the bottom if they weren't there to pick him up on those bad mornings. Their wit and camaraderie made the job infinitely more tolerable.

Karen often joked that all the isms were invented just for her. Mixed-race and gay, she said that, simply by her very existence, she'd been put on this Earth specifically to wind up all the bone-headed bigots. It was a vocation that she took seriously and she could reduce any prejudiced prick (as she called them) to a tongue-tied wreck with a well-aimed put-down. It was a finely-honed skill built out of necessity, she argued.

Karen had a smile that could light up a room, inherited from her mother's side of the family. Passed down through generations, her grandmother told her that 'made in Jamaica' smile had the power to drive men crazy. She was in her mid-teens when she realised that she had no desire to drive men crazy.

Of course, Steve had asked her out soon after they met and, once she'd revealed her preferences, they'd been good friends ever since. It was the only time he'd not taken rejection as a personal slight. – 'You have good reason to turn me down; all the others just think I'm an ugly bastard.' In an attempt to make him feel better, Karen told him she'd have said yes if she were straight. No, you wouldn't, he'd retorted, because if you were straight, you could have any bloke you wanted. Karen admired his tenacity in the pursuit of love, but told him he was trying too hard – let it happen naturally, she advised. Steve said he didn't have that many lifetimes to wait.

Alan, an ostensibly archetypal married man with two kids, was the antithesis of bitterness. Invariably good-natured and happy, he got on with everyone and rarely had a bad word to say; except when anyone had a pop at Karen, in which case he'd politely suggest that, hey, that's not necessary and you're out of order. A dedicated PE teacher and well-built gym-user, Alan usually found that those few words were enough. He treated quiz nights as a laugh – there because he enjoyed the company, not for his intellect. Nevertheless, he sometimes proved invaluable for the sports questions.

It was the most popular night of the week in the Black Swan and the place was heaving with anticipant punters; some who participated every week, others on a more casual basis. They never came last, but there was no way they'd ever catch the Swots, studious and serious in their regular position opposite the toilets. Periodically one of the Swots would disappear into the bog mid-round and upon his return much writing would ensue as they agreed their answers. The suspicion that it wasn't a weak bladder that prompted his dash, but rather an exploration of Google, was never proven.

A convivial and jovial atmosphere was guaranteed and, despite good-natured competition, no-one, apart from the Swots, really cared whether they won or lost. A fine and varied selection of ales either oiled or hindered the cogs of cognition, they were never sure which; and some decent pub-grub was on offer for those who were peckish.

Fortunately, the Black Swan was a spacious establishment, with plenty of nooks and crannies to house the town's quiz-goers. Old black and white photos of the town filled frames on every wall, and each shelf or alcove housed an ornament related to the pub's long and motley history. With décor predominantly burgundy and russet, the place oozed warmth and the landlady welcomed all who crossed its threshold.

Conversations dwindled when a strikingly beautiful and slender lady with a jet-black, shoulder-length bob, made her way to a microphone that had been placed in the corner of the bar area, rustling a sheaf of papers as she went.

'One, two…' she spoke into the mic to ensure it was functioning. Her voice was clear and her diction well defined, as if she'd come from a more refined background than most of the clientele. A plain and flawless orange cotton dress hung from her shoulders and stopped just above the knees; her skinny white legs concluded in a pair of flat, two-tone Vans. With multifarious and unconventional sartorial choices – no-one knew what her look would be from one day to the next; she could probably make a bin-bag look stylish if she so desired.

She hadn't been christened thus, but everyone knew her as Bambi. The nickname, she'd told the landlady at her interview, had followed her from childhood, through an awkward adolescence and into adulthood. As a kid it had been her favourite movie and that, coupled with her large, caught-in-the-headlights brown eyes and gangling gait, was enough to shape her identity.

The pub went quiet in anticipation of the first question.

'It's a general knowledge round to start this week. Question one: What did Percy Shaw invent in 1934?'

'Cat's eyes,' said Trevor.

'What?' said Alan.

'Cat's eyes, those things in the middle of the road; they're called that because he had the idea after seeing his headlights reflected in the eyes of a cat one night. Ken Dodd once said that if the cat had been walking the other way, he'd have invented the pencil sharpener.'

Their uproarious laughter invited stares from the other quizzers. Trevor wrote the answer and prepared for the next question.

Unfortunately, that was as good as it got, and the optimism instilled by getting the first one right was soon curbed by puzzled expressions as the evening progressed. During the break Sarah asked Bambi for some easier questions in the second half.

'Sorry, I don't write this stuff, I just read it out,' said Bambi. 'I learn something new every week.'

They finished tenth out of fourteen.

'Well, that went well,' said Karen, as they made their way outside. 'That's our lowest score for some time.'

'Yeah, but it's harder with just the four of us; there's a narrower knowledge base,' observed Sarah.

'That's true,' said Karen. 'What was your answer to that question, Trev, about which pop star is associated with the Mad range of perfumes? Suggs, you said.'

'Well, I know nothing about Katy Perry; and it was more than you two came up with, sitting there with your blank expressions.'

'Ah well, there's always next time,' laughed Alan. 'Can we give you a lift, Clever Trevor?'

'No, you're OK, thanks; it's a nice evening – we'll walk and get some exercise.'

'See you next week, then,' said Karen, 'and let us know when you get hold of Steve.'

'Will do,' said Trevor, 'but I suspect he just wants to be on his own after the latest knock-back in his lack-of-love-life. This is the last place he'll want to be.'

4. The End of the Track?

As a child he'd stood on this bridge with his father and asked where the tracks went to.

'To London, where I was born,' his father had replied.

'Can we go there?' Steve had pleaded a number of times, but they never did. His mother had explained that Dad had escaped from poverty and a miserable, troubled childhood and had no desire to go back. They appreciated their nice home on the edge of town and aspired to move to the countryside when they retired.

Steve was in his early twenties before he finally made that trip, alone, and he loved it. His senses were overcome by the sheer buzz of the place; the cacophony of traffic on Oxford Street, the shouts of newspaper vendors, the repetitive chant of a line of Hare Krishna followers in flowing orange robes, the myriad eclectic buskers on the Underground; the fascinating sights of historic buildings and bridges that he'd only seen in storybooks and movies, the expansive River Thames, the bustling street markets; the aromas, tastes and varieties of exotic foods from all over the world; and so, so many people of all shapes, sizes and hues. A city full of life and possibility – he'd wanted to share it all with Dad, but he could never be persuaded.

A freight train trundled by, its unknown cargo concealed in boxcars of brown and rust. It seemed to go on forever, the metronomic clatter of wheels on track almost hypnotic. There was a romantic notion of the hobo, hopping boxcars to escape the humdrum and travel to a better life; but that was the domain of folk songs and movies, not of Steve's world. He watched the elongated train disappear into the distance and clambered over – onto the ledge – the same ledge where Peter Groves had wobbled so precariously all those years ago. The high-speed Virgin would be along soon, the one that zipped through without ceremony because it was far too important to stop at the town station.

There's a strange irony to it all, thought Steve, that the track he once believed could take him to Nirvana, could ultimately take his life. He tried once more to see beyond the despair, to focus on the positives of his existence, but the hopelessness was overwhelming.

Then an angel appeared!!

There she stood; a vision of beauty in silhouette against the misty glow of an old lamp that illuminated the path. A hint of shiny blonde ponytail, neatly tied beneath a Police Community Support Officer hat, Steve barely noticed the large, bearded gentleman by her side; her partner in the never-ending fight against crime.

'Good evening, sir,' she said, in a calm, unwavering tone, 'we're not going to do anything silly now, are we?'

Steve wasn't here, his head a muzzy, unconscious mess of scrambled thought. Her words forced a partial return to reality and he ventured some kind of intelligible answer. – 'No, of course not; I just like the view from here.'

'That's all very well, sir, but can you not see it just as good from this side of the railings?'

'No, I'm fine where I am, thanks.'

'Can I ask your name, sir?'

'Steve.'

'Well, Steve, my name's Jenny. Do you mind if I come a bit closer?'

'If you like.'

As she approached, he saw her face more clearly; a kindly face, but with a steely gaze that countenanced no nonsense. She looked him in the eye and spoke quietly, as if it were just a casual conversation.

'Please, Steve, can you meet me half way so we can talk about this?'

He stood carefully and, for the first time, noticed that he was shaking.

'That's good, Steve. Now why don't you tell me what this is all about and I'll see if I can help.'

Steve attempted to mask his panic and embarrassment. He'd been caught out and this wasn't part of the plan. Overcome with a cold and clammy sweat, Steve endeavoured to coherently tell Jenny that no, he wasn't about to jump; he was there to look at the trains and the one he wanted to see was due along soon.

'Ah, yes; the HST Class 43,' she said.

'What?'

'The Virgin HST Class 43 locomotive, if I'm not mistaken.'

Steve was dumbfounded – was she trying to wind him up? – 'Yes, the red one,' he replied at last.

'An interesting hobby, train-spotting,' said Jenny, as if she held conversations like this every day, 'so many variations that it takes a lifetime to tick them all off.'

Steve glanced at the track behind him. If he wanted to go through with this, he had minutes to decide. He sat back down to think – the pull of oblivion versus the calm and reassuring voice of Jenny. She continued to speak, but her words didn't register; they just added to his confusion. He tried to focus and blot out this unwelcome interruption, but he'd never been the most decisive of individuals. What should he do?

Abruptly, Jenny's tone grew in urgency and firmness, as the train's horn blew to announce its approach; and her pleas finally penetrated his thick skull. It was bloody dangerous up there and she'd feel a whole lot better if he'd climb back over – preferably now!! Steve gasped for breath and, with a final glance over his shoulder, complied without argument. He was always a sucker for a pretty lady, especially one in uniform, and of course, he'd do whatever she asked.

As he began his ascent, the whoosh of the high-speed express caught him by surprise and nearly dragged him back into its slipstream. Steve gripped the railings hard, his knuckles white as he fought the force. With a swift lunge, Jenny grabbed his arm, a little tighter than necessary he thought. Her partner quickly joined her and grabbed the other arm; and, as the oblivious express disappeared into the distance, Steve clambered up, trembling and white as a ghost.

It was all he needed, someone to care enough to talk him out of it; even if they were only doing their job. Steve fought against the shivers of shock and tried to present a casual front, as Jenny and her colleague insisted on accompanying him back to town. They spoke nothing of the recent incident; instead, she focussed on the everyday and mundane.

Steve felt ashamed of the shabby nature of his home, as he rinsed a couple of mugs and prepared coffee for his saviours. He poured himself a large whisky, apologised once more for putting them to so much trouble and steadfastly maintained his train-spotter explanation.

Steve could sense their disbelief and felt like a kid again when the possible consequences of his reckless behaviour were pointed out. Jenny wouldn't leave, she said, until reassured that he'd never do anything like that again.

He waved as they walked away. Back in his lonely hovel, he cried himself to sleep.

5. Doctor's Orders

The Doctor's Receptionist enquired what was the problem and whether it was imperative that he see a doctor today. He'd already had the phone to his ear for twenty-five minutes and been told repeatedly that his call was important to them. Steve said he'd rather not go into detail, but that he needed some help and, yes, it was pretty urgent he thought.

'The first appointment I can offer is at 3:50 this afternoon, with Dr Devi.'

'That's fine, thank you.'

Steve had called in sick, his first day off for a couple of years. Normally he struggled on when he got too down and told himself that it was better to keep busy than to dwell on things. But last night was a wakeup call as to how bad it had got and it was time to reach out and ask for help.

He opened the text from Trevor – "Missed you last night. Is everything OK?"

"Not feeling too good. Off work today and going to doctors. Sorry didn't reply last night, was sleeping."

"No problem, hope you feel better soon, will call at the weekend."

Sleeping; that's one way of putting it, thought Steve. Sleepwalking into oblivion was a more appropriate metaphor. He'd been to the doctors when he'd felt down before, but he always got the impression that his problems were not top of their many priorities.

Steve considered how to articulate what ailed him. It must be hard to analyse something you can't see or understand. When someone has high blood pressure there's a machine to measure it; a little torch can reveal a throat infection or a blocked ear; a thermometer shows just how high a temperature can jump; and a broken bone will be revealed by an x-ray. But diagnosis of a troubled mind or a broken heart seems way beyond the expertise of your average practitioner. A disquieting mess of genes, upbringing and life experiences; each person is wired differently and Steve's wiring was in serious need of an overhaul.

A full MOT and service was not possible in his allotted ten minutes however, so Dr Devi prescribed some more antidepressants and set the wheels in motion for referral to a therapist. God knows how long that will take, thought Steve. She signed him off for two weeks and demanded his assurance that he wouldn't repeat his attempt.

'No, I don't think so. I feel better now that I am taking steps to deal with it.'

'Good, but please don't hesitate to come and see me if you need to.'

In limbo again, Steve pondered on how to spend his two-week sabbatical – alone!

6. That's a Good Question

Back in circulation after his fortnight off, Steve felt relieved to be among friends again. Alan told him that it was good to see him and enquired what he'd been up to.

'Just resting as the doctor ordered, a bit of reading and some music now and then.'

'I envy you, you know,' said Alan, 'living on your own. You can play your music as loud as you like and there ain't no-one gonna bust your balls about it. When I was younger it was my parents who kept shouting – "turn it down!" I vowed that, when I got my own place, no-one would be in charge of the volume control except me. Now I get the wife and kids yelling – "turn it down!" And, let me tell you, we're talking about music that was made to be played loud. It's just not the same when you can barely hear it.'

'Yeah, I guess being a sad and lonely old bugger has some advantages,' said Steve, as he turned away to get his round in. He leant patiently, awaiting his turn to be served, conscious that it wasn't just the bar that held him up, the tablets were doing their job too. Next to him, a lady of medium build tapped her foot to the music; Paul Weller's Changing Man – it was one of his favourite songs and he immediately knew that she had good taste. He allowed himself a glance to the right out of curiosity.

At first, he didn't recognise her – that moment when you see someone you think you know but, out of context, can't think where from. And then it clicked. She'd obviously clicked a few moments before, for she smiled and said – 'Hi, how are you?'

Steve could feel the red rising in his face. 'Er, fine thanks. And you?'

'I'm good, thanks.'

'Not seen you in here before.'

'No, this is my first time.' Jenny flicked her head in the direction of a boisterous, mixed group in the corner. 'Some of the guys from the station come once a month, so I thought I'd give it a try.'

Yeah, they're cops alright, thought Steve. – 'So, what's your specialist subject?' he asked.

'Don't have one really; I know a bit about movies, and music of a certain era, but I'm just here for the craic. We have cleverer people than I on the team. I guess you specialise in trains.'

'Er, yeah, but you don't generally get many questions on that; mine's music and movies too.'

'OK, who's next?' said an obviously flustered barman.

'Go ahead,' said Jenny, 'you were first.'

'Thanks.' Steve turned to the barman – 'Three pints of Gnarly Old Scrote and a Coke, please. Can I get you one?' he asked her.

'No, thanks; I have a big round to get in. Who are you with?'

'That's my mob, over there,' he pointed; 'intelligent looking bunch, aren't they?'

'I'm sure you'll do better than us,' laughed Jenny. 'I assume you'll be going to the model railway exhibition at the community centre next Saturday. I'll be taking my dad; not my thing, but he's got his heart set on going and he can't drive anymore.'

'Yeah, definitely, I'll be there; been looking forward to it since I first heard about it.'

Which was a few seconds ago. Steve knew nothing of any model railway exhibition at the community centre, but promised himself that he'd look it up when he got home. He paid for his drinks, blushed again, said he hoped to see her next weekend and, with a barely perceptible spring in his step, went to join his friends.

'Who were you talking to at the bar?' asked Karen.

'No-one, just a lady I bumped into the other week.'

'Oh God, here we go again,' said Trevor, 'a good-looking lady smiles at you and passes the time of day and you fall in love again. It'll end in tears, you know.'

'Don't know what you mean,' protested Steve, 'we were just chatting.'

'No, I've seen that look before – all misty eyed and even more gormless than usual.'

'Leave him alone,' said Sarah, 'a man's allowed to fall in love isn't he.'

'For God's sake, will you give it a rest. She's just an acquaintance; nothing more to it than that. Now, can you concentrate on the quiz and see if we can do better than you did without me last time.'

'We can concentrate if you can,' said Trevor. 'We haven't got any distractions.'

'Well thanks,' said Sarah, 'but I guess it's a long time since I've been a distraction ay, Trev?'

Trevor put his arm around her shoulder. – 'You'll always be a distraction to me, dear.'

Alan addressed Steve – 'See what you've done now; you've started an argument.'

The customary hush of anticipation permeated the pub as Bambi made her way to the mic. She seemed more confident each week, a far cry from the quiet introvert that had appeared from nowhere a few years back. – 'Good evening quizzers; are we ready to quiz? Let's get the serious stuff out of the way first, we'll start with a history round; question one – who was the first woman in the House of Commons?'

Blank expressions all round except for Karen, whose history knowledge was renowned, at least among their close circle. – 'It was probably Mary Mopp, who cleaned the bogs,' she quipped. 'Now, it depends what answer they're looking for – Constance Markievicz was the first woman elected in 1918, but she refused to take her seat. Nancy Astor was the first to sit in the House of Commons in 1919 – nice lady, she believed that Nazism was the solution to the Jewish and Communist problems.'

They all looked at her incredulously. – 'So, what's the answer?' said Trevor.

'Probably Nancy Astor – you won't find Mary Mopp in the history books, and Constance Markievicz was in Holloway at the time due to her Suffragette activity; and, as a member of Sinn Fein, wouldn't accept her seat anyway.'

Trevor shook his head and wrote it down. – 'Just a name will do; we don't need a bloody history lesson.'

By this time Bambi had moved on to the next question, which Karen had to ask her to repeat. Inevitably, she got that one right too, along with seven of the eight remaining in that round. With her specialist subject exhausted, she sat back with a satisfied smile and declared – 'That's my bit done; over to you guys.'

There was no doubt that Steve was a little distracted but, with his team-mates' attention on the quiz, he didn't think his occasional looks in Jenny's direction were noticed. Once, he thought he saw her glance back and smile, but he couldn't be sure.

Then he heard Trevor utter the words that recaptured his attention – the Beatles, a subject on which he considered himself something of an expert. It was a lyric round, starting with one of Lennon and McCartney's many classics. Trevor had immediately recognised it as a fab-four song, but required Steve's assistance in identifying which one.

Bambi repeated the words a second time – 'I can see them laugh at me, And I hear them say…'

Steve had to stop himself singing the next line, the words were so familiar. – 'You've Got to Hide Your Love Away,' he said.

'Thank you,' said Trevor. 'This is the only round where you serve any useful purpose; perhaps you could give it your undivided attention, if it's not too much trouble.'

Steve blushed. 'Yes, of course. I'm all yours.'

Trevor shook his head as Bambi moved onto the next lyric, something about a girl named Wendy dying on the streets in an everlasting kiss…

'The theme to Peter Pan?' suggested Sarah.

'No, it's Springsteen,' said Steve, 'Born to Run.'

'Can't we have something more up-to-date?' said Karen. 'It's all music for old geezers, no offence chaps.'

'I thought you were a history buff,' said Steve. 'This is musical history and you should know all this stuff.'

A few more contemporary lyrics followed, which encouraged Karen to contribute to the round and prompted Steve to look nonplussed. Their combined efforts resulted in a ten out of ten and they were all amazed at how well things were going. Surprisingly, they made a good fist of the remainder of the rounds too and the evening concluded in an unprecedented second place finish, only three points behind the Swots.

Steve was so wrapped up in their relative success, that he failed to notice Jenny and her cohorts slip out quietly. He'd wanted to utter, might see you next Saturday, or some other profound line, but instead contented himself with another celebratory pint. It had been a good, life-affirming, evening.

7. The Train Spotters

Where once there were pool and table-tennis tables, there was endless track, snaking in and out of tunnels, through stations and freight yards; all in minutely-detailed miniature. Buzzing probably wasn't the right word but there was definitely an aura of excitement, as predominantly middle-aged men gathered in groups to discuss track gauges and locomotives.

Steve had once frequented the community centre on a regular basis, in its capacity as a youth club. He hadn't been back here for many years and it rekindled all kinds of mixed memories. He'd been half-decent at pool and table-tennis, and could take on most of his contemporaries and give them a run for their money. He'd garnered a certain amount of respect for his ball-skills in various sports, but he'd have preferred to be with the cool kids who hung with the girls. It appeared a far more glamorous and mysterious world than his, and he longed to be a part of it. But neither the cool kids nor the girls had any time for him it seemed.

He scanned the characterless room in search of any familiar faces; after all, the venue was in the centre of his home town where he frequently bumped into people he knew. Was that his old boss over there, deep in conversation with a fellow fanatic?

Steve's eyes drifted to the periphery and his heart skipped a beat. There, stood Jenny, alone and absorbed in something on her phone. He took a deep breath and sauntered over, attempting to appear casual, but quaking inside. After all these years, he still felt like that kid in the youth club and expected indifference at best.

'Hi there; having a good time?'

Jenny jumped. – 'Oh hi; yeah, this is just how I like to spend my Saturdays.'

'Sorry, didn't mean to creep up and startle you like that.'

'It's fine; I was only trying to pass the time and got lost in Facebook. My dad's over there and he'll be talking with his train buddies all afternoon.'

Steve nodded towards a hatch in the wall, surrounded by a few tables and uncomfortable-looking plastic chairs. – 'Do you fancy a coffee?'

'I don't want to drag you away from the excitement.'

'Oh, I don't mind. There's plenty of afternoon left, I can take a look at the exhibition later.'

'Yeah, OK then.'

Steve grimaced as he took a sip of his coffee – instant, black and bitter. He didn't consider himself a connoisseur, but he liked a decent brew, filtered or percolated at least. Jenny smiled and sipped her tea. – 'Not to your taste, I take it,' she said.

'It's horrible, but I don't know what I expected.'

'That's why I always have tea in this kind of place. There's not so much scope to mess it up. Quite an impressive set-up this, must have taken a while to put it all together.'

'Yeah, it's a good one; they've obviously made a lot of effort.'

'I know all about trains,' admitted Jenny; 'not through choice, but Dad taught me all he knows and that's a lot. Never had any brothers, so he had to pass it on to someone, I guess. Spent most of my childhood watching those bloody things go round in circles. How did you get into it?'

Steve hesitated and felt his face reddening again. Jenny must have thought that was his natural colour and demeanour – permanent embarrassment. He didn't want to perpetuate the lie and his response emerged as a stuttering apology. – 'I-I have a confession to make; I'm not really a train-spotter. I was thinking of ending it all until you came along and persuaded me to come down. Don't know if I'd have had the guts to go through with it, but I might not be alive if not for you.'

'Yeah, I gathered as much, but thought I'd give you the benefit of the doubt. So, if you're not a train fanatic, what are doing here?'

Steve blushed some more. – 'Er, because you told me you were coming. I'm sorry, you must think I'm some kind of stalker; I'll leave now.'

He found it hard to reciprocate as Jenny looked him in the eye. 'No, it's fine,' she said, 'at least finish your coffee first. I suppose I should be flattered really.'

'I don't normally do this kind of thing, I promise.'

'So, how are you now? You must have been pretty desperate the other week.'

'A bit better, thanks. I've been to my GP and she's arranged for me to speak to someone. I'm really sorry to have put you through that experience; and thanks; again.'

'All part of the job, I guess. My cousin killed himself last year and seeing you up there brought it all back. No-one knew there was anything wrong – he was always laughing and joking; then his wife came home one day and couldn't wake him. He'd taken an overdose. A little less messy than what you were contemplating, but the same result and the family were devastated. I still can't believe he's gone.'

'I'm sorry.'

'You know that suicide is the biggest killer of men under forty-five in this country; and all because you guys won't talk about your problems. It's such a waste. That's why I was determined that you weren't gonna jump off that bridge.'

Steve was immediately transported back to that night and its rainbow of emotions – desolation, fear, embarrassment, relief. He shivered as he considered just how close he'd come. – 'What can I say? I'll be forever in your debt.'

'Well, the important thing is you're still here and trying to turn your life around. Please, don't ever let it come to that again. There are always people who can help.'

'You already have; just by caring and taking the time to talk.'

'What about your friends on the quiz team? They looked like a decent bunch, I'm sure they would be supportive if you asked.'

'Yes, they're all good friends.'

'Then open up; there's no shame in asking for help. We all get down sometimes and life has a habit of throwing all kinds of crap at us. I'm sure you'd be there like a shot if the boot was on the other foot.'

A smartly-dressed, grey-haired man in his seventies strode over, sporting a green tie with a red loco-motif over a pristine pressed white shirt, above grey trousers and shined black shoes. – 'So, who's this then?' he asked Jenny.

'Steve, this is Dad, Dad, this is Steve. We met through work a few weeks ago.'

Steve stood and shook his hand.

'So, which are you, then; cop or criminal?' said Jenny's dad.

'Neither,' said Steve, a little unnerved by the bluntness of the question. 'I was in a bit of bother and your wonderful daughter came to my assistance.'

'Ah, yes, she's always doing stuff like that; so busy looking after waifs and strays, that she neglects her own happiness. Hope you treat her better than the last fella.'

It was Jenny's turn to go a lurid shade of red. – 'Dad, please! Steve and I are just acquaintances. There's no need to embarrass the poor man.'

'Looks like it's you that's embarrassed, not Steve,' said Dad, 'I'm sure he has a sense of humour. Time I got back to the boys; just came over to check that you weren't getting too bored, but I can see you're fine.' He winked at Steve as he shook his hand once more. 'Pleasure to meet you, young man.'

'Sorry about that,' said Jenny, shaking her head as she watched her dad re-join his friends. 'He's always winding me up like that.'

Steve laughed – 'No problem. Seems a bit of a character, your dad, although he needs to get his eyesight checked; he called me young man.'

'That's what he calls anyone younger than him.' Jenny nodded affectionately toward her father's animated entourage. – 'He's happy as a pig in the proverbial, look. I really don't mind missing my afternoon's shopping to see him like that. He's not been himself since he lost the independence that driving gave him; although he's still driving Mum crazy, stuck in the house all the time.'

'Why did he have to give up?'

'When he was younger, he used to rant and rave at older drivers, said that a lot of them were bloody dangerous and shouldn't be allowed on the road. He made me promise to tell him when he got like that and to take away the keys. He'd had a few minor bumps, and his driving and reactions were getting slower and slower, so I told him the time had come. Think he knew it himself too, so he didn't argue.'

The afternoon flew by and, before he knew it, Steve realised they'd been chatting for over two hours. Jenny didn't mention again the circumstances of their first meeting, the conversation natural, flowing and covering a plethora of subjects, like movies, music and holidays. He couldn't recall when he'd spent such a pleasant afternoon, all in the most basic of surroundings.

'Well, you've been here all afternoon and you haven't spotted one train,' said Jenny, 'I must apologise for distracting you from the entertainment.'

'Well, it's not the first time you've dragged me away from the trains,' said Steve. 'Sorry, that's in bad taste. I've had a great time and I'd rather talk to you than watch trains go round a track.'

'Thanks, I've had a nice time too.'

Silence reared its head for the first time that afternoon, as Steve stumbled over what to say next. It was now or never and he hoped his cold sweat wasn't too noticeable. He glanced up to see that Jenny seemed lost for words too. OK, he thought – here goes. 'L-look, I hope you don't think me too forward, but there's a comedy night at the theatre on Friday; no-one famous, but I've been to a few before and they can be good. Do you fancy coming?'

Jenny thought for a moment, obviously unsure how to respond, before declaring – 'I should probably check the PCSO handbook first, to see whether it's appropriate to socialise with someone I've met in the course of my duties, so to speak.'

'So, is that a yes, or a no?'

'It's a yes, I think. A comedy night sounds fun and I could do with a laugh.'

They awkwardly swapped phone numbers for confirmation of final details and went their separate ways, exchanging waves as Steve exited. A slight detour to the Black Swan on his way home, Steve indulged in a pint of dark mild, which had the added bonus of washing away the taste of that awful coffee, as well as quenching his thirst and slipping down quite nicely. He often popped into the pub on his journey home; it was far too convenient and infinitely preferable to his empty house. Steve wasn't exactly a major contributor to the landlady's pension fund, as he rarely drank more than a pint or two, but he was a regular and always welcome. He felt good, but wary of another false dawn; after all he'd had so many of those.

'Same again, Steve?' asked Bambi.

'Probably, but you never know. This time could be different.'

8.   I Want to Hold Your Hand

All manner of folk milled around the theatre bar prior to the show. Most were in couples and, for once, Steve didn't feel out of place. He didn't even care about the extortionate price of a pint, for Jenny stood before him and seemed pleased to be there. They found a space to chat and Steve was chuffed that the conversation flowed as naturally as in their last encounter. It was time to discover more about each other.

Jenny told him that she'd once been in the Army and was a divorced single mum. Her current PCSO work gave her the flexibility to look after her son, George, but she aspired to be a proper cop one day.

'Now, what about you?' she said. 'Tell me about the man behind the mask.'

'You've already seen some of what's behind the mask. Much more than I would have chosen to reveal. In fact, I can't believe you're here, given what you already know.'

'Never met anyone who doesn't have some kind of problem,' said Jenny. 'We all have insecurities and a history to deal with, don't we? Sometimes it all gets too much. What do you do for a living?'

'I'm a teacher, at the college. Specialise in English, but we have to cover all kinds of things these days. Love the job, but the paperwork and bureaucracy drive you crazy.'

'A teacher! No wonder your quiz team does so well. Are they all teachers?'

'Ha, that's a good theory. The night you were there was our best ever score. Believe me, it's not always like that. We're a bit of a mixture really – Alan teaches sport; Karen is the college transitions co-ordinator – supporting the special needs kids when they move from school to college; Trev and Sarah own a local brewery; and I know a bit about some things and not a lot about most things.'

Steve would have been happy to talk all night, but the announcer said the show would start in ten minutes – it was time to take their seats.

The stand-up comedian stood up and thanked the few-hundred punters who'd ventured out this evening. He held a newspaper before him – 'You're in for a proper evening of jollity folks, as this review from last night's show testifies. It says here – "There are two essential facets to becoming a successful stand-up comedian and there's no doubt that this guy has mastered the first bit – he can stand up." A bit unfair, I thought, but I'll do my best to crack the second bit for you tonight.'

And he did. Much laughter ensued as he regaled the audience with bizarre tales of his childhood and clumsy journey through adolescence. Steve was happy to see Jenny laughing and, apparently, having a great time. When their hands brushed together on the arm that separated their seats, Steve left his there and Jenny entwined her fingers in his. As if an electric shock had travelled up his arm and entered his body, the tingling sensation took him by surprise. He turned to Jenny and smiled; and she smiled back.

As they often did, The Beatles permeated his consciousness – "I Want to Hold Your Hand" – recorded long before Steve was born and yet another classic from his Uncle Roy's record collection. He loved its simplicity and innocence, born of less complicated times. It was all he wanted, nothing more than that connection. A gesture that said so much, without the need for words.

As the stand-up comedian sat down to warm applause, Steve still had that inane grin on his face. 'Well, he was pretty good,' he said. 'What did you think?'

'Yeah, very funny. Thanks for inviting me; I've had a great time.'

The evening had flown by and was everything Steve had hoped; a relaxed atmosphere, plenty of laughter; all without the awkwardness that usually accompanies a first date and the stilted conversation between two people who barely know each other. The comedy was a good ice-breaker and Jenny said she'd like to come again. It all augured well for his idea of dinner on Saturday, to which Jenny agreed without too much hesitation.

Could things finally be looking up?

9. The Therapist

Steve wasn't looking forward to his visit to the therapist; he didn't really see the point. He'd always indulged in a lot of soul-searching and self-analysis and, deep down, thought he knew what was wrong with him. A potentially lethal combination of sheer loneliness and negativity, and more than enough time on his hands for it all to ferment into despair.

Would it help to talk about it? Perhaps for a while, but ultimately, he thought he knew the solution – to eradicate the loneliness; to find someone to care for, and someone who cared about him. It wasn't much to ask, he saw them all around him, happy couples, happy families. He wasn't naïve enough to believe that all of these allegiances were the epitome of blissful contentment, but at least they had each other.

He approached the characterless surgery with trepidation, a typical 1960s-built single-storey block of stone that fitted in perfectly with the surrounding estate. The receptionist asked him to take a seat in the waiting area and he questioned his habit of turning up at least ten minutes early for all appointments. He hated being late, but it gave him time to wonder once more why he was here; how had it come to this and should he just get up and leave? No, he'd come this far, he would go through with the first session at least.

Finally, he was called into a soulless white room, with a simple desk housing a PC, an overflowing folder, pens and strewn papers. The man who greeted him had made a little more effort with his own appearance than with the tidiness of his desk. Smartly dressed, tall and with a completely shaven dome, he oozed confidence as he proffered his hand.

'Mr Brent, is it Steven or Steve? Please take a seat.'

'My friends call me Steve.'

'Then I will too, if I may. My name is Philip Jacobs and I'm here to do all I can to help. Now, there are a few formalities to go through before we begin, I'm afraid.'

As they completed the necessary paperwork, Steve began to feel more relaxed. Philip must have been at least ten years his junior, but he had an aura that engendered comfort and security. He immediately felt that he could talk to this guy and he would be non-judgemental and sympathetic.

Steve noted Philip's tie, a dark blue number, completely covered in cockerels. He wondered what unfortunate events had led him to choose such a life of misery. Was it an affliction inherited from his father? Had he been attracted by the legend of Jimmy Greaves, a man who'd honed his craft in far loftier climes? Or maybe he simply lacked taste, a theory backed up by the fact that he was wearing that tie in the first place. Still, at least Philip would be able to empathise with Steve's own predicament – a life lived in permanent disappointment, full of unrealistic aspirations and false dawns. For, as it is with a man unlucky in love, such is the perpetual lot of a Tottenham fan.

After a brief summary of recent events, Philip asked Steve how he was feeling now.

'I feel as if I'm wasting everyone's time, to be honest. There are others far worse off than me; people in poverty, people with disabilities, people who've lost loved ones.'

'But just because a problem isn't visible, it doesn't mean it's non-existent. Take someone with a hidden disability for instance and how they are often challenged when parking in a disabled space – "you don't look disabled," the great British public will say. The same applies to our mental health – we all have it and we all go through difficult times. We need to take the time to look after our mental wellbeing, otherwise the negativity festers and leads us to despondency. It's just as important as our physical health. Besides, if there were no psychological issues, then I'd be out of a job.'

'So, people like me keep you in employment. It's good to know I'm useful for something and not a drain on resources.'

'Absolutely not,' said Philip, 'it's what I'm here for. Now, let's get to the nitty-gritty. Would you like to tell me what nearly brought you to the point of no return?'

Steve had considered this question so many times but, now the time to talk had arrived, found it difficult to begin. His hesitation said it all.

'Ah, the travails of love and relationships, we all find that hard to address. If it helps, then I can tell you that I've heard it all before. There's nothing you can say that will shock me.'

'Am I that easy to read?' said Steve.

'Just a good guess; it is at the root of most people's problems and why they come to see me. Tell me; how you have been driven to the depths of despair and who is responsible?'

'That's a bit harsh, isn't it? Why should anyone but I be responsible?'

'Most people blame others for their misery. I have heard so many stories of mistreatment and pain; you rarely hear both sides of the story. It's usually one particular experience that's at the root of things. Tell me about her; did she lead you on?'

'That was my interpretation at the time, but I guess she just liked to talk. Look, I'm not the first bloke to make an arse of himself over a beautiful woman, and I won't be the last. Happens to us all, doesn't it?'

Steve could tell that Philip was being deliberately provocative in an attempt to get a reaction. In some respects, he was right; Steve blamed her for leading him on and leaving him low but, ultimately, he attributed his loneliness to no-one but himself. Yes, it was unrequited love a couple of decades ago that had ripped out his once warm heart and replaced it with a heart of ice, but it was he who fuelled its refrigeration and maintained its distance from any source of thaw. Whatever the root of his discontent, he felt as if his body and soul resided at the core of a bloody Chi-Lites song; and he was utterly sick of it.

'You know that rejection, in one form or another, is the most common cause of unhappiness,' said Philip.

'But I have been rejected so many times, that I can only conclude that I am the one at fault.'

'And to what do you attribute this repeated rejection?'

'That's the problem, I don't really know. I am fully aware that I'm not the best-looking geezer in the world, but I see plenty of blokes in relationships who look equally unlovable. I've often wondered if it's a confidence thing; like when you go for a job interview – if you can master the ancient arts of bullshit and blarney, you stand a much better chance.'

'But if you bullshit in a job interview you soon get found out when you start the job,' said Philip. 'The same applies in a relationship – we can't pretend to be something we're not indefinitely. Have you tried just being yourself?'

'That's all very well if you want to be yourself. We all put on some kind of act, don't we?'

'But an act is not sustainable. Sooner or later the façade will slip.'

'I am kind of seeing someone,' confessed Steve; 'someone who has already seen a fair bit of what's behind the façade.'

'Well, that's good news, isn't it? May I ask who?'

'I told you about the PCSO who talked me down from the bridge; her name's Jenny.'

'Interesting,' said Philip. 'We are naturally drawn to those who show us kindness, whether it be the nurse who dresses our wounds, or the barmaid that pulls our pint; but the woman who saved your life will stimulate strong feelings indeed.'

Steve flinched at the mention of the barmaid who pulled his pint. It was as if Philip could see into his very soul. His thoughts returned to Jenny. – 'Experience has taught me not to have strong feelings for anyone; you only end up getting hurt.'

'But those feelings still exist, no matter how hard you try to repress them. How long has this been going on?'

'Not long; we've met a couple of times socially and we're going out for a meal on Saturday. It's early days yet, but I like her a lot. It feels so natural when we talk.'

'But you're worried about messing things up again; am I right?'

'I'm worried about raising my hopes too high, only to have them dashed to the ground. It's happened too many times.'

'It's always an interesting dilemma; if we express our feelings too soon, we risk scaring away the object of our affection. However, if we say nothing it is assumed that we're not interested. Very few of us manage to strike the right balance.'

For a moment Steve wondered which of them was the therapist; with a wistful expression, Philip gave the impression that he was speaking from experience. Nevertheless, it was good to talk about such things and get it all out in the open. How many years had he been alone, wondering what was wrong with him? For too long he'd lived in the shadow of his past, his imagination his only respite. He'd reached the stage where his fantasies replaced a cruel, monotonous reality. But oh, how he longed to reside in the real world.

'You have taken the first steps to deal with your issues by coming to see me,' said Philip. 'I would suggest that you see how things go, let them happen naturally. If it's meant to be then the relationship will develop. If not, and she doesn't feel the same way, then let it go and move on. And try be yourself – we've only just met, but you come across as a decent bloke and there are plenty of women looking for one of those. Has this session helped?'

'Yes, I think so. Thank you for your time; it's certainly given me plenty to think about. When you put it all in perspective things could always be worse – I could be a Spurs fan too.'

Philip smiled as they shook hands. – 'Touché! Look forward to seeing you next week, then.

As Steve left the building, he wished the receptionist a good weekend and emerged into a pleasant, warm afternoon. He assumed that Philip had used the same strategy on countless others but, for the first time in ages, Steve sensed the existence of some seeds of optimism. Would they sprout and grow? Well, that was up to him.

10. Scene of the Crime

Steve turned the corner to be met with a crime scene, like something from a TV cop show. The usually welcoming Black Swan was swathed in police-cordon tape and cops were everywhere. All the familiar quiz-goers milled around outside; their voices combined to produce a subdued drone. Steve spotted Trevor and Sarah. He wandered over, an inquisitive look on his face that asked without the need for words – what the hell's going on?

'No quiz tonight,' said Trevor. 'The word going round is that someone's died; they think it's Bambi.'

Steve reeled in shock. Trevor often quipped that the criteria required to become the subject of Steve's affections was to be female and in possession of a pulse. This theory had some validity, given the desperation of his permanent bachelor status, but Steve had genuinely liked Bambi. She was invariably friendly to everyone, even the obligatory awkward customer, a smile on her face regardless of how busy or hassled she was.

'She's dead?' he gasped.

'It seems so,' said Trevor, 'and the fact that the place is swarming with the old bill, indicates that foul play is suspected.'

The fragility of human mortality hit Steve hard. His own brush with death still fresh in his thoughts, this awful news brought it all back. Would he have traded places? Would a world without him be preferable to a world without Bambi? Aesthetically, yes; there was no question. He couldn't believe that anyone would want to harm such a beautiful person.

Steve noticed that some of the cops were positioned behind the pub's thirsty clientele, presumably to ensure that no-one left the scene. It appeared that they were all to be questioned before they would be permitted to go on their way. Karen and Alan arrived and expressed their utter disbelief. Karen was particularly upset; she and Bambi had engaged in a long conversation the previous week after Karen had enquired about Bambi's unique fashion sense.

'It'll be some bastard of a man that's done this to her,' she fumed. 'Was there any sexual assault?'

'No-one knows yet,' said Sarah, 'the cops are not saying anything.'

It was to be a long evening, with each punter asked to join one of four lines. At the end of each line an officer read from a script and took a statement from all present. Steve was shaking by the time his turn came and he gave his name, address and contact details. As the inquisition began, he felt his body tense with every question.

'Why are you here this evening, sir?'

'For the quiz night.'

'Are you aware of what has happened in there?'

'From what I've been told, someone has died.'

'And did you know the person in question, sir?'

'She served me with beer and we had conversations at the bar. It's such a tragedy; she was a really nice lady.'

For the first time, the detective looked up from his script. – 'But I haven't told you who is dead, sir.'

'It's all round the place,' said Steve, 'everyone knows it's Bambi, unless they are mistaken.'

'Can you tell me your movements today please?'

'Been at work all day, then walked into town and picked up a few things for dinner. Showered and shaved, and then came here.'

'Can anyone vouch for that?'

'My work colleagues and the check-out girl at the supermarket, I guess.'

'And last night?'

Steve had to admit that he was spending far too much time in the Black Swan. – 'I was here till about 11:00 then went home. In fact, you could probably call this place my second home. When did all this happen?'

'We won't know until the post-mortem is complete. Do you have any objection to taking a DNA test, sir?'

'None at all.'

'Very well, if you could join the queue over there, please; thank you for your time.'

'No problem; and I hope you catch the scumbag that did this.'

'Oh, we will, sir.'

11. Life Goes On

The following week, and Steve was working on autopilot. The Black Swan community and the town in general were still in shock that such a tragedy could occur in their midst. This was a peaceful neighbourhood. Things like that didn't happen here; did they?

A coffee, that's what he needed and the morning break couldn't come a moment too soon. Steve retreated to the staff room, sat back in his usual chair and took a deep breath. Around half-a-dozen staff took advantage of the brief hiatus, before that teenage onslaught would begin again.

Even the customary banter between Karen and Alan had been more subdued since last week's awful revelations. Quiz nights would never be the same again; there would always be a void where Bambi once stood.

'You OK, mate,' said Alan.

Steve shook his head – 'Still can't believe it.'

'No, me neither. Don't suppose they've caught anyone yet.'

'Not that I know of. Haven't been able to bring myself to go back to the pub yet. Must be terrible for the landlady and the other staff.'

'Yeah, and something like that is not exactly good for business, is it?' said Alan.

Steve glanced up to see Donna, the college receptionist at the door; two ominous dark shadows lurking through the frosted glass behind her. Donna pointed at Steve and the dark shadows emerged and turned into bulky policemen with serious expressions.

'Mr Steven Brent?'

'Yes.'

'Is there anywhere we can speak in private, sir?'

'Yes, of course; what's this all about?'

'All in due course, sir.'

'What's going on?' said Alan.

'No idea,' said Steve. 'Better go and find out. I'll catch up with you later.'

With a feeling of trepidation, Steve led them to an unused classroom. – 'We'd like you to accompany us to the station for questioning, sir, in relation to the murder of Ms Emma Forrester.'

'But what's that got to do with me?'

With gravitas in the officer's tone – 'That's what we'd like to discuss.'

Steve shivered. He didn't like the sound of that. – 'Can it wait till later? I have students waiting for me.'

'I'm afraid not, sir.'

'So, am I under arrest?'

'If necessary, but we'd rather you came voluntarily.'

It all happened in a blur as they flanked him along the corridor. Breaktime had finished and the other teachers and the students were all back in lessons by now. There was no-one to come to his assistance and say – hey, you've got the wrong man; no-one to offer support and say – we're here for you, Steve; but thankfully, there was also no-one to witness his fear, indignity and embarrassment.

Only the receptionist saw him escorted through the front doors. Steve looked over his shoulder as they left. – 'Er, Donna; could you arrange for someone to cover my classes today, please? Something's come up.'

In a state of shock, he stared through the police car window, as they left behind his life, his sanctuary – the only place where he felt useful.

12. Jenny

'What happened to that fella you were seeing?' asked Dad. 'You know, the one I met at the model railway exhibition; seemed like a nice chap.'

'Well, you can be wrong about people,' said Jenny, 'and I got this one very wrong. You heard about that barmaid at the Black Swan? Well, Steve has just been arrested for her murder.'

'What!! Jeez, you sure know how to pick them; first a wife-beater, and now this. And are you OK?'

'No, not really; I really liked Steve and can't believe how I could have been so naïve. On the plus side, I suppose you could say I've had a lucky escape.'

A boisterous, be-freckled boy of eight bounded into the living room, the door visibly vibrating in his wake. Jenny ruffled his unruly hair and smiled. No matter how often she combed it, the mop had a life of its own and always reverted to its naturally anarchic state within minutes.

'Why are you crying, Mummy?' he asked. He was a gregarious, caring and loving lad and, whenever Jenny felt down, she knew she could count on George to cheer her up.

'I'm OK,' she lied, 'just heard a sad story, that's all.'

George seemed satisfied with her answer and his attention turned to the reason he'd entered the room. – 'Grandad, can we take Sandy for a walk?'

'OK, but it's your turn to pick up the poo.'

'No, it's your turn. I did it last time.'

'Toss you for it; heads or tails?'

'Tails,' cried George and he stood back as the coin span in the air, before landing on the back of Grandad's hand. George waited in anticipation as Grandad teased him and kept it covered. Eventually the fifty pence piece was revealed.

'Tails it is,' said Grandad, 'that means you have to pick up the poo.'

'That's not fair; I won, so that means you have to do it.'

Sandy, the placid golden Labrador, lay contentedly on the rug, oblivious to the squabble over the consequences of her bowel movements. What was all the fuss about?

Jenny shook her head; she'd witnessed this ritual many times and knew they'd be arguing for ages yet. She excused herself and retired to her room; the same room in which she'd grown up. Yes, she'd redecorated it since she'd returned home three years ago, but it still occupied that familiar setting and vista, the conker tree through the window more majestic with each passing year. Her dad had recently introduced George to the ancient combat sport of conker-fighting. Dad was incredulous when George had got into trouble at school after encouraging his friends to join in. Jenny had to explain to both of them that you weren't allowed to do that anymore. 'The world's gone mad,' said Dad.

She studied that old pine wardrobe, with its knots of dark brown that used to stimulate her vivid imagination in childhood. Those knotted shapes were still there; the scary spider, the flying saucer, the face beneath a graduate's mortarboard, and the binoculars that she'd once covered with a poster of 101 Dalmatians. Of all the images conjured, the binoculars scared her the most, for she had visions and nightmares of a man behind the door, watching her every move. It hadn't helped to quell her terror when she'd read the Chronicles of Narnia, its depictions of another life behind a wardrobe door feeding her fears. Even in the naivety of childhood she knew it was irrational and stupid, but her imagination was a wild and untamed beast back then.

Jenny felt tired and sluggish, her every step around the house viewed head down through half-closed eyes. Whenever she laid back on her bed with time for thought, she reflected upon how far she'd regressed; the independence she'd earned denied by circumstances beyond her control. When she'd left home to join the Army there was no turning back. Dad had encouraged her to follow her dreams, though Mum had expressed reservations as to whether her little girl would be tough enough. Jenny was determined to prove her wrong and she'd pushed herself to thrive amid the mud of field-craft and survival exercises, before rising to the rank of Lance Corporal in the Royal Military Police.

Then she'd met Johnny, a handsome young squaddie with a roguish smile and sociable demeanour. Everyone liked Johnny and she relished that he not only took notice, but pursued her relentlessly until she agreed to be his girlfriend. A blissful courtship followed by a joyful wedding, they moved into decent Army accommodation close to the base. She couldn't have been happier, in a job she loved and with a man she loved even more.

And then it happened; Johnny was posted to Iraq. At first, Jenny barely noticed the changes when he returned on leave and he seemed little different to the outgoing young man she'd married. George was conceived during his third period of leave and they were both ecstatic at the news, their future plans taking shape, with the promise of a new life to nurture and cherish.

In stark contrast to the bright new dawn of hope instilled by George's birth, the nightmares grew worse and Johnny would often awake in fear and rage – Jenny the nearest thing to strike out at. For years she tried; she made excuses for the bruises; she'd walked into a door, or tripped on the stairs. She knew it wasn't Johnny's fault and that it was a classic case of post-traumatic stress disorder. This wasn't the real Johnny, the man she'd married; he was a victim of a misguided and irresponsible decision to send our troops into that hell. The war had destroyed the man she loved and turned him into an emotional wreck, with no control of his temper and haunted by visions that no man should see.

There was little help from the army or the government; instead, they referred him to various charities, set up to repair the untold damage to his body and soul. They had intermittent success and there were long periods when the old Johnny would return. It was why she'd stayed so long, to try to support him through the therapy and give him something solid to hold on to. But ultimately there was no going back and a particularly violent episode, witnessed by a four-year-old George, made the heart-breaking decision for her. No matter how many times that Johnny said he was sorry, that it wouldn't happen again and he wanted her back, she had to move on to create a safer world for her and George.

And, of course, the next man she chose to take an interest in was Steve, a murderer! Dad was right; she sure knew how to pick them. With an uncontrollable sob, Jenny buried her head in the pillow and resolved to stay where she was. Despite the fears of what lay behind that wardrobe door, it couldn't be any worse than real life.

13. Let's Get Quizzical

Some weeks later and it was Jenny's mum that persuaded her to arise from her solitary cocoon and venture out again. – 'I'm not having you moping around the house all the time feeling sorry for yourself,' she said. 'You've proved before how strong you are; it's time to prove it again and get back out there.'

Perhaps the quiz night at the Black Swan wasn't the best choice of venue for her re-emergence, but it was convenient and the company congenial. Besides, she wanted to overcome the natural reluctance to venture anywhere that was a reminder of her mistakes, face her demons head-on. None of her colleagues knew about her clandestine liaisons with Steve as they'd been careful to keep it low-key, so the conversation about the case was candid and they congratulated each other on the conclusion of a successful investigation. Rob, a popular detective, was singled out for particular praise.

'If you hadn't sussed out that he'd been sniffing around the victim and she'd blown him out, then we'd never have suspected him,' said Dave.

'I didn't do much,' said Rob, 'It was the DNA that got him. It's one of the easiest cases I've ever been involved in; means, motive and opportunity.'

Jenny kept quiet and lost herself in the quiz, mining the deepest recesses of her brain for answers. It had been an emotional introduction from the landlady, as she'd paid tribute to Bambi and dedicated tonight's event to her memory.

'Which letter in the alphabet does NOT appear in the name of any U.S. state?' she asked the first post-Bambi question.

'It's got to be Z or X, hasn't it?' said Rob.

'Arizona, New Mexico and Texas,' said Jenny.

'OK, clever clogs; what's the answer then?'

'Give me a couple of minutes to think about it.'

The next few questions were answered by Dave, before Jenny grabbed the paper and wrote down the letter missing from the U.S. states.

'Ah, yes, of course,' said Rob.

The evening drifted by in a pleasant way and Jenny was glad she'd taken the first step back to civilisation; until, during the break, she was furtively approached whilst waiting at the bar by a balding man with thick black glasses.

'Sorry to intrude,' he whispered, 'I'm Trevor, a friend of Steve's. You probably don't want to speak to us, but my friends and I wondered if you would join us at the end of the evening. We have a few things we'd like to discuss with you.'

Jenny said nothing, but nodded imperceptibly and returned to her table. If she'd have known what the future held then Trevor's request might have been ignored, as it should have been in her professional capacity, but her curiosity had been aroused. What could they possibly want to speak to her about?

As the quiz drew to a close and her colleagues began to leave, she made her excuses and retired to the toilets while the rest of them dispersed. A peek out to ensure no-one remained, and she made her way to Trevor's table. After brief introductions Trevor came straight to the point – 'We think Steve is innocent and there's been a dreadful mistake.'

'And do you have any new evidence to back that up?' asked Jenny. 'The case for the prosecution was pretty conclusive.'

'No, but Steve wouldn't kill anyone,' proclaimed Sarah, 'he's one of the sweetest guys you'll ever meet.'

'I think any one of us could kill,' said Alan, 'if we have reason to do so. I admit that, in Steve's case, it's unlikely, but just saying.'

'But this is Steve, we're talking about here,' said Karen. 'I refuse to believe that he'd do such a thing.'

'So, what do you think I can do about it?' said Jenny.

'You went out with him a few times,' said Trevor, 'you must have liked him too. Can you make some further investigations?'

'But I'm only a PCSO. I'm not even a proper cop. Besides, they've closed the case; I can't simply walk into the station and start snooping around.'

'Then how can we help him?' said Sarah. 'None of us are private detectives.'

'I think you should know that Steve had some problems,' said Jenny; 'he was going through a lot of turmoil in the lead-up to the murder. We should maybe question whether he was himself at the time, whether he was thinking straight.'

'We know about his periodic depression,' said Trevor, 'but he'd seemed much happier in those last few weeks; after he met you in fact.'

'Well, I suppose I should take that as a compliment.' – Jenny looked up to see a collection of expectant eyes, all trained on her. She felt cornered, these fervent appeals on Steve's behalf, in contrast to her desire to forget about the whole sorry episode and move on. Some kind of response was required, however. Eventually, Jenny shook her head in befuddlement. – 'I'll think about it and come back to you. Firstly, I need to consider what use I could be, and secondly the possible impact on my career. I'm thinking of training to go full time and will not jeopardise my prospects on a lost cause.'

'So, imagine how impressed they'll be when you solve the case,' ventured Trevor.

'Hmm, not sure the Chief would see it that way. There are protocols to follow when you sign up, you know.'

Jenny said she admired their loyalty to their friend and stood to leave. Then she saw it – the advert on the door – BAR STAFF WANTED. PLEASE SPEAK TO THE LANDLADY IF INTERESTED. Now there's a thought – it may be time for a little undercover work.

14. Bambi

Jenny's first stint as a barmaid at the Black Swan was devoted to training. She'd briefly experienced bar-work before, in order to reacclimatise to Civvy Street after leaving the army, but this pub was very different to the upmarket establishment of her previous employment. She already knew that she'd prefer it here; it was much more down-to-earth and friendly.

'Call me Ruby,' said the landlady, 'and anything you want to know, just ask. So, let's see how well you pull a pint.'

Jenny pulled the handle smooth and steady, and the tilted glass gradually straightened in her other hand as it filled with dark velvety liquid. A quarter inch foam head completed the perfect pint of Guinness and she held it up to the light. It looked and smelled so good that she was tempted to drink it, but thought that might give a bad impression to her new employer.

'Hey, you're a natural,' said Ruby, 'it won't take you long to settle in.'

'It seems I have big shoes to fill,' said Jenny, 'I hear that Bambi was very popular with the customers.'

'She was good at her job, and I'm sure she was the reason that half the blokes came here in the first place.'

'Such a tragedy. Had she been here long?'

'A couple of years, but it wasn't till she went that we realised we knew nothing about her. You know that form you completed with emergency contact details and everything? Well, when we tried to contact Bambi's, the phone was unobtainable and the email undeliverable. It was as if she never existed and had no-one to mourn her passing.'

'It was amazing, what you did,' said Jenny, 'that crowd-funding thing to pay for her funeral. You didn't have to do that.'

'Well, she lived with us here in the pub, you know. We had a spare room and she said she was new to the area, so it seemed the logical solution. There was no-one else to give her a decent send-off; and I felt bad that the bastard that killed her was one of our regulars. Not that any of us could have seen that coming. I'll leave you to it then; just shout if you need anything.'

It was fairly quiet at the beginning of the evening, so Jenny chatted amiably to Shaun, her fellow bar-operative. It seemed that he too was equally uninformed about the mysterious and enigmatic Bambi.

'She wasn't my type, if you know what I mean,' said Shaun, 'I go for a more muscular sort. We got on well enough, but she was never much of a one for conversation. I once asked where she was from and she replied "another world". I tried to delve further, but it seemed she wished to remain a woman of mystery.'

This is going to be harder than anticipated, thought Jenny as she began to question the wisdom of taking this job, on top of her PCSO duties. The extra cash would be welcome, but it appeared that there would be few clues to further her quest. Her brief exchanges with Ruby and Shaun had raised more questions than answers. Why had her police colleagues not been able to find any next-of-kin either?

A lesson in bar-craft followed when a customer returned his half-empty beer glass, with the complaint that there was a hair floating in it. A shaven-headed Shaun inspected it seriously, as if analysing its source. He glanced at Jenny. – 'Not one of yours, is it?' he enquired.

Jenny took a look. – 'No, it's black; not my colour.'

Shaun raised his eyes to the dark-haired customer and grabbed a clean half-pint glass. – 'Well, I think the jury's out on the previous owner of the offending item but, in the interests of goodwill, I'll replace what's left,' he said.

'Thank you.'

'Think yourself lucky it wasn't a curly one, Dear,' said Shaun, as he handed him the glass. The man scurried quickly back to his table.

'Well, that's a new one,' laughed Shaun, 'but I don't think he'll be pulling that stunt in here again.'

∞∞∞∞

Over the next few weeks Jenny probed gently whenever the opportunity arose, but little information was forthcoming. The landlady had concluded from Bambi's personal details form that she was thirty-seven years old and had previously worked in various retail jobs.

'A couple of years younger than me,' said Jenny. 'Such a waste.'

'But, bearing in mind that her emergency contact information was incorrect,' said Ruby, 'who knows the truth about her age and employment history? She probably made the whole lot up.'

'Perhaps she had a past that she wanted no-one to know about,' said Jenny.

Ruby looked askance at Jenny, as if a penny had dropped. – 'And, what's your interest? You've done nothing but ask questions about her since you started work here. Shaun said the same too.'

'Is it really that obvious?' Jenny squirmed.

'Well, you're not exactly subtle about it.'

Jenny hesitated, then decided to come clean. – 'Steve's friends asked me to investigate. They think he's innocent and, as I'm a PCSO and knew Steve too, they thought I might be able to find out something that would clear his name.'

'So, you tricked me into taking you on,' said Ruby.

'Yes, I guess so; but I genuinely like working here. I've enjoyed every minute of it.'

For an instant Ruby's expression tightened, a flash of anger that Jenny assumed would result in her immediate dismissal. She apologised profusely and asked if Ruby wanted her to finish her shift or leave now. Then Ruby's eyes softened as she sighed – 'I must admit that I found it all hard to believe too. Steve's been coming in here for years and he's the last person I would have suspected.'

'So, will you help me to get to the truth? If Steve's guilty, then he deserves to be where he is; but if there's evidence that was missed then I'd like the chance to find it.'

Ruby thought for a few moments, then nodded. – 'OK; what do you want from me?'

'Has her room been disturbed since it happened?' said Jenny.

'No, I keep meaning to give it a deep-clean but, whenever I think of what happened in there, I can't bring myself to go in. I was going to get it redecorated professionally to erase any trace of Bambi, but hadn't got round to it yet. Besides, it seems somehow disrespectful to do it so soon.'

'Then do you mind if I take a look around? There's probably nothing there, but it's worth a try.'

'Yeah, I guess there's no harm. I'll ask Shaun to hold the fort.'

Jenny followed Ruby up a narrow, creaky staircase, the carpet old and threadbare, in keeping with the decor. She hadn't had cause to venture into the living-area of the pub before and was surprised at the contrast to its meticulously crafted public face. Beige wallpaper peeled at the edges, tired blue paint cracked on skirting-boards, and cobwebs hung from dusty lampshades.

'I must apologise for the state of the place,' said Ruby. 'All our time and money goes on the pub and we're just about afloat. It's hard keeping a place like this going these days, but I wouldn't want to do anything else.'

As they approached a door at the end of the landing, Ruby retrieved a bunch of keys from her pocket. She hesitated before picking the correct key and placing it into the lock. – 'Do you need me to come in with you?'

'It's up to you,' said Jenny. 'You can leave me to it if you like, but I may have some questions if I find anything.'

Ruby took a deep breath. – 'OK, I'll wait at the door.'

Jenny entered a dark, stuffy room, curtains closed and the air stale and still. – 'Can I open the window?'

'Yes, might be a good idea.'

Once she'd pulled back the heavy, crimson curtains, Jenny took in the view as she struggled to release the stiff catch. Eventually it loosened and the window slid and shuddered open. The room looked out onto the street, an intermittently busy thoroughfare with a dentist and solicitor's office opposite. A welcome gust of wind freshened the room a little and Jenny turned to take in the scene of the crime.

The bed had been stripped, the duvet and sheets presumably removed for forensic evidence. A large mahogany-effect wardrobe stood in one corner, a matching dressing table in the other and, beside the bed, a random oak cabinet with a blue-shaded reading lamp. Ruby stood silently, framed in the doorway, as Jenny decided where to start.

'Do you know if they went through her clothes?' said Jenny.

'I just showed them in,' said Ruby. 'It was me that found the body and called the police after Bambi didn't turn up for her shift. I was too traumatised and they sent me downstairs with a nice lady police officer to calm me down. I assume they were thorough and looked through everything.'

'You poor thing, it must have been awful.'

'It's not something I've ever experienced before – a dead body. Look, can you just get on with it please? This is bringing it all back.'

'Yeah, sure,' said Jenny, as she opened the wardrobe doors. 'Sorry, this must be really difficult for you. Wow, she liked her clothes; there's plenty of choice in here.'

'She was renowned for her dress-sense, but it's all from charity shops. She always said we didn't pay enough for her to afford first-hand designer-label gear.'

Jenny pulled out a yellow cotton dress and commented on the simple, yet sophisticated style.

'Yes, and Bambi could always pull it off', said Ruby; 'she had the elegance of a model and a natural grace.'

Jenny placed it gently back on the rail and began the intrusive process of searching any item of clothing with pockets. It felt disrespectful to her colleagues, who should have already gone through this routine procedure in the course of the original investigation, but she needed to satisfy herself that nothing was missed. With so many outfits it was a time-consuming job, but Jenny persevered till the end. She was about to give up and move on to the other furniture, when her fingers touched something in the pocket of a pair of Levi's. The folded slip of paper was so small that she could see how anyone might have overlooked it, but there it was – a phone number. Jenny surreptitiously put it in her pocket and determined to decide what to do with it later.

She moved to the bed-side cabinet, carefully removed its contents and laid them on the bed. She wasn't expecting to find a diary that detailed every aspect of Bambi's life, but any kind of clue would be a start. There was no ID like a passport or driving licence, but Jenny assumed that anything like that would have been removed in the initial investigation. Instead, there was the usual paraphernalia that resides next to a lady's bed, within easy reach should it be required; Paracetamol, an inhaler, some other unidentified tablets; and a jewellery box containing various rings, necklaces, earrings and bracelets. She examined the jewellery in case any piece was personalised, a name or initials, anything that might hint at a relationship. Sure enough, engraved inside a gold ring embedded with three tastefully small diamonds, the barely visible initials EFS & ROC. Who were these people; deceased parents, grandparents perhaps? Was it a wedding ring? It looked expensive, yet it had a stylish subtlety that didn't scream ostentatious. She carefully placed it in her pocket to join the phone number.

Jenny was sure that Rob and his team had already supposed that none of these objects were worthy of further examination, but one other item on the bed caught her eye. A hardback copy of Lorna Doone by R. D. Blackmore stood out among the trivia of existence that lay scattered around it. Its red, gilt-lettered cover worn and its pages well-thumbed, it looked loved because it had obviously been read many times; but by how many and whom? Was it an original copy? It certainly looked old enough. Had it been purchased from an antique bookshop or handed down through generations of the same family?

Jenny picked it up and carefully opened its cracked, weak-hinged cover; its yellowing pages felt fragile in her hands. An eighteenth edition from 1881, a cryptic message on the inside cover read – "To Emmeline – take a look in the mirror. Who do you see? From Beatrice xx"

She studied the inscription. Was it as old as the book itself, intended for its original or a subsequent owner, or was it written for Bambi? Lost in conjecture, Jenny jumped as Ruby asked – 'Have you found anything?'

'Possibly; can I take a couple of things with me to check them out?'

'Don't see why not. I assume you'll be handing in what you've found to the police.'

'Yeah, of course,' said Jenny, 'but maybe not just yet. I want to know if it means anything first. They've closed the case, so may not welcome me dredging up further evidence.'

'Whatever you think is best. What on Earth am I going to do with all this stuff? Should I give it to charity or wait in case you find her family? I could do with renting out this room again as I need the income, but I doubt if anyone will take it once they know what happened in here.'

'You'll be surprised; people are always looking for somewhere to live, and they have short memories. If the clothes all came from charity shops, then maybe take them back. I'd keep hold of the jewellery for now; some of it may have sentimental value for someone.'

'Makes sense,' said Ruby. 'Thanks for making me face what I've been avoiding. I had to open this door sometime, but it's been easier with you here.'

Jenny carefully placed the book in her bag, respectful of its aged fragility, and made her way to the door. Before leaving, she turned and took one more look at the bric-a-brac on the bed. – 'Not much to show for a life, is it? Regardless of whether Steve did this or not, I intend to find out more about her; to find someone who cares enough to want to know what happened.'

15. The Professional Opinion

'So, is this an official visit?' asked Philip. 'No offence, but they wouldn't normally send a PCSO.'

'I'm just making further inquiries,' said Jenny. She didn't know why, but she felt as if she were the one under scrutiny.

'I was surprised that I wasn't asked any questions after it all happened,' said Philip.

'No-one came to see you?'

'Not even a phone call. I can't tell you much – patient confidentiality and all that.'

'OK, but in your professional opinion, do you think Ste…, er, Mr Brent, is capable of murder?'

Philip's answer sounded cold, as if read from a textbook on the subject. – 'We're all capable of murder, given the right provocation; but I didn't have any specific concerns in his case.'

'Look, I'll be straight with you,' said Jenny; 'I'm not here in any official capacity. Steve and I had seen each other socially a few times and I'm finding it hard to believe that he's a killer.'

'Yes, he told me about you. I find it hard to believe too, but my years in this profession have taught me not to make assumptions. We all have hidden depths and our public face often disguises turmoil within.'

'But his friends, who have known him far longer than I; they also say he couldn't have done it.'

'So, you are questioning the conclusions of your colleagues in this case.'

'Yes; oh, I don't know. They said there was overwhelming evidence.'

'DNA, is what I read in the paper,' said Philip, 'that's hard to argue with. Perhaps you are questioning your own judgement too, and you're angry with yourself that you fell for the wrong man.'

'Hey, you're good. How much are you charging for this consultation?'

'You can have this one on me. If it's any consolation, Steve really liked you; said you saved his life and he was feeling a lot more positive since he met you. That's why it came as such a shock when I heard what he'd done.'

'Well, that's nice to know, I think,' Jenny blushed. 'Thanks for your time. I'm more confused than ever now.'

'All part of the service,' said Philip, 'my rates are reasonable if you need to talk some more.'

'I'll bear it in mind,' said Jenny, as she shook Philip's hand and turned to leave. She hesitated – 'Do you really think he did it?'

'To be honest, no; but then I'm no cop, judge or jury.'

16. Amateur Sleuths

Jenny had convened this meeting to discuss what she'd found out so far, which admittedly wasn't much. In order to protect her potential career, she also intended to suggest that the quiz team do some of the donkey-work. Jenny laid out the evidence on the table before them.

'Is that it?' said Karen. 'What the hell are we supposed to deduce from this?'

'That's all there was,' said Jenny.

Karen gently opened the copy of Lorna Doone, as if afraid that it would fall apart at her touch. She read the message aloud – "To Emmeline – take a look in the mirror. Who do you see? From Beatrice xx"

'Well, we know that Bambi called herself Emma Forrester on her job application,' said Jenny. 'There's a chance that Emma may be short for Emmeline.'

'But this thing is so bloody old that the inscription could have been written in the 1800s,' said Trevor. 'How do we know the message was for her?'

'No, it's written in ballpoint,' said Karen, 'so it must be more recent than that.'

'Hey, well done,' said Alan, 'you're good at this.'

'Still not much to go on, though,' said Trevor.

'From Beatrice, it says,' said Karen. 'Emmeline and Beatrice are not names you hear where I grew up, and Bambi was quite well-spoken. Could be that she came from a more privileged background than the rest of us.'

'You speak for yourself,' said Alan, 'I woz brung up proper.'

'You lived on the next estate to me,' said Karen, 'and went to the same school. Don't go putting on your airs and graces with me.'

'What about the story of Lorna Doone,' said Jenny; 'I'm not familiar with it, but could there be any relevance?'

'I've read it, a long time ago,' said Karen. 'As I recall it's about a farmer who falls in love with a beautiful girl named Lorna, not realising that she is part of a family called the Doones, who are notorious and ruthless outlaws. Turns out that Lorna was kidnapped by them as a child.'

Karen delicately picked up the ring, studied its majesty and placed it on her finger. – 'Wow, it's beautiful; whoever gave her this must have thought a lot of her.'

'Take a look inside,' said Jenny.

Karen tried to remove it, but was pained to discover that it was firmly stuck. No matter how hard she pulled it wouldn't traverse her knuckle and, the more she tried, the immovable object became more fixed.

'Here, let me try,' said Alan, and he twisted and turned it while Karen complained that he was being too rough and that a more subtle approach might be required. – 'Go and ask at the bar for some butter,' she suggested.

Jenny did as requested and headed for Shaun.

'What on Earth do you want that for, Dear?' he laughed.

'My friend has a ring stuck on her finger.'

'Ah, yes; in my experience butter usually does the trick.'

Jenny returned with the requested lubricant, pleased that she'd provided some amusement for Shaun. The butter was applied and, after a little manipulation, the ring finally came free. Karen wiped it clean with a serviette and squinted at the inside, where she struggled to identify the lettering. – 'I have the wrong glasses on,' she complained and passed it to Trevor. 'You should be able to read it through those things.'

Indeed, Trevor could, aided by the enhanced magnification of his prescription spectacles. – 'It says, EFS & ROC. What are we supposed to glean from that?'

'EF may be Emma Forrester,' said Karen, 'but what about the S; and who is ROC?'

Sarah had contributed nothing so far, but had a more pragmatic approach. – 'Let's not get carried away with speculation. What do we have here? If we assume that Emmeline and Emma (a.k.a. Bambi) are one and the same; we also know that she knew someone named Beatrice, who was familiar enough to sign off with two kisses when she gave her this book, could be family or a good friend; the name Emma Forrester could either be real or made up, or even her married name; then we have this slip of paper with a phone number, which is our only concrete lead. How about I give this number a call tomorrow and find out who's on the other end?'

'Sounds like a good plan,' said Jenny, who was grateful for Sarah's practicality and willingness to take some of the responsibility from her shoulders. 'We also know that Bambi gave false personal information, which could indicate that she didn't want anyone to know about her past. Maybe she was running away from something, or someone.'

'Don't the police have a missing persons' register?' said Trevor. 'I assume your mob would have checked that out.'

Jenny felt obliged to defend 'her mob'. – 'It depends how long ago she went missing. These days it's hard to just vanish; there's CCTV everywhere and we all have a digital footprint through social media, or generally using phones and computers; but it wasn't always like that. If someone wanted to disappear without trace, even as recently as the 90s, it was much easier to cover their tracks.'

'Well, I'm not impressed to be honest,' said Trevor; 'we've got further sitting round this table for the last half-an-hour than the original investigation.'

'They're busy suburban cops,' said Jenny, 'not Sherlock Holmes. They took what Forensics gave them, which was Steve's DNA all over the scene of the crime, and reached their conclusions. The judge and jury agreed, so it wasn't just the police who put him away.'

'How about we meet up again at the end of the week to review progress,' said Sarah. 'I'll let you know how I get on with that phone call, Jenny.'

Once everyone had drifted away, Jenny brought Ruby up to speed. – 'It's not much, but it's a start,' said Jenny. 'It'll all probably lead nowhere.'

Ruby looked distracted, far away, as if trying to retrieve something from the recesses of her mind. Eventually she spoke – 'I overheard her on the phone once, thought nothing of it at the time, none of my business, but she was arranging to meet someone. Must have been some distance, because she was talking about train times; completely slipped my mind until now.'

'Did she say where she was going?'

'No, she saw me nearby and took herself off to her room. Had that weekend off, but wasn't herself when she came back; seemed upset about something. I asked if everything was OK, but she just said she was fine.'

'How long ago was this?'

Ruby furrowed her brow in thought. – 'Must have been about a month before she died.'

'Thanks; if only I had access to all the police resources, I could check out CCTV for the weekend in question and maybe find out who she met.'

'Then why don't you tell them what you're up to?'

'I will,' said Jenny, 'but I was hoping to present them with something worth investigating first. All we have at the moment is guesswork.'

Jenny left the pub with more problems than solutions echoing round her brain. What were the next steps? Should she be getting involved? Who could she turn to for advice?

17. Once a Cop...

Jenny's mum loved to read George his bedtime story, said it was her favourite part of the day. It was Jenny's too, but George often asked for Nanny to do it, so she conceded defeat and retired to the living room. There was so much familiarity to this room that it was at once comfortable and stifling. Echoes of her childhood would last as long as she called this place her home; from the porcelain figurine that she'd broken as a child, glued meticulously back together by Dad; to the haunting stares of the family portrait on the mantelpiece, like ghosts from a past life.

Jenny tried to relax in the comfy old armchair, her grandmother's home-embroidered antimacassar still in situ. She glanced at her dad for any sign that he would be in the mood for a chat. The news had just finished; yet more doom and gloom to add to yesterday's depressing outlook. There were plenty of good things that happened in the world and Jenny often wondered why they weren't given more prominence over the endless tales of conflict and rancour.

She bit the bullet and broached what was on her mind. Dad was a seasoned ex-copper with many a case cracked in his long and illustrious career. He was unimpressed when Jenny told him how she'd spent the recent weeks. – 'You could lose your job and scupper any chances of becoming a fully-fledged police officer. Is this fella really worth it?'

'It doesn't matter whether he's worth it or not,' said Jenny. 'If he's been wrongly convicted and I know stuff that could put that right, then it's my duty to investigate.'

'So, you'd do this for anyone, would you?'

'Of course.'

'Hmm, I don't believe you. And what about the officer in charge of the original investigation; Rob wasn't it? I worked with him before I retired; he's a good cop.'

'Well, I disagree,' said Jenny, 'I don't think he's been very thorough in this case.'

'OK, then convince me. What do you have?'

Jenny proceeded to bring her father up to speed on the efforts of the Black Swan Detective Agency, as he condescendingly christened them. As she recounted all they'd found, she wondered if there was enough there to warrant re-opening the case, or whether her judgement had been clouded. After all, it wouldn't be the first time.

'So, you've concocted this alternative story on this flimsy evidence,' said Dad. 'What about Steve's DNA being found at the scene; how can you explain that?'

'I can't, yet. Steve was adamant at the trial that he'd never been to her room, so there must be some other explanation. I'll work it out. I want to follow up these other leads and see if they take us anywhere. What I'd like to know is whether you think I have enough to take it to the Chief Inspector.'

Dad took another look through Jenny's notes and eventually concluded – 'If you want my advice, I'd let sleeping dogs lie and move on. If you want a career in the police it doesn't help to ruffle the feathers of a respected officer. Rob has been at the station for years and he's trusted by the Chief. I know you mean well, but you've got to look after number one, and PCSOs are expendable.'

This wasn't what Jenny wanted to hear and the disappointment showed in her face. – 'You know, I always looked up to you as a kid. My dad was an important man in the community. He went after the bad men and protected the good ones. Surely that's what it should be about and, if it's not, then I don't want a career in the police. I intend to examine this case properly, with or without your approval.'

Dad frowned. – 'You don't need my approval; you've always made up your own mind anyway. I just want you to be happy. I know you had your heart set on joining the police and I don't want anything to jeopardise it, that's all. You'll have my support, whatever you decide.'

'Thank you, but I'd rather have your blessing as well as your support.'

'Look, it's all very well being idealistic, but you have your future to consider. Mum and I aren't going to be around forever and, sooner or later, you'll have to stand on your own two feet. It's a good job, being a cop, and it'll set you up with a decent salary and pension. Do you really want to throw that away for some loser?'

'You don't even know him.'

'And nor do you, very well. You should also consider what you're getting into. In the unlikely event that you are right, then there's another cold-blooded murderer out there that you're proposing to go after. Promise me that you won't go anywhere alone if you start digging around.'

'Don't worry; I'll have the Black Swan Detective Agency as backup.'

'Well, that's very reassuring. Just be careful is all I'm trying to say.'

18. The Plan

Jenny nibbled on her breadcrumb-encrusted fried camembert, dipped in sweet chilli sauce; absolutely delicious, she thought. With no time to go home after her PCSO shift, she'd decided to eat at the pub prior to catching up with the others. Ruby told her that she looked knackered and wondered whether she wasn't taking on too much, to which Jenny responded that she was fine and ordered a well-earned dessert. Her role involved a lot of walking which prevented her from piling on the pounds, so she allowed herself the occasional indulgence. Ruby was right though, she was exhausted.

Gradually the motley crew that constituted Steve's friends wandered in, selected their libation of choice and gathered round the table. After exchange of the usual pleasantries, they got down to business.

'It was a genealogist, the number on the paper,' said Sarah.

'Well, that's a dead end then,' said Alan. 'I guess all ladies have to get their bits checked out now and again. Nothing suspect about that.'

'Not a gynaecologist, you moron,' said Karen, 'a genealogist; someone who looks into family trees and ancestry.'

'I knew that,' said Alan. 'And what did they say?'

'Oh, I didn't ask any questions about Bambi,' said Sarah, 'just established what their business was. I thought we should work out a strategy before wading in. They're not going to give me information on a client over the phone, are they? I thought we could devise a way of convincing them that we're working in an official capacity, or on Bambi's behalf.'

'And where are they based?' said Jenny.

'North Devon,' said Sarah, 'around Exmoor, I think.'

'Lorna Doone country,' said Karen. 'So, the book *is* linked to the mystery. It's getting more interesting with each new piece of information.'

'You're enjoying this, aren't you,' said Alan. 'It's all still just speculation, though.'

'Every mystery is speculation until it's solved,' said Karen. 'Why don't you make yourself useful, find out where this place is and how to get there. A good time to try out your new toy.'

Alan pulled a brand-new shiny phone from his pocket and, with a confused expression, attempted to fathom its buttons and screen. Eventually he was ready to enter the location.

'It's all very well owning a smart phone,' said Karen, 'but a smart phone is only as smart as the person who's using it. What's the name of the place, Sarah?'

'Lynton, it's called; up on the coast, I think. Googled it yesterday and it looks charming. Nice place for a long weekend if anyone's up for it.'

'I can't leave the brewery at the moment,' said Trevor. 'You know we've just expanded the business and everyone's after the new brew.'

'I can't get away during term-time,' said Alan, 'and I don't think the missus would be keen on being abandoned with the kids. It's alright for you, Karen. They're a bit more flexible with you admin bods.'

'There's a bit more to my job than admin,' said Karen, 'as well you know.'

'I'm in,' said Jenny, 'as long as I can get my parents to look after George.'

'Looks like it's just us then, girls,' said Karen.

'Are you sure you'll be OK?' said Trevor. 'You could be getting into some dodgy territory if there is a murderer still out there.'

'Yes, we're all grown-ups and we'll be careful,' said Sarah. 'Gone are the days when we needed men to hunt for food and provide protection.'

'Looks like we've been made redundant, Alan,' said Trevor. 'Not much point to our existence anymore.'

'Oh, you do have your uses, occasionally,' said Sarah. 'I'm more concerned about how *you'll* cope without me.'

'We should do it by public transport,' said Jenny. 'Bambi didn't drive and we could follow in her footsteps.'

'Yes, but I'd rather not end up in the same destination,' said Sarah, 'I'm too young for the graveyard. How about the weekend after next? I'll arrange the accommodation, and train and bus times.'

The plan was agreed in principle, along with a commitment to confirm availability the next day. Jenny felt good that she was contributing something to what she considered a just cause, whether that be proving Steve's innocence or honouring the memory of Bambi. She'd not known them long, but Jenny genuinely liked

Steve's disparate group of mates and warmed to their good humour and loyalty to their friend; whether or not it might be misguided.

She wondered if Steve was aware that he had such faithful friends and if he realised how lucky he was. It's only in adversity that you find out who you can rely upon, she thought. Who would be there for her if she ever needed anyone? Her ex-army colleagues were spread far and wide, and old friends had disappeared off the radar long ago. She had her parents and her son. Maybe it was time to reach out and make new acquaintances. Jenny was already looking forward to a weekend away with these total strangers; whatever their adventure may bring.

19. The Visitor

Steve had been in prison for the best part of six months, a mere fraction of his sentence, but it already felt so long that he was becoming institutionalised. Those around him, fellow inmates and prison officers alike, assumed he was culpable and treated him accordingly. The relentlessness of their accusatory eyes made him question his own innocence too. Could he have done it – had his medication caused a blackout and erased an act of murder from his consciousness and memory? There wasn't a day went by when he didn't ask himself whether, perhaps, he was guilty and really deserved this punishment.

He was told he had a visitor, which came as something of a surprise. Trevor had made the long trip a couple of times in the early months of his custody, but it seemed his friendship and patience had waned of late. His mother had disowned him and didn't want to hear his protestations of innocence, or excuses as she called them. Besides, she had his father to look after, a good man who was more deserving of her love. So, who else could it be?

Among the rest of his family, he was known as the man who fucked-up Christmas, due to a particularly fractious game of Monopoly one Boxing Day. Cousin Donald always played everything to win and took it as a personal affront to his competitive nature when Steve wilfully went against the spirit of the game.

Steve had accumulated a couple of modest properties on Fleet Street and gained the kudos of a hotel on Park Lane, after which he thought he'd have some fun, at Donald's expense. Cousin Michelle was virtually bankrupt when she landed on Park Lane and had resigned herself to an early exit from the game. Steve, however, had an interesting proposition. He'd decided to run his property portfolio as a co-operative he declared and, in return for a fraction of what Michelle owed, he would offer her a stake in his hotel, providing that she made a reciprocal arrangement when he landed on one of hers. That way, he argued, they'd both benefit from any profits accrued and mutually prosper. As the game progressed, Steve was surprised when a couple of other players opted to participate in the scheme, whilst Donald steadfastly declined and grew increasingly annoyed at its viability and growing success.

'That's not how you play the game,' he ranted, 'you're nothing but a damned communist.'

Mum too had complained that, if it carried on like this, the game would go on forever and there would never be a winner; whilst Steve replied that, with his way, everyone was a winner.

'That's all very well,' said Mum, 'but I have the dinner to get ready.'

She needn't have worried, for in the next moment Donald had upturned the board and stormed out, after Steve accused him of deliberately miscalculating the sum of his dice to avoid landing on the Supertax square. For months to come, they would find Monopoly money in every nook and cranny of the living-room.

All in all, he couldn't think of anyone who would go to the bother of coming to see him. The apparent desertion of all his friends and family combined to diminish Steve's self-worth, and added to the shock of seeing Jenny when he entered the visiting area. Subconsciously, he brushed back his unkempt hair in a futile attempt to make himself look more presentable. He approached with a quizzical expression and sat opposite her at a perfunctory booth with a reinforced glass screen – a momentary awkward silence, before Steve spoke first.

'It's great to see you, but what on Earth are you doing here?'

Jenny smiled. – 'It's good to see you too. How have you been?'

How to answer a question like that? Desperate, lonely, bereft of hope, depressed? No words seemed adequate. – 'Oh, you know, I've been on better holidays. The accommodation is basic, to say the least, and the food could be better. Going to write a strong letter of complaint to the travel agent when I get back. And how are you?'

'Not so bad; still trying to keep the peace and stop people doing anything stupid.'

'I can't tell you how much it means to see a familiar face; but why? I wouldn't think that you'd want anything to do with me.'

'You have some good friends out there,' said Jenny. 'The guys from your quiz team, they still don't believe you would kill anyone and they asked me to look into the case.'

'So, if they have that much faith, why has no-one been to visit, apart from Trev about four months ago?'

'Don't be too hard on them; this place is quite a distance, and in the middle of bloody nowhere.'

'Yeah, I guess you're right and they have their own lives to lead,' sighed Steve. 'I'm sorry, but this existence does tend to make one a little cynical. Have you found any new evidence, then?'

Jenny hesitated, as if she didn't want to give him false optimism. – 'Not hard evidence as such, but we have a few leads that we're going to follow up.'

'So, you think the cops may have missed something?'

'I don't want to be dismissive of the efforts of the officer in charge, but it's possible that he may have been a bit lazy in his investigations. As far as he was concerned it was an easy collar, a feather in his cap and it made the station figures look good. On top of that, DNA matches are a major factor in most convictions.'

'Well, it's reassuring that they have the interests of justice at heart,' said Steve.

'I'm not suggesting that they deliberately covered up evidence that would have presented other options, I'm merely saying that they didn't look too hard in the first place. Look, I don't want to raise your hopes too high, but we're going to do some digging and try to get the case reopened. My superiors may not be too happy though, as all my inquiries have been off the record. I'm just a PCSO remember, not a proper cop, and they won't welcome the embarrassment if they've got it wrong.'

'That would be amazing if you could get them to look at it again, but if I didn't do it, then someone else must have. Are there any other suspects?'

Jenny shook her head. 'We're working on it, but we don't have anything yet.'

Overwhelmed by this unexpected brief encounter, Steve could feel the tears behind his eyes. He tried to hold them back, but one escaped and rolled down his cheek. – 'No-one has ever shown this much belief in me before. Why are you going to so much trouble?'

'Your friends were pretty convincing with their character-references, and I hate injustice. If we've got the wrong man, then it's our duty to put it right.'

'And I thought it might be because you liked me.'

'I do, but that's for another day.' Jenny looked him in the eye. 'If you did it, then you should be honest with me now and stop wasting my time.'

Steve returned eye contact; clear blue and beautiful eyes that he would never forget. – 'No, I swear I'm innocent.'

'Then that's good enough for me. 'I'll do all I can to get you out of here.'

'Do you have the ladder with you, then?' Steve whispered.

'Within the constraints of the law, I should add.'

Steve placed his hand on the glass. – 'Thank you so much.'

Jenny hesitated then mirrored his hand from her side.

'Time's up,' shouted the guard from the back of the room. Jenny stood and said goodbye for now. The visitors and prisoners went their separate ways once more. Most wore expressions of resigned inevitability; but not Steve this time. Was there really a remote possibility that he could be exonerated?

20. Go West

Jenny was there first; she found a bench outside the railway station and plonked herself down on its uncomfortable slats to wait for Sarah and Karen. Jenny had hardly slept, with the excitement and uncertainty of the forthcoming adventure playing on her already troubled mind. It had been a tearful farewell with George; he wasn't used to Mummy going away for weekends and had clung to her neck, until she'd managed to calm him down with the promise that she'd bring him back a present.

Barely a cloud in the sky, but still very chilly in the early morning, Jenny was glad she'd decided to wear her puffer-jacket. She was beginning to regret her suggestion that they travel by public transport, as it would mean trains in and out of London and a couple of bus changes at the other end. They wouldn't get there till mid-afternoon, despite their early start. Nonetheless, she was looking forward to a change of scenery and was pleased to see Sarah and Karen come round the corner.

'You're cutting it a bit fine, aren't you?' said Jenny.

'We have ten minutes yet,' said Sarah. 'I got the tickets yesterday, so all we have to do is get on the train.'

'What about my coffee, though?' said Jenny. 'I don't function in the morning without a shot of caffeine.'

'No, me neither,' said Karen. 'Come on, we've still got time.'

With minutes to spare and coffees in hand, they boarded the sparsely populated carriage, hoisted their cases onto the rack and made themselves comfortable. As the train left the station, Jenny sighed, sat back in the worn upholstery and took her first sip of the day. – 'Ah, that's better; I'm awake now. How are you both?'

'Fine thanks,' said Sarah. 'Trev's got his instructions on how to survive without me, but I doubt he'll remember any of it. He was quite apprehensive about me going on this trip; said we could be in danger if we unearth anything about the real murderer.'

'Yeah, my dad said pretty much the same,' said Jenny. 'They could be right; we'll have to be on our guard.'

'That's the advantage of only having yourself to worry about,' said Karen. 'There's a lot to be said for independence.'

'Have you not got anyone in your life?' said Jenny.

'Not at the moment, but I'm open to offers. What about you?'

'It's a long story, but I'm divorced and better off that way; I've been through hell and come out the other side and have no desire to go back.'

'But you must like Steve, or you wouldn't be here,' said Karen.

'Yeah, I think I do. My dad thinks I'm mad to get involved and he's probably right. Whatever we find out it's going to be a long, drawn-out process to prove his innocence, launch an appeal and get him released.'

'So, you're convinced he didn't do it, then,' said Sarah.

'I went to see him last weekend and yes, I think he's innocent.'

'You didn't tell us you were going,' said Karen.

'No, but I wanted to hear it from him before I committed to this trip.'

'And how is he?' said Sarah.

'He didn't look too good. Said it was a nightmare in there. We didn't get long, but I told him we're trying to help, seemed to buck him up a bit. Think he was just pleased to have a visitor.'

'Oh, God,' said Karen, 'poor Steve. He's never going to fit in and he's bound to get picked on.'

'He'll be a different person when he comes out.' said Sarah. 'You can't go through an experience like that without it changing your perspective on life.'

It was the beginning of rush-hour when they arrived in the capital and people were everywhere, all going about their daily business with little thought for their fellow travellers. With a deep breath, they entered the throng and descended to the underground. After a relatively short hop to Paddington, they boarded the train to Exeter.

Jenny tried to relax and catch up on some sleep, but she never could switch off when travelling. Instead, she grabbed her Kindle and continued to read Lorna Doone, while Sarah got lost in her phone, and Karen in the sounds on her iPod. In the interests of research, Jenny considered it her duty to delve into the slaughter and romance of this historical novel that may or may not be at the heart of the mystery. At first, she had struggled with the archaic prose and long, cumbersome sentences but, after a while, began to marvel at the descriptive language and lost herself in the story. Jenny tried to blot out the rampant sexism and primitive class values that infused each chapter, telling herself that these attitudes were from a different era and that more people had an enlightened outlook these days. Or was it just concealed beneath a cloak of political correctness, still very much there, but afraid to speak its name aloud?

The countryside came to life; the bleak and lonely landscape of Exmoor seeping through every page, as the tale of murder and love unfolded. Jenny wondered how much it had changed since the days of John Ridd and Lorna. Hopefully the roads were more navigable and there were no longer outlaws behind every rock, waiting to ambush innocent travellers. But at least back then their wickedness was palpable and the residents of the moor knew to be on their guard. Bambi's murderer was more insidious and hid behind a mask of anonymity, their weapon an everyday item of clothing, rather than a blunderbuss.

Karen too had revisited the book in recent weeks, in case it had any significance in Bambi's life. Half-an-hour into the journey she broached the subject with Jenny, whose furrowed brow told of great effort and concentration.

'It's a bit of an epic, isn't it?' said Karen. 'What do you reckon – a fine wine to be savoured one sip at a time, or a tough old steak that takes forever to chew?'

'A bit of each, actually. I've just read another of the many references to women knowing their place and being respectful to men – those bits make my blood boil but, apart from that, I suppose it's a decent yarn.'

'That was the way they thought back then,' said Karen, 'and some men still do. All that crap is handed down from father to son and it takes generations of education for it to change.'

'I just wish that misogynistic bastard, John Ridd, could sit with us now,' said Jenny. 'We'd soon put him right.'

Karen laughed – 'Yes, it would be interesting to talk to all kinds of fictional characters. But do you think the book could hold any clues about Bambi's life and death?'

'All we know is that it was in her possession, and that she visited a genealogist near where the story is based. I doubt that it's a coincidence, but we won't know till we find out why she went there.'

'I've made us an appointment with the genealogist tomorrow morning at ten,' said Sarah. 'Mr Heritage, his name is, would you believe? Seemed to fall for our little lie and said he'd be happy to help; sounded like an obliging chap and I felt a bit guilty about deceiving him.'

'No point in us all going,' said Karen. 'I'll take a walk round town while you're there, see if I can find the library. We may need to access local info and archives.'

Conversation was sparse as the train sped on to its destination, Jenny absorbed in the story and speculation as to its relevance, Sarah watching the scenery wiz by, and Karen intermittently dosing off. Once on the bus to Lynton, the landscape began to reflect the vivid descriptions in Lorna Doone. Jenny wondered at the skills of the author; she'd never been here before, but already felt as if she knew the area, its wild and windswept ways, its beauty and dangers. Little did she know how the splendour and perils would come to manifest. If she had, she may have jumped on the next train back.

They climbed wearily off the bus, the early start catching up with them. Jenny was looking forward to finding somewhere to eat, a local pub perhaps, and an early night. Sarah and Karen wholeheartedly agreed and added that a few drinks would slip down nicely too. But first they had to find their B & B.

Sarah had booked a secluded and homely-looking place online, arguing that they should remain as inconspicuous as possible. – 'Word gets around in a small town,' she said, 'and, if our killer is about, we don't want them to know there's a bunch of strangers asking questions.'

'That's all very well,' said Karen, 'but where the hell is this place?'

They'd walked the narrow streets for ten minutes, the small wheels on their cases designed for airport terminals, rather than the uneven and steep pavements of Lynton. Sarah had already complained that it was all uphill and that she wasn't built for climbing. – 'It's the next path on the left, I think,' she said at last.

It was a chilly afternoon and a gradually saturating sea-mist added to their eagerness for warmth and sanctuary. Eventually they found the Victorian guesthouse and rang the doorbell, to no answer. Sarah had been sent an email with codes for a key safe, in the eventuality that there was no-one in to welcome them. They entered and called hello, to nothing but an echo. The place appeared to be deserted.

'Guess we better find our rooms and make ourselves at home,' said Sarah. 'I'm sure someone will be around later.'

Karen and Jenny were to have the twin room. Sarah had told them that she snored rather loudly and that, if they wanted any sleep, it would be inadvisable to share with her. Jenny suspected this was a ruse to gain the single room, but was happy to concede as Sarah had organised the trip. Besides, she could do with the company and found Karen an amiable companion. The rooms were comfortable and clean, with biscuits, tea and coffee laid on. A foot between Karen's bed and Jenny's, her time in the army had accustomed her to sharing accommodation and Jenny could sleep anywhere. It felt strange at first to be the only guests in an empty house, but at least they had each other.

Once freshened-up and changed, they wrapped up warm and headed out again in search of the Crown, recommended by all the online forums on such matters. The busy old coaching inn had been there since the mid eighteenth century and was the perfect place for the refreshment of exhausted wanderers. Walls adorned with the amazing anthropomorphic art of Mick Cawston, his animals characterised in poses of pub clientele and musicians, it all added to the warm and welcoming atmosphere. Decent local ales and classic pub grub with good vegetarian options for Karen, served with genuine bonhomie and washed down with a few glasses of their chosen beverage, it was a couple of hours well-spent in agreeable company.

The customers comprised a broad mix of holidaymakers and locals, their conversations merged in a constant background hum of cordiality. Jenny studied every face, wondering if the murderer was among them; then she returned to reality and tried to keep her imagination in check. The evening meandered by in a pleasant manner, as they got to know each other better. Jenny expertly fielded questions about her marriage and what went wrong. It had been four years now, but it still felt as raw and distressing as when she and George had walked out of their home for the final time.

Instead, she steered the subject to how they could spend the weekend productively. Could they find out if Bambi came from this area? If so, were there any more family around and did they know anything? It was concluded that, after their meeting in the morning, a plan would emerge based on information gathered. The rest of the evening was consumed in honing their story and queries for Mr Heritage.

Suitably revitalised and relaxed from fine food and drink, they headed back to their accommodation. Disconcerted to find that they were still alone, they made their way up the creaky staircase to their rooms and locked the doors. It had seemed eerie enough when they'd arrived, but now it was dark too.

The day had been long and, despite their uneasiness, the weary, wary travellers snuggled down in the comfy beds. Despite her tiredness, Jenny found it hard to get to sleep. She missed George and felt alone, a fundamental part of her so far away. She tried to justify her absence. Was it a quest for justice, or had Steve got under her skin?

Her prison visit had brought it home – how lost and isolated he must be in there.

21. Calaboose

It had been a rude awakening for Steve, a new low among all the lows in his sorry existence; but here he was, in calaboose and it wasn't a bad dream. A minimum of fifteen years, the judge had specified. It hadn't sunk in at first; that a black-robed man in a grey, curly judicial wig had passed a sentence that would terminate his freedom for such a long time, but gradually the gravity dawned. This was to be his life until he was at least in his sixties and it panned out before him in all its uniformity.

He'd not only been condemned by judge and jury, the press had been rampant too, as they'd delved unscrupulously into his private-life and character. They'd plunged the depths to invent stories for the titillation of their gullible readers, in pursuit of the destruction of a previously unblemished man. There were quotes from people he barely knew; neighbours who said he'd kept himself to himself, but they thought there was something dodgy about him; ex-employers who said he'd had time off for stress and mental health issues; they'd even gone back to his school days and youth club to paint a picture of a withdrawn and lonely lad with few friends. The papers and TV news reports had been so thorough in their character-assassination that, even if his innocence had been proven, he wouldn't be able to show his face in public again.

As he'd entered the prison, his thoughts had drifted back to that evening on the railway bridge and he wished that Jenny had let him jump; now he really had nothing to live for. Those simple freedoms that he'd taken for granted, the liberty to move at will through the world, now had immeasurable value. No longer would he be able to stop for a pint on his way home, go for a walk in the countryside, enjoy evenings with friends, or engage in banter with work colleagues.

He was advised to do his time without fuss or rancour, keep his nose clean and stay out of trouble. – 'You don't give us any hassle and we won't give you any.'

The discussion had turned to how he could spend his time constructively whilst he completed his sentence. He was going to be incarcerated for at least a decade and a half, and he wanted to know how the other prisoners filled their days. After being told that it wasn't a bloody holiday camp, he was given his options. Apparently, you could learn new skills, work at making clothes or furniture, engineering or gardening. There were opportunities to study for qualifications too. He was asked what his interests were and he'd replied that he was an avid reader. Did they have a library? Yes, but that was the job everyone wanted.

Steve was to share a cell with a chap named Martin, a burly and surly fellow with close-cropped hair and numerous tattoos. Martin had immediately made it clear that he wasn't here for the social life, hated small talk and had no desire to get to know his fellow prisoners.

The cell was about the size of the spare-room in his previously under-appreciated house, and contained a bunk bed (Steve was to have the top), a sink, a toilet, a table and a couple of cupboards. The loss of privacy would be punishment enough and Martin was probably feeling the same. So far, each step Steve had taken into the prison had deepened his despair, but the sight of this room and the unwelcoming nature of his cellmate plunged him deeper still.

He wasn't expecting Martin to hang up the bunting and throw a party, but some basic civility and cordiality would have been nice. Any questions Steve had about prison life were met with a grunt or single syllable answer and, apart from that, he was to discover that Martin snored like a chainsaw, punctuated by heavy breathing worthy of a seasoned pervert. This was going to take some getting used to. He'd barely slept for the first three nights and only on the fourth due to exhaustion.

But adapt he did and, in the absence of scintillating conversation, he'd immersed himself in any reading material he could get his hands on. After a few months of acclimatisation and familiarisation with the Draconian prison routines, he'd been summonsed to the office – some lucky sod had done his time and there was a vacancy in the library! Was he interested?

Steve had smiled as a surly prison officer showed him in. Books – loads of them. A bastion of civilisation in such a hostile environment; a butterfly on a turd; a spring-flower on a slagheap; virtue among evil. Jayden would show him the ropes.

'You're privileged to get this job,' Jayden told him. 'I've been after this job for years and only just get it; for good behaviour they tell me. Then a white man who's been here for five minutes walks straight in. Wha' your qualification?'

'I just told them I like reading.'

'Ha, I tell them that too. What conclusion do you reach from that?'

'That there's racism in here.'

Jayden clapped sarcastically. – 'Ten outa ten. Why should here be any different? There's racism everywhere. So, what's a fine, upstanding citizen like you doing in a place like this?'

'I thought that subject was off limits,' said Steve.

'Yeah, it's not my business what you did, man; it's just that you look so out of place; like you don't belong in here with all these bad men.'

'I was convicted of murder, but I'm innocent; I didn't do it.'

Jayden smiled. – 'They all say that, man. "It wasn't me, wrongful arrest, mistaken identity," all the excuses under the sun; but if you're in here, you must have done something bad.'

'We've all made mistakes in life, but I'm not a murderer.'

'Tell me mind yours if you like, but who you supposed to have killed?'

'The barmaid at my local. She was a lovely lady; they called her Bambi.'

Jayden nodded. – 'So, Bambi knocked ya back and ya got mad.'

Steve recalled how he felt when Bambi had told him she wasn't interested; it was more resignation and hopelessness than anger. Jayden was obviously street-wise and probably knew much more about human nature than he, but Steve couldn't get used to the fact that his fellow inmates immediately assumed that he was guilty.

'How did you know I'd asked her out?' said Steve.

'By the way you chat about her, the look on your face.'

'So, you like to read people as well as books. What about you, how come you ended up here?'

'I stabbed someone; no excuses, I did it. He was just a youth like me when it happened, 16 years old; and if I don't knife him he woulda knifed me. A fuckin' waste of his life, and mine too.'

'What was the argument about?'

'Just some petty gang stuff, turf and drug war, that kinda thing; normal life where I come from. Not a day goes by when I don't see the fear on his face as his life drain away.'

'So, it was a tough neighbourhood, where you lived,' said Steve.

'Yeah, it was tough, man. A youth have no choice but to fight to survive.'

'What about your parents; didn't they try to stop you going down that path?'

Steve noticed Jayden's expression change, as if he were explaining something to a child. – 'Ha, you come from a different world, man. I never knew my father; he split before I leave the womb. My mother had to work all hours to keep me and my sister, so she was never there much either.'

'So, you had no-one around?' said Steve.

'There was Simon from the youth centre, before they shut it down. Closest thing I had to a father. He was the only one who cared. He cared about all of us, man, and try to show us the right way. But the government take away the money, so the place had to close. Last time I see Simon, he was begging in a shop doorway. I buy him fish and chips that night, but I never see him again. They take his living, they take his pride, his purpose and dignity. They throw him out of his flat, cos he can't pay the rent or feed his family. In the end even Simon had no choice, and all the youth he used to help are back on the street.'

'That's a really sad story.'

'It's real life, man; it happens all cross London, and other cities too. We're on the street cos that's where they want us; that way they keep us in our place. They don't want us to succeed or have opportunities; they keep us oppressed and then say we're all criminals.'

'You've obviously given it a lot of thought, about your situation,' said Steve.

'Nothing else to do in here, man, is there?' Jayden pointed to a trolley full of books. – 'We have to put those back on the shelf in alphabet order; think you can manage that?'

'Yeah, I'll give it a go; and thanks, this is the first civilised conversation I've had since I've been here.'

'Who do you share a cell with?'

'Martin.'

'What, big Martin with the tattoos? You're not likely to get any conversation there, but Martin's harmless. He looks a lot scarier than he is. You may not think it now, but you'll find out there are worse dudes you could be shacked-up with.'

'Yeah, I've yet to meet some of the prison's more colourful characters.'

'Don't be in too much of a hurry. Trust me, there's some you need to stay away from.'

It was good advice. If only Steve had listened!

22. A Can of Hornets

Bed and Breakfast, it had said when Sarah booked. The beds were extremely comfortable and they'd all slept very well; even Jenny when she'd finally drifted off. Now it was time to ascertain whether anyone actually lived here; and would they be around to prepare and serve their breakfast?

They need not have worried because the landlady welcomed them heartily, explained that she and her husband had been visiting friends the previous day, and they were expecting further guests later that day. Their apprehension evaporated immediately and the extensive menu only cheered them further. Far from the foreboding establishment of their first impressions, their hosts couldn't have been more accommodating; and the breakfast was something else!

Suitably refreshed and full of good food and optimism, Jenny and Sarah made their way to their morning appointment, sun glinting on gentle waves below and birds singing from verdant treetops. They'd left Karen at the library and it was a further fifteen-minute walk through narrow streets to their destination.

'Ah, welcome to my humble abode ladies,' said Mr Heritage, 'please come in. I was very sorry to hear of Ms Forrester's passing; under terrible circumstances I gather. A real tragedy, she seemed utterly charming.'

A grey-haired, smartly dressed man, James Heritage oozed charisma and dignity. He ran his business from a pretty and well-maintained cottage in its picture-postcard setting, complete with immaculate garden and magnificent view across the bay. It was hard to imagine a more idyllic location. After formal introductions, he led Jenny and Sarah through to a comfortable, cosy living room, with display cabinets full of antique vases and trinkets against three of the walls. The other was occupied by a splendid oak bookcase, filled with ancient tomes. Jenny and Sarah admired the array of exquisite items, while he fetched two teas and a coffee from the kitchen.

'What a stunning collection,' said Sarah, upon his return.

'Thank you, it's just a little hobby of mine; taken years to accumulate, but I sometimes wonder if it's a sin to lock such beautiful objects away, where only I get to enjoy them. So, how can I be of assistance?'

Sarah took a sip from the fine-china tea-cup before answering – 'We are solicitors working on behalf of the Public Administrator's office as executors for the late Ms Forrester. At her place of employment, the emergency and next of kin details she gave were unobtainable, so we are trying to find any family she may have. One of the items found during the investigation into her murder was a slip of paper with your number; we wondered if you might have any information that could help.'

Jenny nibbled on a delicious luxury biscuit, covered in thick white chocolate; bet these are from Waitrose, she thought. She observed that Sarah looked uncomfortable in the delivery of her prepared preamble and hoped that Mr Heritage hadn't noticed. She too, fidgeted in her chair and felt as if it were obvious that it was all a pack of lies.

James Heritage looked at them askance. – 'You know, in my line of work you are obliged to take care with client confidentiality, even if the client is deceased. I was intrigued when I received your email and made a few basic checks on your company; just normal procedure and no offence intended. May I ask why you have no website, unheard of in this day and age; or no registration with the Solicitors Regulation Authority?'

Jenny wasn't surprised at this question. After all, investigation was his business; it involved a lot of digging and verification, not necessarily taking things at face value. James was obviously a shrewd man of integrity and, to be honest, it wouldn't have taken a great deal of effort to unravel their flimsy ruse. Despite her anticipation of his suspicion, she couldn't bring herself to utter the words she had ready. Jenny glanced at Sarah who, going by her hesitation and inability to look him in the eye, was apparently feeling the same. Jenny decided to come clean, endorsed by a nod from Sarah.

'OK, it's a fair cop; and we probably don't look much like solicitors anyway.'

'On the contrary, you are both very convincing; your fake company, however, is not. So, what is your real interest in Ms Forrester and her family?'

Another nod from Jenny, and Sarah spilled the beans. – 'She was the barmaid at our local, and the man convicted of her murder is a friend of ours. We believe he has been wrongly accused and imprisoned. We're simply trying to uncover evidence that may clear his name and, possibly, in the process, find the actual murderer.'

'Intriguing,' said James, 'I am quite partial to a good murder mystery. And you are completely certain of your friend's innocence?'

'Absolutely,' said Sarah.

James Heritage joined his hands together with forefingers extended, creating an Eifel Tower shape beneath his nose, deep in thought as he considered these extraordinary revelations. Eventually he looked up. – 'OK, then persuade me. What evidence do you have?'

Meticulously, Jenny recounted the whole story, with the occasional interjection from Sarah. From the discovery of the body; through the inadequate police investigation and the results of her own search of Bambi's room, to the unanimous character references for Steve. In conclusion, she lay out on the coffee table the meagre evidence gathered from Bambi's room, the slip of paper with James's phone number, the engraved ring, and the ancient copy of Lorna Doone, with its cryptic message within.

After retrieving a magnifying glass from a drawer behind him, James studied the ring carefully. He nodded knowingly, as if the initials within meant something. Next, he turned his attention to the book, which he picked up cautiously, his gentle hands displaying a reverence for all things antique. A glint in his eye, he stared at it for at least a minute before speaking.

'I have handled many copies of Lorna Doone in my time, but this must be one of the finest specimens I have seen. It is probably worth a lot of money.'

Jenny thought about the time when she'd plonked it on the table in the Black Swan for everyone's perusal. What if one of them had knocked over a glass or bottle and soaked its ancient pages in beer? She considered how she'd transported it here, in the bottom of her case alongside a plastic bag containing a pair of mud-encrusted sturdy walking shoes. She vowed to treat it with more respect in future.

James carefully opened the book and read the message inside its cover. He shook his head with an expression of sadness. – 'Now, that's a real shame. It breaks my heart when someone scrawls across a precious item such as this in ballpoint pen. Not only does it decrease its value, but it is a desecration of a work of art.'

'But do they mean anything to you, the words they wrote and the initials on the ring?' said Sarah.

James hesitated before answering – 'I have to consider the implications if I decide to help you. Your story is a credible one and I admire your loyalty to your friend, but there are others who will be affected if we start digging; those who will be unaware of Ms Forrester's sad demise for a start. And trust me, from my research thus far, there is a can of worms beneath all this that may be better left unopened.'

'So, what do you suggest?' said Sarah. 'One way or another we are determined to uncover the truth.'

'I would suggest that you don't go steaming in like a runaway train. This must be handled sensitively and cautiously. If I am to contribute to your cause, then I must insist that you allow me time to speak with a few people first; primarily out of respect to the family of the deceased, but also to prepare them for the inevitable questions that will follow.'

'So, she did have family in this area,' said Sarah.

'Yes, she was born and grew up not far from here. That is all I am prepared to tell you at the moment. Can we meet again when I've consulted the family?'

'But we go back on Monday,' said Jenny, 'we're only here for the weekend.'

'Then you must weigh up the value of your friend's liberty against how much time you are willing to spend. It is way too complex to solve in a weekend. I will try to make contact with them this afternoon. It is not going to be a pleasant task, but I will come back to you tomorrow. I think it best, at this stage, that I don't mention your part in all of this and that you remain inconspicuous. This is a small community and rumours spread quickly. Thereafter, I recommend that you make arrangements for another visit to our beautiful part of the country, and preferably for a longer stay.'

Jenny and Sarah shook his hand and thanked him as they left the cottage, his handshake as firm and sure as expected.

'My pleasure, ladies,' he said. 'Hopefully we can look forward to some stimulating conundrum cracking ahead.'

∞∞∞∞

As arranged, they met Karen in the increasingly buzzing Crown, in perfect time to sample the lunchtime menu; pizzas all-round the unanimous decision. Whilst waiting, they brought Karen up to speed with details of their meeting.

'It's obvious that he knows a fair bit,' said Jenny, 'but he won't tell us anything yet.'

'Understandable, I suppose,' said Karen. 'And can we trust him to be discreet? We don't want anyone to suspect why we're here.'

'I think so,' said Sarah, 'seemed sincere enough to me.'

Jenny concurred and enquired how Karen had spent the morning. She looked rather pleased with herself and Jenny could tell that she was itching to get something off her chest.

'Well, it's possible that I may have solved part of the mystery already,' said Karen.

'What!' Jenny and Sarah cried in harmony.

'They have a brilliant section in the library where you can research if you're interested in family trees. They have birth, marriage and death records, as well as local census documents going back hundreds of years; all saved on computer. I punched in Emma Forrester and the only match was a 93-year-old woman from a small village about twenty-five miles away. That was obviously a dead end, so I started looking through old newspaper headlines and cuttings, and that's when it started to get interesting.'

'How did you know what dates to look for?' said Sarah.

'Well, as we believe that Bambi was in her late thirties, I began by searching stories from the last twenty-five years. It was a longshot, but I thought that, if anywhere, I might find something about her in the local rag. Took me all morning, but eventually I found something that may match our girl.'

Impatient to get to the crux of the matter, Jenny suspected that Karen was milking the story for dramatic effect and suggested she get to the point.

'OK, OK, give me a chance. While you two have been relaxing in a cosy cottage with tea and biscuits, I've been working hard, you know. One story I found concerned the disappearance twenty years ago of a 19-year-old named Emmeline O'Connell. She went out walking on Exmoor, as she often did, and was never seen again. Obviously, there were major searches carried out, involving the police, the army with helicopters, and hundreds of volunteers, but they found nothing. After exhausting every avenue, they finally gave up and classified it as a 'missing, presumed dead' case. The official police statement said that it was likely she met her end on the moor, either through accident or foul play, but a body was never found.'

'So, what makes you think that this girl was Bambi?' said Sarah.

'Well, this is where it gets a bit speculative, but it does fit together with the evidence we have. When Emmeline went missing, she was recently married to a local businessman named Richard O'Connell. Her maiden-name was Emmeline Foster-Smythe – EFS & ROC – the initials in the ring and the Emmeline written in the book cover, perhaps? That's as far as I got – I'd like to go back and follow this up, but it's closed now till Tuesday.'

The wonderful smell hit them a moment before the waiter arrived, with three succulent-looking pizzas just waiting to be devoured. A grind or two of black pepper, a sprinkle of chilli-oil and Jenny was ready to go; but, before the first mouthful, a high-five for Karen. – 'Hey, well done; you have been busy. That all sounds plausible and it's something to investigate further.'

'Yes, I know,' said Karen, 'there are other leads to try. If it is her, then we now know her maiden name; we can find out where she's from and any family that's still around. We can also look up this Richard O'Connell chap. I would have stayed there all day, but it closed at lunchtime and they had to kick me out.'

'Let's leave it for now and see what Mr Heritage comes back with,' said Sarah. 'He warned us about blundering in and stirring up a hornets' nest.'

'A can of worms,' said Jenny.

'What?'

'A can of worms, he said; there was nothing about a hornets' nest.'

Sarah grabbed the bottle of chilli-oil and good-naturedly threatened Jenny's pizza with it. – 'Don't be so pedantic; it means the same thing, doesn't it?'

Jenny pushed the bottle away and turned to Karen. – 'We've got no chance,' she laughed. 'How are we supposed to solve a complex mystery such as this, when we're working with someone that can't tell the difference between a worm and a hornet?'

'Well, either way,' said Karen, 'I reckon the worm will turn and there'll be a sting in the tale.'

Jenny and Sarah groaned in unison. – 'Someone's been reading too many murder-mystery books,' said Sarah. 'Let's just call it a can of hornets.'

23. It's Against the Law

They spent the afternoon in exploration, before deciding to take the cliff-railway down to Lynmouth; "the highest and steepest water-railway in the world" – they'd read in the leaflet from the Tourist Information Centre. One thing to which they could testify is that it was bloody steep. Jenny held on to the rail inside the cabin as it trundled down the cliff, and hoped that the breaks were regularly serviced. A bright spring day, the view was stunning as they made the almost sheer descent among trees and beneath bridges.

The seaside still evoked that childish excitement in Jenny and she vowed to cherish that feeling forever, as they strolled among the old fishing cottages and watched boats bob gently in the harbour. Karen too, seemed overcome with childlike wonderment, for she cried out loudly at the sight of an ice-cream van. – 'You can't come to the seaside without having an ice-cream,' she said, 'it's against the law.'

'That's not in any of the police training books that I've read,' said Jenny.

'No, Karen's right,' said Sarah, 'it's in the same section as you can't have fish and chips without salt and vinegar.'

With a lick of the lips and salivating taste buds, Jenny approached the van and placed her order; a classic cone filled with the finest creamy Devonshire ice cream. Eyes as wide as her inner-child's, she waited in awed anticipation as the smooth mixture spiralled into the cone; a piece of magic that would never grow old.

'Do you want a flake in that, love?' said the jovial man behind the counter.

Jenny didn't like being called 'love' by anyone, but let it slide. – 'Yes, please; you can't have an ice-cream without a flake, it's against the law.'

Sarah and Karen burst into laughter, much to the confusion of the ice-cream man – it wasn't that funny. Silence prevailed as they savoured the age-old delight of a seaside tradition; the knowledge that it wasn't good for you, temporarily forgotten in a tongue-tingling taste beyond resistance. It was always an argument between the conscience and the appetite and, on this occasion, it seemed inevitable which would come out on top.

Jenny considered how life's simple pleasures get lost among the stresses and strains of everyday life and decided to make more time for her and George to enjoy such indulgences. She felt it her duty as a mother to ensure that George had all the fun of childhood, before real life came along to spoil the party. After all, those innocent years are passed way too soon.

A cool and gentle breeze filled their lungs with fresh sea air as they sat on the small shingle beach. It really was a beautiful setting, but still Jenny felt restless; frustrated to come all this way just to encounter a roadblock. Hopefully, the traffic would begin to flow again tomorrow after the call from James Heritage and they could resume their investigation; but Jenny knew that he was right, this was a mystery that would not be unravelled in a long-weekend.

'What are your plans for the summer holidays this year?' she asked.

Sarah didn't appear surprised at the question. – 'I was thinking the same thing.'

'Why, what did you have in mind?' said Karen.

'Haven't really thought it through properly yet,' said Jenny, 'but maybe we could all do with a seaside break. There must be loads of places to stay round here and it would be good cover. Nobody would suspect a thing; we'd just be a bunch of holidaymakers. I could bring George too; and there'd be Sarah and Trevor, Alan, and you, Karen – The Black Swan Detective Agency.'

'Trev and I don't have anything booked,' said Sarah. 'The business is expanding, but we could both do with a holiday and I could plan deliveries in advance to cover a couple of weeks off. The difficulty might be getting Trev to relinquish responsibility for the brew, but there are a few perfectly capable assistants who we could leave in charge.'

'I'm answerable to no-one but myself,' said Karen, 'so count me in. Not sure about Alan, though; he has a young family.'

'He could bring them with him,' said Jenny. 'That would make us even less conspicuous. It would be great for George to have some other kids around too.'

'Bloody hell; how big a place are we going to need?' said Karen.

'Four tents at the most should do it,' said Jenny.

'Ugh, camping,' said Sarah. 'Only been once; Trev loved it but I hated it – pissed it down all week *and* the tent leaked. I know you were in the army and are used to all that survival stuff, but I prefer a little luxury.'

'You can camp in luxury these days,' said Jenny, 'there are all kinds of accessories you can get; glamping they call it.'

'Yeah, chandeliers and everything, I've heard,' said Karen.

'What about showers and toilets?'

'That's no problem,' said Jenny, 'they're generally a pretty high standard on most campsites.'

'But they're still communal, and you have to leave your tent in the middle of the night and find them in the dark. And believe me, when you've been camping with Trev after he's had a few beers, tripping over your sleeping-bag in his efforts to get out of the tent, it would put you off for life.'

'It's character-building,' said Jenny, 'and you can have a laugh about it afterwards.'

'Hmm, there are a lot of things in life that are character-building,' said the sceptical Sarah, 'most of which I have no desire to repeat. When someone says something is character-building, it usually means it's unpleasant.'

'But you shouldn't let one bad experience put you off,' said Jenny. 'There's nothing to beat the smell and taste of a fry-up, cooked over a camp-stove in the mornings.'

'A vegetarian's paradise,' said Karen.

'You can have veggie fry-ups,' said Jenny, 'mushrooms, tomatoes, hash-browns, baked beans, fried bread etc.'

'You've got an answer for everything, haven't you,' sighed Sarah. 'OK, I'll contact Trev and Alan, see what they think; plant the seeds and then we can discuss it further when we get back.'

They passed a bunch of loud and lairy lads, perched on the harbour wall. – 'Well, I still would!' Jenny heard one of them say.

'You wouldn't know where to start,' she retorted, much to the amusement of Karen and Sarah.

'Let's face it,' said Sarah, 'that's the way most men think. Those lads just haven't developed the maturity to hide it yet. I wonder which of us they were referring to.'

'Shall we go back and ask?' said Jenny.

'No, you're OK,' laughed Sarah. 'We'd frighten the life out of them if we did.'

As the cliff-railway made its rattling ascent, Jenny reflected upon how comfortable she felt in the company of Sarah and Karen. It wasn't that long ago they'd invited her to assist in their fight for justice and she wondered aloud how the object of their mission was doing in prison, while they were enjoying a weekend by the seaside.

'Well, all we can do is our best,' said Sarah. 'Steve's got no-one else on his side, has he?'

Back at the guesthouse and Jenny made her daily call to George. Excited to hear her voice, he told her in great detail what he'd done that day – his goal in football training in the morning, and where he'd walked Sandy with Nanny and Grandad in the afternoon.

'Where are you, Mummy?' he asked.

'Somewhere really nice,' she said, 'and next time you might be able to come too.'

'When are you coming home?'

'Monday evening, but it will be past your bedtime.'

'I'm going to stay awake and look out of the window.'

'But it might be very late and you'll have school on Tuesday.'

'I don't care. I have super-powers and I don't have to sleep.'

'Wow, that's cool – I wish I had super-powers too.'

'You do, you're a Super-Mum.'

'You really think so?'

'Yes, you're the best mum in the world.'

'Ah, thank you,' said Jenny, with a tear in her eye; 'and you're the best little boy in the world. Love you, see you on Monday.'

'Love you too; bye.'

'Everything OK?' said Karen.

'Yeah, I guess so. Never been away from George for this long before; but at least we know that Steve's gonna be fine. Apparently, he has Super-Mum on his case.'

24. Filbert

Steve liked his job in the library, even if it essentially consisted of retrieving books from the small store room and placing them on the shelves in genre and alphabetical order. Jayden took care of any customer interaction with prisoners returning and borrowing. He listened to their analyses, made recommendations if asked, and provided a professional and genial service. It was obvious that the library was a refuge for some, a safe-haven away from the day-to-day stresses of prison life. For Steve it was an escape from the monosyllabic Martin and the unescapable stench of that toilet in the corner of the cell. He couldn't get used to the lack of privacy afforded by a waist high screen and the inexorable soundtrack.

In the library Steve also enjoyed spending time with the likeable Jayden and was grateful for the sage advice that belied his youth. – 'You wanna stay safe, there are some dudes you need to avoid. First is Filbert; they call him the Doctor – he's a, what you call it, a psych something or other.'

'A psychologist? Is that why they call him the Doctor?' said Steve.

'Nah, a psychopath; they call him the Doctor cos he's in charge of all the pills in here. He's the man who controls this place, cos he controls the drug supply. Then there's Van Gogh.'

'I take it that's not his real name.'

'Yeah, that's his real name; we get a lot of post-impressionist painters in here. He's called Van Gogh for obvious reason when you see him, but he can get a bit distressed if you ask him why his glasses keep falling off.'

'They sound like interesting characters,' said Steve.

'Interesting is one way of putting it,' said Jayden. 'Those are the bad guys, but everyone's a little crazy; it's what this place does to you. There's some who shouldn't be here; people who need help, not prison. Let's be honest, if a dude loses his mind, he ain't likely to find it in this hell-hole.'

Despite his best efforts, Steve found it difficult to follow Jayden's advice and avoid Filbert, and his presence was all pervading. It seemed that the continuation of drug supply in prison was a constant battle with the powers that be; and Filbert had to develop increasingly creative methods of procurement and concealment. Steve was aghast that Filbert's latest wheeze apparently involved him.

'This isn't a request,' stated Filbert, 'I'm telling you how it's going to happen.'

Steve quaked in fear and wondered why an ordinary chap like him warranted such intimidation. Filbert was an undeniably threatening bloke and the two thugs that flanked him looked equally scary. The scheme was enthusiastically relayed to Steve in all its genius and involved the cutting of a recess into the pages of certain books in order to hide drugs.

'The customer borrows the book from the library and everyone's happy,' said Filbert, with a smile to emphasise the brilliance of his idea.

Steve was far from happy. Damaging books went against every fibre of his soul, not to mention the fact that he was trying to keep his head down and stay out of trouble. He pointed out that a sudden interest in reading among Filbert's clientele might appear suspicious in the eyes of the authorities, but Filbert would countenance no opposition. He told Steve that he'd be in touch soon with the finer detail of the plan.

'I'll look forward to it,' said Steve, as he walked away to find Jayden.

'Yeah, he asked me to do it too,' said Jayden.

'But if we follow his instructions, we could lose our jobs in the library.'

'And if we don't follow his instruction, we could lose far more than that. Don't know 'bout you, but I'm quite attached to my body parts. Have a word in Van Gogh's good ear and he'll tell you the cost of crossing Filbert.'

Steve winced at the thought, but still insisted that he wouldn't do it.

'Then I can't help you no more,' said Jayden. 'It's been nice knowing you.'

25. Mansion on the Hill

The landlady hovered by their table as they viewed the early morning options. – 'And what can I get you ladies this morning?'

Jenny considered again the tempting choices on offer. So far this weekend she'd consumed a chilli con carne, a couple of breakfast fry-ups, and a pizza, not to mention the desserts and yesterday's ice cream. She observed Sarah who, judging by the guilty expression, was feeling the same. Only Karen, with her healthy vegetarian diet, seemed at ease.

'I'll have the smoked salmon and scrambled eggs please,' she decided at last. Sarah nodded and asked for the same, whilst Karen went for the continental – all muesli, fruits and yogurts.

James Heritage had been in touch to say that he'd made contact with the family and was in a position to further discuss Bambi's case. He was to pick them up at ten and said he'd prefer to drive somewhere out of town in order to maintain their anonymity, for the time being at least. – 'Now that Ms Forrester's demise is known, there will be some fallout. It's best that your involvement and motives are not revealed at this stage. I know the very place where we won't be disturbed.'

'Is this a good idea?' said Karen, as she brushed her hair ready for the day ahead. 'I trust yours and Sarah's judgement implicitly, but I'm about to get into a car with a man I've never met and he's going to take us to a place outside of town, where we won't be disturbed.'

'I suppose it does sound a bit dubious when you put it like that,' said Jenny, 'but I think he's above board. Besides, there's three of us and only one of him; and I reckon he's in his seventies. Anyway, we're going to need his help and local knowledge to get to the bottom of this.'

'Hmm, I was doing pretty well with just one morning in the library, but I suppose it won't do any harm to listen to what he has to say.'

James arrived right on time, of course, insistent upon opening the door for each in turn, as they climbed into his magnificent vintage Jaguar MK2, in a meticulously polished racing-green. After some debate Sarah took the seat next to James in the front, while Jenny and Karen sunk into the luxurious cream upholstery in the back.

Immediately unnerved by the intense smell of leather and petrol, Jenny was whisked back to her wedding day, when she'd chosen a similar conveyance to the ceremony. She recalled how she'd felt on that journey, nervous but exuding radiance and optimism, with her proud father at her side. Jenny said nothing, a torrent of past expectation and present regret whirling around her head in an unstoppable stream of consciousness. She was shocked that a simple aroma could bring it all flooding back, and angry that it could still affect her so easily.

'See what you mean,' whispered Karen, abruptly bringing Jenny back to the real world, 'I trust him already.'

Sarah chatted incessantly with James – what a beautiful car to go with his charming cottage, what a wonderful life he must have with his antiques and fascinating occupation…

'Yes, I suppose I have a lot to be grateful for to lead such a privileged existence, but it's not the same since I no longer have anyone to share it with. My wife, Anne, passed away two years ago now, and I still miss her every day. Damned cancer is such a cruel and indiscriminate predator.'

'I'm sorry,' said Sarah.

'Don't be. This is exactly what I need; something to take my maudlin mind off things and to get my teeth into. It gets me out of the cottage in charming company; and a mystery to be solved is always a welcome distraction.'

'So, where are you taking us?'

'Now, that would spoil the surprise, wouldn't it?'

'OK, then how far is it?'

'Only about six miles; we'll be there in no time.'

James's only mobile antique, the elegant and graceful Jaguar, purred as it climbed gently out of town to the countryside beyond. The narrow roads wound among ancient woodland, sunlight flickering fitfully through trees and undergrowth; Jenny, Sarah and Karen silent now, in pensive speculation as to their destination.

Eventually, Jenny noticed the click, click of the indicator and James veered right, through rusty, rickety gates onto a pot-holed drive. Well, this is off the beaten track, she thought; doubt if anyone's ventured this way for a while. She wondered what could be at the end of this seemingly never-ending path, as James drove on for at least another three quarters of a mile.

Finally, they emerged from the trees into a large gravelled crescent, behind which stood a magnificent, but derelict, old mansion, its windows smashed and hanging in the breeze. Everything around was overgrown, the once landscaped gardens now bursting with rambling bushes and wild flowers.

Their feet crunched on the weed-covered gravel as they emerged from the car, a deafening sound among the stillness that caused a murder of crows to fly raucously from the roof. James appeared calm, as if he were on familiar territory, whilst Jenny gazed in awe at the dilapidated elegance of the façade. Sarah and Karen looked jittery, starting at every noise.

'So, why have you brought us here?' said Jenny. 'It's very impressive, but I'm sure there are quiet places closer to home.'

'This is where Ms Forrester grew up,' said James, with arm outstretched. 'You wanted to know where she came from; well, this is it.'

'You mean, Emmeline O'Connell, ne Foster-Smythe,' said Karen.

James looked at her with an air of shocked disappointment, tinged with irritation. – 'Who have you been speaking to? I explicitly asked you to remain under the radar, until I'd spoken with the family. It was only a day, for God's sake.'

Jenny spoke on Karen's behalf. – 'We haven't talked to anyone. While we were with you yesterday morning, Karen was busy in the library rummaging through archive newspapers; she found the story there.'

James's annoyance subsided as quickly as it came as he remembered his manners. – 'Ah, I see, very resourceful, yes; my apologies.'

'So, they are the same person,' said Karen.

A pregnant pause of anticipation as James considered his response. Eventually he spoke – 'Yes. She revealed her true identity when she came to see me, in complete confidence I hasten to add. Came as quite a shock, I can tell you. I didn't recognise her at first; changed a lot since I last saw her.'

'And why did she come back?' said Jenny.

'My late wife was Emmeline's piano teacher; taught her since she was a child and they became quite close. She was a talented musician and could have gone far, but gave up when she was about sixteen; other distractions I suppose. Anne was devastated when everyone assumed that Emmeline died on the moor. Took her years to get over it; don't think she ever did, really. Emmeline wanted to see Anne to apologise for putting her though all that grief. She seemed genuinely upset when I broke the news that Anne was gone. But that wasn't her only reason to return. She wanted to know about her family. Where were they, what were their circumstances etc.? I got the impression that she'd fallen on hard times and was enquiring to ascertain if there was any inheritance due. Both parents are recently deceased and she must have found out somehow. As far as I am aware, her sister, Beatrice, is the only one left now. Their estate, such as it is, will all go to her.'

'And no-one knew why Emmeline disappeared, or had heard from her since?' said Sarah.

'No; there were all kinds of stories and theories going around when it happened, but never anything but gossip and rumours.'

'What about Richard O'Connell,' said Karen, 'is he still around?'

'Hmm, you have been busy,' said James, 'may I congratulate you on your aptitude for research. Richard's is an interesting story, which we can talk about later. In the meantime, shall we take a look inside? Give you a feel for the environment from which Emmeline emerged.'

'You seem to know this place,' said Sarah, 'as if you've been here before.'

James looked wistfully at the old manor. – 'In its prime, this was a pretty impressive setting. The Foster-Smythes generally kept themselves to themselves, but there was a tradition, passed down through generations, to invite selected pillars of the local community to a summer ball. I moved in such circles back then and was fortunate, or unfortunate enough, to be summoned each year. Can you imagine it; the clink of glasses, the canapés, the buzz of conversation between all the upwardly mobile pretenders, each vying for advantage over their fellow high-flyers? Yes, exactly; it was ghastly and I hated every minute of it. On the upside, this is where Anne and I met, so I have a grudging affinity for the old place. She felt the same, so we used to grab some food and drink and walk in the grounds for hours, until the party was over. My father always asked what business connections I'd made, but I was young and much more interested in the connection between Anne and I.'

'Seems that being here brings back some mixed memories,' said Jenny. 'Are you OK?'

'Yes, I'll be fine. I came back after Anne passed away; visited all our old haunts in fact. It was upsetting at first, but it helped in the end; made me realise how lucky we'd been to have so many wonderful years together.'

'Doesn't anyone own the property now; aren't we trespassing?' said Karen.

'No; the family got into financial difficulties and, ultimately, couldn't afford its upkeep. One day, they simply sold what remained of their assets and moved out. It's been left to rot ever since. So, shall we step inside or not?'

They all nodded and followed James to the magnificent oak front door, its brass handles corroded and loose. Inevitably, it creaked noisily when opened, amplified by the echo of the cavernous hallway. No coat stand, no paintings on the wall, no chandelier, no butler to welcome them; nothing but cobwebs hanging from the ceiling, and from the banisters on the broad staircase at the end of the hall. As James said, it had been stripped of anything that made it a home, anything that could be sold. Cautiously they entered, each looking up, down and into every nook and cranny. What they expected to see, not one of them knew, but it felt to Jenny like they shouldn't be there.

'Do you think it's haunted?' said Karen.

'You've seen too many episodes of Scooby Doo,' said Sarah.

'Nonetheless, it is pretty spooky,' said Jenny. 'Is there any reason why we need to be here to discuss Bambi's origins?'

'You wanted to know everything about her,' said James. 'When someone comes to me looking for answers about their ancestry, I often visit the places they inhabited. I get to know them almost, and the client appreciates the effort if you can give them a rounded picture. Anyone can find out dates of birth, marriage, death; but what people really want to know is who they were. Where did they go to school, what did they do for a living, what were their beliefs, what were the achievements or scandals in their life? If we want to know what happened to Emmeline, then it starts here.'

'OK, I can see the logic behind that,' said Jenny; 'but there's nothing here anymore.'

'We don't know that until we've undertaken a thorough search,' said James. 'You can't simply walk away from a place without leaving a trace; particularly if it's the ancestral home. These walls can tell so many stories; just imagine what they've seen.'

'Yes, but unless they can talk, they won't tell us anything,' said Sarah.

James picked at a piece of peeling flock-wallpaper. – 'There are the lives of generations beneath the surface; we simply have to scrape it away.'

Jenny looked at James and, for the first time, saw him as a troubled and vulnerable man; so different from the self-assured and confident front that he presented to the world. His profession was an extension of himself, she thought. What better way to hide from the present, than to study the past?

'Are you suggesting that we strip what's left of the wallpaper, in the hope that we might find a clue?' she said.

'No, of course not, but there will be something here. I can feel it.'

They followed him slowly up the broad, grandiose staircase, the echo of the creak of each stair, loud enough to wake any slumbering ghosts that may reside. The ceilings high and stately, a reek of privilege unearned and status taken for granted. How the mighty are fallen, thought Jenny. There must have been at least eight bedrooms, just in this wing of the house. They split to save time, but a search of each room revealed nothing, until a shout of excitement from Karen prompted a reunion.

'Look, there, on that window blind,' said Karen.

All gathered round to stare at a hinged wooden louvre screen, upon which were scratched the initials EFS & JR. Although faded with time, the engraving was still legible; but what did it mean? Jenny reflected on what might be a bygone relic of teenage girl's dream or infatuation; a hope for the future, perhaps. A tinge of sadness, when she considered what became of that girl. It seemed that Richard O'Connell wasn't her first or only love; but who was JR?

'Perhaps she was a 'Dallas' fan,' said Jenny.

'Or it could be John Ridd, from Lorna Doone,' said Karen. 'Have you never fallen for a character from fiction?'

'I once had a crush on Lady Penelope,' said James. 'I suppose if one can fall for a puppet, then anything's possible.'

Jenny looked at James for any hint that he was joking, but his face remained expressionless. Nevertheless, Sarah and Karen couldn't resist a little chuckle.

'OK, so it looks like this was her bedroom,' said Sarah, 'but I can't see any other clues around. It's just an empty room.'

'We haven't even started looking yet,' said James.

He checked each side of the screens, but no more messages. Next, James turned his attention to the floor; the threadbare and patterned red carpet probably housed all kinds of bugs. He pointed to one corner of the room. – 'Over there; that carpet's been pulled back.'

'Probably mice,' said Karen.

'One way to find out,' he said, as he got down on his haunches, grabbed a handful of carpet and tugged. A plume of dust caused him to cough, but undeterred he pulled it back to reveal the floorboards beneath. Dark and grimy, there was no sign of any recent activity, but one board was a little loose to his touch. Much as he tried, he was unable to get his fingers in to shift it. Ever prepared, Jenny passed him her Swiss army knife. She'd never once had cause to remove anything from a horse's hoof, but many of the other attachments had come in handy over the years. James levered and pried until it eventually lifted, to reveal; not a lot. A shocked spider scuttled through a crack, leaving nothing but a couple of upturned, deceased woodlice. He reached beneath, as far as his arm would stretch, fingers feeling and probing.

'Anything there?' said Karen.

'No, I don't think so. Ah, hang on; damn it!! I felt something, but I've just pushed it further away. No, it's no good, I can't quite reach it.'

It was agreed that Jenny had the longest and thinnest arm, so she was encouraged to give it a go. God knows what's under there, she thought; we've already seen one spider. Nevertheless, she got down on her knees and, with a little manoeuvring, managed to reach what felt like a small metal box. With the tips of her fingers, she moved it closer, until it nestled in the palm of her hand. Triumphantly, she stood and held it out for all to see. James took it carefully from her and placed it on the window-ledge, in order to shed some light on their discovery. He looked at it from every angle, not just any metal box, but ornate and inlaid with stones of indeterminate value.

'Damn, it's locked,' he said.

Jenny noted the second time James had used the word 'damn' in his last few sentences; probably the closest he ever came to a swear word. They all took a look and concurred that it was, indeed, impenetrable. Jenny was dispatched for another rummage beneath the floorboards, but no key was forthcoming.

'We'll take it with us,' said James. 'I have some tools at home that may prise it open. It's a beautiful piece though, and I don't want to damage it.'

'Seems wrong, somehow,' said Karen. 'Whatever is in there is obviously private, otherwise it wouldn't have been so well hidden.'

'Well, she won't have any use for it now,' said Sarah. 'Don't know about you, but I kept all kinds of rubbish when I was a teenager. There's probably nothing of any significance in there anyway.'

James asked Sarah to carry the box in her bag. – 'Yeah, why not?' she said. 'What else is a lady's bag for, other than to carry everyone else's crap?'

As they made their way downstairs, Jenny reflected upon the passing of time and the effects of decay. This old place must have been a hive of activity through generations, where liaisons transpired, where empires arose, where adults conspired, and where the dreams of children grew and shattered. She'd seen enough period dramas to picture the scene; orders barked at servants, children raised by nannies, the comings and goings of the self-important – those confident of their status in the world and distraught when the whole lot came tumbling down. In the end it all came down to one thing – money!! In their world, once it's gone, you're cast out to make your own way, forgotten and disowned.

And what of their legacy? A derelict building, a family torn asunder, ancestry irrelevant, a daughter disappeared, a scattered workforce and an unsolved murder…

26. Upstairs, Downstairs

Jenny was keen to leave, the shivers down her spine nothing to do with the dampness and cold of the uninhabited mansion; the place gave her the creeps. Sarah and Karen agreed, but James persuaded them to explore a little more. – 'We still have downstairs to uncover.'

A thorough search of all the ground-floor rooms proved fruitless; just empty shells – they really had stripped everything bare. Despite protestations that it was a waste of time, James was insistent that they visit the kitchens below – where the real people worked, he proclaimed. As they contemplated the dark descent, Karen pointed out that they probably wouldn't be able to see anything anyway.

James pulled his phone from his pocket. – 'These things come equipped with torches, you know. Thought you young people would be up with the latest technology.'

They followed reluctantly down groaning stairs, the walls on each side stained and decayed with damp. Invisible cobwebs stuck to their faces, and fingers were brushed through hair to repel any unwelcome arachnids, whilst all but James questioned whether this was really necessary.

At the bottom a sturdy wooden door opened into an enormous kitchen area where, surprisingly, much of the old equipment was still in place. Perhaps this stuff was too heavy to shift, thought Jenny, or nobody wanted it. She considered how many extravagant banquets must have been created here – of pâté and salmon and grouse and quail and steak, followed by desserts so exquisite as to induce mouth-watering over-indulgence. Despite these succulent musings, a rank smell of eggs invaded her nostrils, so strong that they all commented upon it at once.

'It wasn't me,' said Sarah.

'Probably some dead rodents decomposing,' said James.

'Well, thank you for that thought,' said Karen. 'For God's sake, there's nothing here; can we go now?'

'Just a quick look around.'

James made his way along uneven flagstones, opening and closing dusty cupboards as he went, with phone-torch in hand to expose every shadowy crevice. It all looked pretty spooky from where Jenny, Sarah and Karen were standing; his face illuminated intermittently amid the shadows. Suddenly, he stopped and exclaimed – 'Now, this is interesting!'

'What is it?' said Jenny.

His answer was precluded by a stifled scream from Karen, as they heard the sound of footsteps on the stairs behind them. Hurriedly, they scurried to join James at the other end of the room as the footsteps grew louder and a sporadic dull glow filled the doorway. James switched off his light and they all huddled together, fearful of who or what might emerge from the gloom.

'Who be there; what be thy bisness ere?' The booming, gruff voice emerged from the ether. Behind an ancient lantern's flickering flame, through unkempt grey hair and beard, the piercing eyes of an aged and rugged countenance searched the room. In the darkness Jenny could feel Sarah and Karen shake beside her. The face seemed to be suspended in mid-air, unattached to a body, its twitching nose a ruddy riot of burst capillaries.

'Good God!!' said James. 'Trossard, is that you? I thought you were long gone.'

'Who be that? How thee know ol Trossard.'

James fumbled for his phone and switched the light back on. – 'It's me, Trossard, James Heritage; you remember? But maybe you don't, it was so far back.'

The visage hesitated, as if delving the depths of memory. Eventually, his answer came. – 'Ay, I recall. You be the one that use to hide in the gardn wi Miss Anne. Ad to tell thee off for tramping o'er the flower beds and undoing me hard graft.'

'Time hasn't blunted your memory,' said James.

'Nout else to do but remnisce round ere, be there?'

'Well, we're sorry to intrude, but it's wonderful to see you, after all these years. Allow me to introduce some friends of mine – this is Jenny, Sarah and Karen.'

That nose of substantial proportions emerged first, followed by a flushed face immersed in that long grey bush of hair. A man of imposing stature, but stooped with age, his clothes ragged and worn, he eyed them with suspicion.

'Don't need no vis'tor, I fine by meself. Ye can go back to where ye come from.'

'We don't mean any harm, Trossard,' said James.

'So, what be ye ere for? Ain't no-one left; jus me an the odd critter.'

'Can we talk upstairs?' said Jenny. 'It's too dark and cold down here.'

'I don't ave nout to talk about.'

'We have news of Emmeline,' said James.

With a pensive expression and his curiosity finally aroused, Trossard reluctantly agreed to listen to what they had to say. Upon Karen's insistence on daylight, they silently followed this enigmatic old man back upstairs, along the hallway and through the front door once more. Blinded by the midday sun, it took a few minutes to adjust, before James led the way to a drystone wall, shaded beneath a row of poplar trees. A welcome breath of air to rid them of the staleness within, it was a relief to escape that dungeon of a kitchen.

'What news be thy ave? Sweet Emmeline lost pon the moor an age ago. Why come ye here to open up old wounds?'

'We think she may be the same person that worked in our local pub,' said Jenny. 'We knew her as Bambi.'

A look of shock and hope briefly overcame Trossard, before he regained his composure. – 'It was me give er that name. From when she was a tiny thing she run free in the grounds, and always me that find er and bring er home. Always knowed where she be – she like to watch the deer in the woods. She was so quiet, she could get so near – a few foot away. Then she scold ol Trossard for scaren them away.' His distant expression returned to reality and he raised his eyes. – 'So, if she din't die, where be she now?'

Jenny took his gnarled old hands in hers. – 'I'm sorry, but she was killed recently. Our mission is to find out who did it.'

Tears filled those olden eyes; eyes that must have seen so many born and perish, but this was news that obviously resonated deep within. The tears of grief, soon turned to anger. – 'We mourn er passin all them year ago; and now thee come to make I mourn again. What thee want from me?'

'We had no idea you were here, Trossard,' said James. 'I brought these ladies to look for clues about her past. Now we know that she didn't die on the moor twenty years ago, there must have been a reason why she disappeared. There may be no connection, but I'm willing to wager that there's someone round here knows a lot more than they said at the time.'

Trossard looked at once devastated and thoughtful. After a short time, he spoke – 'It may be so, that there be someone that knows; it be true then, and it be true today. We were all asked questions back then, but the answers were as empty as the moor where sweet Emmeline loved to roam. Get more sense from listnin to the wind, what say only one thing; that she's gone.'

'But you know more about the comings and goings of this place than anyone,' said James. 'Won't you help us solve the mystery and avenge her killer?'

A cloud blocked the sun and stole the warmth of the day. Jenny glanced up to see that it was the only one in the sky and that it would soon pass. Trossard, however, seemed to take it as a sign that he needed to think before he shed any further light on the subject. With click of joints and a low moan, he raised himself slowly from the wall and wandered back toward the house. James signalled to let him be and they observed, as he stood before the mansion and surveyed its faded splendour. The old man's head pivoted side to side, up and down, as if in remembrance of all he'd witnessed. Body gnarled and twisted through all he'd endured, he shook until Jenny could watch no more. She rushed to his side, supported his weight and led him slowly back. Through the layers of his ragged clothes, she could feel the brittle bones and rattle of his laboured breathing. He deserved warmth and comfort in his dotage, not this lonely, godforsaken and derelict life.

From his inside pocket, James retrieved a hip-flask, opened it, and handed it to Trossard. – 'It's a fine single malt,' he said, 'here, take a drink to aid your thoughts.'

Trossard took a deep swig and gasped as the whisky's warmth slid down and fired his belly. – 'This be the first in many a year. Thank ee.'

'Please, keep it,' said James, as Trossard handed the flask back. 'I have others at home and I'll bring another bottle or two to top it up.'

A cough and a wheeze, before he spoke – 'Don't know what I can tell ee that I din't tell police twenty year ago. It be right enough that this ere place be in me veins; my father be the gardener and dogsbody ere too, and his father before him. It's all ol Trossard know, and the first an last time I leave Foster Gables was to search for Emmeline. She always say come visit when she wed that O'Connell fella, but he want nout to do with likes of I.'

'So, you didn't approve of their marriage,' said Karen.

'Weren't my place to say, were it? But as much a young lady be free to roam where she please, she ought be free to choose who she wed. T'was all arranged, for O'Connell's money to save the house.'

Trossard took another swig from the hip flask and studied each of them in turn, his tired eyes resting first on James, before moving on to Sarah and Karen, then Jenny. – 'S'pose ye look well enough like honest folk. Ol Trossard ain't much longer for this world; p'raps it's time someone knowed the truth.'

'Take your time,' said James, 'you can trust us with your story.'

'Ay, maybe so, and there ain't no-one left it can hurt no more. This is how it be…'

27. A Reckless Act of Principled Indignance

The first punch took him by surprise! Steve instinctively curled up in a ball and fell to the floor with his arms around his head. This could have been a mistake as his prone position seemed to invite a series of hefty kicks from four prison-issue size tens. He considered how useful Filbert's thugs would be in the central defence of the prison football team, before whimpering and begging for mercy.

In a reckless act of principled indignance Steve had declined to be party to Filbert's hare-brained scheme and it was time to pay the consequences. The beating was unrelenting and brutal. Not since school had Steve suffered such indignity and pain, the memory of those bullies coming back to him as he feared for his life. He sneaked a peek from beneath his arm and gasped as the flash of a blade caught his eye. He'd heard all the stories of what Filbert did to his victims, but had never believed them; until now, that is. Which body part was he to lose?

'OK, that's enough; you can stop now,' came a voice from the shadows.

'But don't you want a souvenir, Boss?' said one of the henchmen.

'Not this time; I think he's learnt his lesson.'

'If you say so, Boss; but you don't want people thinking you've gone soft.'

'I don't think there's any chance of that. It looks like you've done a pretty good job.'

A final boot for luck and they turned and left, as quickly and quietly as they'd come. Steve moaned in pain and tried to stand, but to no avail. His shattered leg bent beneath him, he was simply too weak to move and he wondered how long it would be before anyone would come to his assistance; there were never many visitors to the library stockroom. Steve drifted in and out of consciousness, he knew not for how long, before he heard the familiar, and for once welcome, voices of two prison officers.

'This is the bastard that killed that barmaid. Pretty thing, she was; why don't we just let the scumbag die?'

'Because we're professionals and we must behave as such; that's what they told us on that course, isn't it? That we shouldn't let our prejudices get in the way of our duty.'

'Yeah, I guess you're right. He looks in a pretty bad way; suppose we better call an ambulance.'

28. Homeward Bound

The following morning saw a thoughtful trio retrace their tracks, the rhythm of the train an accompaniment to all kinds of speculation and theories. It was the start of their journey home, after a weekend of revelations that none of them could have envisaged. In contemplation of Trossard's story, all agreed that they hadn't been expecting that!

That Emmeline had been forced, or at least enticed, to marry for money to rescue their ancestral home, was entirely believable. Old Foster-Smythe must have been in a desperate place; his previously assumed and honoured position in the world under threat, he could see no way out. His money was all gone, the result of ill-advised investments. The prospects for profit were high, but the risks even greater; and the result inevitable.

Trossard told of Foster-Smythe's fury once the con had been unravelled and he knew that he could do nothing to reverse his fortunes. What he'd done was barely legal, if that; his offshore accounts and dubious tax arrangements negated any possibility of recourse through the courts, and he knew he'd been well and truly had.

He'd limped on for a few years, propped up by Richard O'Connell's charity, which came with a number of ever-increasing provisos. Then the whole arrangement came to an abrupt halt upon Emmeline's disappearance. O'Connell no longer had a vested interest and he'd delighted in the Foster-Smythes' eventual fall from grace.

It wasn't this age-old tale of greed and conniving that had surprised them, it was Trossard's own part in the saga. They could see the inner-turmoil from his expression, a secret he'd kept from the world for so long and none too sure if he should reveal it now. It had taken a lot a coaxing and a few more swigs from James's hip flask to finally loosen his tongue.

'Twern't my idea,' he'd said, 'twas the Lady what come up with it. Twasn't an unpleasant experience for me, but she didn't seem to enjoy it much.'

There followed the disclosure that the Lord of the Manor was unable to father children. He'd tried for years to produce an heir to his fortunes and had ultimately blamed his wife for the barren results. It was at this point that she had confided in Trossard that she knew it wasn't her and that she'd had tests to prove it. Her proposition had initially shocked Trossard, but he'd been a humble servant all his life and it wasn't for him to refuse, was it?

'You be the first to know; ain't tell no-one else. Ol' Foster-Smythe go to him grave not knowing, and sweet Emmeline too. I be her father!'

Jenny stared out of the train window and watched the blur of countryside speed by. She imagined how hard it must have been for Trossard to reveal his secret to them, three strangers that he'd only just met, and James, a minor character from his distant past. But then she thought, how much of a burden to keep such a secret hidden for so many years. It must have eaten him up inside and he appeared a little lighter once the tale was finally told.

Of course, there had been no end of questions. James enquired what of her sister; was Trossard her father too? No, he'd said; the Lady had grown tired of him by then and the butler had been invited to do the honours. Lord Foster-Smythe remained oblivious throughout, but was disappointed when both were girls; he'd craved a son to continue the family name. Hence, he'd had little time for the sisters and had hardly any input into their upbringing; the vile lure of the hunt and grouse shoot seasons, seemed of greater import.

With a tear in his eye, Trossard had gone on to tell of a natural bond between he and Emmeline. As soon as she could walk, the outdoors had been like a magnet and Trossard was forever tasked with her search and rescue. He recounted the time when he'd found her asleep among a small herd of curious deer, and had christened her Bambi. It meant so much that she had still used that name until her tragic demise.

He'd asked if she was happy and all were ashamed that they couldn't answer honestly; none of them had known her, any further than an occasional cordial chat at the bar. She was a popular member of the Black Swan community, was all they could tell him; which seemed to offer some comfort at least.

'So, what happens now?' said Karen. 'We've read Lorna Doone; do we have to read bloody Lady Chatterley's Lover too?'

'We've learnt a lot this weekend,' said Jenny, 'but we're no closer to solving the mystery, are we?'

'All we've unearthed is more questions,' said Karen. 'Even that box we found under the floorboards; when James finally got it open there was nothing there but a slip of paper that said – "the butler did it". All we have are a few echoes from Bambi's past; no hard and fast leads.'

'Wish we could have stayed longer to quiz Trossard some more,' said Jenny, 'but I think we'd worn him out by the time we left. Bet he's not spoken to anyone for years.'

'I wouldn't be so sure about that,' said Sarah. 'James said that when he'd opened that kitchen cupboard it was far from bare. Trossard told us that he lived self-sufficiently, didn't he; eggs from chickens, meat from snared rabbits, foraging for mushrooms and berries, digging potatoes and veg from the ground. But that doesn't explain the Tesco bags that James found in that cupboard, does it? He's either been nipping out to the shops, or someone's been delivering his groceries. Think there's more to that old codger than meets the eye.'

29. A Tale of Two Filberts

Steve awoke in a prison in-patient bed. He knew where he was by the smell of disinfectant, the hoist holding up his broken leg and the presence of a bored-looking screw at the door. He had no idea what time of day it was, as he'd fallen asleep from exhaustion upon his return from the hospital. There had been little sympathy from the two prison officers who'd accompanied him and they seemed to consider his pain and discomfort an inconvenience, an unwelcome interruption to their routine.

As it had a number of times since his imprisonment, Steve's mind drifted back to that evening on the bridge and he wondered once more if the world would be a better place without him. At least he would have been put out of his misery and, let's face it, his quality of life hadn't exactly improved since then. He would obviously be on pain-killers for a while and he considered whether he could accumulate enough to finish the job.

With some difficulty, he sat up, reached for the water on the bedside cabinet and surveyed his accommodation. There were a few other surly-looking prisoners in the room, none of whom he knew. I'd best get used to it, thought Steve, as he took in his plastered leg and winced at the pain induced by a few simple movements. Look upon it as an opportunity to catch up on some reading perhaps.

He was allowed a visitor and it was good to see Jayden's friendly face as he pulled up a chair by Steve's bedside and enquired – 'How you feeling, man?'

'Pretty crap; how do you think I feel after a beating like that? It's outrageous that they can attack someone whenever they wish. The prison has a duty of care to all its inmates and I will be registering a complaint with the appropriate authorities.'

'Doubt you'll get very far. Filbert has all the top-brass in his pocket. He knows that everyone's got something to hide. No matter how respectable they look on the surface, they all have a skeleton in the closet. He simply exploits their fear of getting caught out.'

'So, Filbert can do whatever he wants with impunity?' said Steve.

'Pretty much, yeah; but it woulda been a lot worse if I hadn't stopped them,' said Jayden.

'You stopped them?'

'Well, not directly, but I had a quiet word with Filbert.'

'Hey, thanks; but what influence do you have with Filbert?'

Jayden took a furtive look around to ensure no-one was listening.
– 'I read him a bedtime story every night.'

'What?'

'It all come about cos the prison has no money to employ anyone
to come and teach English. Filbert can't read or write and he told
them he wants to learn. The Governor looked for prisoners with the
skills and, cos I work in the library, I got the job.'

'Hope it pays well.'

'Ha, it pays nothing, but they say it looks good on my record. We
have to start with the basics so I read to him one night while he
followed my finger on the page. Next thing I know he's snoring and
asleep like a baby. Turns out that his mama used to read the same
story when he was a kid. She died when he was six, but he still
remembers.'

'So, you're Filbert's surrogate mother,' laughed Steve.

'As long as he don't suck 'pon me nipple I can handle it,' said
Jayden. 'I provide a public service – when Filbert gets a good night's
sleep this prison is a happier place. He's even more unhinged when
he doesn't sleep.'

'Well, I've heard everything now.'

'You keep this to yourself, if anyone finds out I'm in big trouble.
Don't forget that it's me who saved your ass. You're lucky, I hear
there's only one appendage left that he doesn't have in his
collection.'

Steve grimaced. – 'Listen, thanks for preventing Filbert from
inflicting any further damage, and for coming to see me.'

'You're welcome. Now, enough of this shit; how long are you
gonna be in here for? There's some books that need sorting and
someone has to mop up the blood from the stockroom floor.'

Steve had all kinds of injuries and every bone in his body ached.
The bruises were evident, multi-coloured and very painful to the
touch. He tried to put on a brave face. – 'I'm in plaster for six weeks,
but should be hobbling around on crutches in about a week.'

'Cool; and is there anything you need?'

'Something to read would be good. You choose it for me.'

'And would sir like his book with or without drugs?'

'That's not funny.'

Jayden chuckled. – 'You're OK, I think Filbert decided that it wasn't such a good idea after all.'

'Great, so I went through all this just for him to change his mind anyway.'

'Yeah, but it coulda been worse; it coulda been me.'

30. The Return of Super-Mum

The pirate-ship kit wasn't just for George; Jenny knew that his grandad would enjoy it just as much. They would spend hours together to ensure that its intricate rigging was just right, that its cannons were fixed in place, and that it was painted authentically. Her father would research its history, tell George of its crew and the battles they fought. George would lap it all up, even the bits that Grandad made up; then he'd excitedly recite it all to Jenny at bedtime.

Jenny realised these days were precious, that George wouldn't always be so thrilled by her homecoming and see her as a Super-Mum. It had only been a few days, but still she felt guilty about leaving him. It soon became apparent though, that she hadn't been missed that much; for Nanny and Grandad had been to watch him play football, taken him to the zoo, and let him walk Sandy on the Common four times.

It was good to be in the warmth of home, back on familiar territory and far away from cold, deserted mansions. Jenny reflected upon how lucky she was to have a loving home to return to, whenever she wanted. So different from Bambi's supposedly privileged upbringing in luxury, with money no object. She had been used as a bargaining tool for financial gain, and didn't even know who her real father was. No wonder she'd run away.

Of course, Dad was curious as to what she'd discovered in Devon; had it been a wild goose chase and complete waste of time as he'd predicted? There was no hiding the astonishment in his eyes when Jenny relayed the story so far. – 'Impressive, you're turning into quite the detective,' he said.

'It wasn't just me,' said Jenny; 'Sarah and Karen were brilliant, and James Heritage is a natural investigator. You'd get on really well with him.'

'Almost makes me want to come out of retirement. So, what's the next step?'

'James is going to do some more digging into the family – talk to Bambi's sister some more and piece together the history. We've barely scratched the surface and there's a twenty-year gap between when she disappeared and her murder.'

'What about you? Not sure if you can achieve much from here.'

'The rest of us are looking into a camping holiday this summer,' said Jenny. 'There will be quite a few of us and it will be good cover for what we're really up to.'

'And you'll want us to look after George again, I presume.'

'No, he'll be coming too. Alan's got kids of a similar age and it'll do George good to get away for a while. He's not had many seaside-breaks like we used to; and it's an essential part of childhood, isn't it?'

Dad looked concerned. – 'Are you sure it's safe to combine a family holiday with a murder investigation? And you hardly know the crowd you're going with.'

'I'd never do anything to put George in danger; and I need to get back out there too. I've been too long moping over my marriage break-up. It's time to move on with my life – make new friends and have some new adventures.'

'And this guy, Steve; is he part of the adventure? You're sure going to a lot of trouble on his behalf.'

Jenny tried to appear noncommittal. – 'Don't know; we'll have to see how things pan out. In the meantime, I intend to go visit him again, let him know what progress we've made.'

'It will change him, you know. Prison is a ruthless environment and, from what you've told me, he doesn't sound like the kind of chap who'll find it easy to survive inside. Weren't so long ago that you stopped him from killing himself.'

'Which is all the more reason we need to get him out of there as soon as possible.'

'It's not that simple, you know,' said Dad. 'As far as the authorities are concerned, he's a convicted murderer. You'll have to convince the police to reopen the case, go through the appeals process, get it reheard in court and hope that they uphold the appeal. Could take years.'

'Then it's my job to convince him that there's hope. Given something to live for, he could prove more resilient than you give him credit for.'

'Well, wish him luck from me. If I still have any influence with the force, I'll use it to get them to reconsider their conclusions when the time is right.'

Jenny hugged her father. – 'There, you see, I knew you were one of the good guys.'

Back at the station, Jenny was immediately called into the Chief Inspector's office upon her return to work. Rumbled already, she thought; so much for my powers of concealment. She'd been careful to keep her rendezvous with Steve's friends secret, along with her prison visit, and short break in Devon. Now it seemed her efforts had been wasted and she stood nervously to attention and awaited her punishment.

'You wanted to see me, sir.'

'Yes, Jenny; thought it was about time we caught up. How long have you been with us now?'

'Nearly three years, sir.'

'And you enjoy the work I gather.'

'Yes, sir, I find it very rewarding.'

'I've heard nothing but good things about your performance. Your colleagues speak very highly of you and your professionalism.'

'Thank you, sir.' Jenny waited for the 'but', but it didn't come.

'And how's your father? I knew him well in his days with the force; and exemplary officer.'

'He's well thanks, sir. He misses the day-to-day involvement, but is trying to keep busy in his retirement.'

'And now it seems his daughter is following in his footsteps. Have you ever considered becoming a full-time cop? The force needs people like you.'

'It is an ambition of mine, sir, but it's not practical at the moment. I have a young son who needs his mum and wouldn't be able to give my full commitment to the role. Maybe, when he goes to secondary school, I can think about it, but I need the flexible hours right now.'

Jenny had mixed feelings. She was relieved that she hadn't been called in for a reprimand, but felt even more uncomfortable about her covert investigations. Should she come clean and lay her theories on the table? There could only be two outcomes – given the praise she'd just heard the Chief might take her seriously; or he might be angry that she'd gone behind his back. She was about to speak, when an unexpected opportunity arose.

'How about if we offer you more training,' said the Chief. 'You could continue with your current hours, but learn on the job. That way, when you're ready to commit, you'll be better prepared for the exams. I'd like you to do some work-shadowing with Rob, give you more of a feel for the job. What do you say?'

Work-shadowing with Rob! The investigator in Steve's case. What better way to get behind the scenes, to find the flaws in the case? Steve's quick conviction had been the highlight of Rob's career so far; he wouldn't need much persuasion to boast about how he solved it so swiftly. Jenny could bring up the subject in casual conversation whilst they cruised the neighbourhood in search of criminals. It was perfect, wasn't it?

So, why did she feel so guilty when she accepted the proposition?

31. Hope

He used to have hope. No matter how numerous the knock-backs, Steve always hoped the next time would be different. Youth had that essence of expectation, an almost blind optimism that can only be blunted by the passing of time and the realisation that it's getting late. It was a realisation that had driven him to the edge; to a teeter on the brink of oblivion.

Now the lady who'd pulled him back sat before him once more and spoke of hope. And, in the midst of the most hopeless place he'd ever been, he believed every word. Within the constraints of prison visit time, Jenny summarised their recent trip to Devon and the plans to return to continue their investigation. Steve listened in silence; it wasn't just her words, it was the timbre of her voice that inspired confidence that it would all turn out right in the end.

Despite that Jenny warned of no guarantee they would solve the mystery, or that the real murderer could be found and brought to justice, and that any inquiry and appeal could take years; Steve was contented that, for the first time, someone believed him worthy of the effort. And not only Jenny, but his friends too. They say that it's only in adversity that you find out who your real friends are, and Steve was chuffed that he had so many who cared.

Steve revealed nothing of his recent exploits; he didn't want Jenny to worry. His injuries were mostly on his lower body and his good-looks remained intact. Too soon, their time was up. The visit cruelly short and curtailed with so much more to say. Nonetheless, Steve returned to his cell with a spring in his step. He expected no welcome from cellmate, Martin, but he didn't care; the promise that Jenny would be back was enough.

Jayden's comment the next day – that it was all very well falling in love, but it weren't much use to no-one in their circumstances – still couldn't dampen his spirits. Steve went about his business with assurance and vigour, the insults and slurs a minor irritation that could hurt him no more. If it wasn't for the minor inconvenience of his incarceration, Steve could almost aspire to happiness!

He thought about his old home – a modest, underappreciated abode, from which he'd often ached to fly, to explore exotic climes and cultures. He'd only seen a fraction of that huge world out there; but now he'd give anything to return to that little hovel.

He had his Uncle Roy to thank; his father's solitary bachelor brother. As a child, Steve spent a lot of time with Uncle Roy. A bolt-hole from Dad's foul moods and constant disapproval, Roy was always there to listen and to talk to. It came as no surprise when Roy passed away – he'd been going downhill for years. What did come as a shock was that he'd bequeathed his house to Steve. The will said it all – he had no-one else and Steve was the closest to a son that he could wish for. And so, Roy's lonely bachelor pad became Steve's lonely bachelor pad. A parting of the ways with Dad and a respite from the endless conflict of his late-teens, Steve gave thanks through his grief.

The house was damp, grubby and cracked when Steve inherited it. His uncle had died from loneliness, alcohol and self-neglect – in that order. Steve had watched him deteriorate, cleared up the mess when necessary and tried to care for him as best he could; but ultimately, he was powerless to help this fundamentally good man.

When Steve moved in, he sorted the place out; spruced it up, redecorated in brighter colours. He filled it with the optimism of youth – pictures, music, books; and his proudest possession – a solitary football trophy, the spoils of his team's unlikely cup run. The final had seen a heroic rear-guard action by he and his teammates, before Steve had ventured forward for their late and only corner. He'd risen like a salmon, as he always told it, to head home the winner. In reality it had hit him on the nose and trickled over the line. No matter, it was a rare victory for the underdog, both in terms of the team's lowly status and Steve's footballing prowess. Happier days!

But, as time elapsed, the house turned grey again, as Steve gradually lost the lustre, the will and motivation to maintain the façade. Was he crumbling, just like that old house, destined for the same sad and lonely life as his uncle?

Now, as he suffered the rasping snores of Martin once more in that soulless cell, Steve longed for the solitary confinement of his previous existence. In an attempt to blot out reality, he buried one ear in the lumpy pillow, wrapped his arm around the other, and wondered where his dreams or nightmares would take him tonight.

32. On the Beat

A bit of a Jack the Lad, but harmless enough and a decent copper. If you took a poll of his colleagues, that's how they would have described Rob. He fancies himself, thought Jenny, as they drove round one of the local estates. Pleasant and well mannered, but Jenny couldn't help but get the impression that he was trying to impress her with his tales of bravado and heroism. He probably thought it was his lucky day when they told him he'd get the chance to cruise the beat with that 'hot' PCSO.

Not that she thought of herself as such, but that's what she'd overheard in some station banter among the blokes a while back. Jenny wasn't one to scream sexual harassment, but it made her feel uncomfortable to be objectified in this way. Yes, these attitudes were institutionalised and would take a meteor to shift, but Jenny was more than capable of standing up for herself if anyone were to try it on. From his opening conversation, Rob obviously fancied his chances.

'So, you've been sent to learn some real police work, then,' he said. 'Don't worry, I'll look after you.'

'Thank you,' said Jenny, 'but I don't think that will be necessary. I did train with the Military Police in the Army, you know – Lance Corporal by the time I left.'

'Oh, sorry, didn't realise you were ex-services. Respect. A lot of the girls who join up as PCSOs don't get what's involved. They can get a bit squeamish when we get to the front-line stuff, but I guess you've been around a bit.'

'Well, I wouldn't put it quite like that, but I have seen a few things that I'd rather I hadn't. It does prepare you for some of the more unsavoury sides of the human condition. What's the plan for the day, then?'

'We have a route to follow and we keep our eyes peeled for anything that looks dodgy, or for anyone that needs assistance,' said Rob, as they turned into a particularly run-down area. 'It's usually pretty quiet round here, as they make themselves scarce when they see us coming. There's probably all kinds of shit going on behind those closed doors. At some point we'll be called to attend an incident or two; could be a domestic, or another junkie O.D. We watch out for each other – people are not always pleased to see us.'

'So, why do you do it? What gets you up in the morning?'

Conversation cut short, the radio crackled and ordered them to a nearby location. Jenny gripped the sides of the seat, as Rob swerved through traffic with lights flashing and siren on. She could feel the power when people moved aside to let them pass, the unwritten understanding that they were doing an important job and must be allowed free access. It took less than ten minutes to reach their destination, where they found two men of middle years in a fervent altercation over a minor traffic incident.

'You see those little lights on each corner of your car,' shouted one of the gentlemen. 'Well, if you move that little stick by your steering wheel then they flash on and off. They're called indicators and are designed so that other road users don't have to guess where the fuck you're going.'

Jenny observed and admired Rob's skill at diffusing the situation. He ascertained quickly what had happened, ensured that they exchange insurance details, and even persuaded one of them to admit liability based on their statements. To conclude, he reprimanded them both about the fuss caused and told them that the police had better things to do. Both went on their way with tails between their legs.

'A bit of light relief to break up the day,' smiled Rob. 'It may have been trivial, but I do enjoy winding up BMW drivers.'

They'd only just got back to the car when another call came through. – 'Anyone near the High Street? Apparently the 'coptor's spotted two women sunbathing naked on the roof of M & S. God knows how they got up there.'

'We'll take that one,' said Rob, before anyone else had the chance to volunteer, 'we're only five minutes away.' He turned to Jenny and grinned – 'Never know what you're gonna get in this job.'

Another wailing white-knuckle ride, which Jenny thought unnecessary given the nature of the incident, and they screeched to a halt, with curious bystanders aplenty. They probably thought it was some kind of terrorist threat. Once inside, the store manager showed them to the stairs that led to the roof. As they reached the door, Jenny intervened. – 'Do you think I should go out first, so the two ladies can preserve their modesty?'

Rob looked disappointed, but conceded that, yes, it would probably be more appropriate for Jenny to check things out. As she emerged, she wondered why on Earth anyone would choose such a location to top up their tan; it was a sunny day, but far from tropical, and a bit breezy up there. It didn't take long for her to find them, along with another young lady standing above them with a spray can. That doesn't look like sun lotion, she thought.

'Can I ask what you're doing?'

The young lady jumped and screamed. Jenny read the name on her badge, apologised to Rachel for startling her and repeated the question.

'These manakins; I've been asked to spray them flesh-coloured,' Rachel explained. 'They looked a bit creepy when they were white with staring eyes. Would have been ok for a Halloween display, but not for the summer range. I'm doing it out here, so the shop doesn't stink of paint.'

'Bet that wasn't in the job description,' said Jenny.

'No, but it's better than working on the tills.'

'Are you ok, Jenny,' shouted Rob; 'what's going on?'

'Better get out here quick,' said Jenny, 'they're not moving, Rob.'

The door slammed open and Rob was there in a split second. – 'Stand aside, I'm trained in first aid; you take one, I'll take the other.' He fell to his knees and grabbed the nearest hand to check for a pulse, only to quickly realise he was covered in paint. 'Shit, that's not funny. Look at the state of my trousers.'

'I'd just finished that,' said Rachel, 'now I've got to do it again.'

It took Rob a while to see the funny side, but eventually he admitted that it was a good one. – 'You better watch your back,' he said, as they emerged into the High Street, 'I will get my revenge.'

'I'll look forward to it,' said Jenny. 'I guess that was a bit different from your famous murder rap.'

Out to impress again as they got back into the car, Rob needed little encouragement to elaborate further on his most celebrated case. – 'All pretty straightforward really. It was forensics that did all the hard work – if it wasn't for the DNA, it may have been a bit harder to make it stick. We had CCTV of him in the vicinity of the Black Swan on the night in question, but it didn't show him actually entering the building.'

'You had CCTV?' Jenny checked herself. She didn't want to arouse suspicion that she knew too much about the case. Fortunately, Rob didn't notice and continued.

'Yeah, he walked by there, twice in the space of half an hour. Came up with some bullshit about how he couldn't sleep and how his therapist had told him to get up and go out. Who the hell goes walking at that time of night, unless you're up to no good?'

Jenny thought back to the evening she'd persuaded Steve not to jump off that bridge. She knew he was a troubled man, but how many other times had he wandered the streets in turmoil? This was new information and she was shocked that CCTV had placed him near the scene of the crime. For the first time she began to doubt whether Steve had been honest with her. Why hadn't he mentioned his nocturnal stroll? What more was he hiding?

'In answer to your question, that's what gets me up in the morning,' said Rob; 'knowing that bastards like that are off the streets and he can't hurt anyone else. Bet you wish you'd let him jump that night, now you know what he would go on to do.'

'I was doing my job. Felt great at the time, that I'd potentially saved someone's life.'

'Yeah, you weren't to know. There's scum on these streets; but it's not easy to tell the good from the bad. He wasn't your archetypal murderer, whatever that is.'

'What about the victim?' said Jenny. 'That must be the hardest part of the job, notifying the next of kin.'

'Well, that's where it was a bit strange. There wasn't anyone – no-one knew anything about her; where she came from; who she was. We tried to do some traces, but nothing. It was as if she never existed – sad really.'

At the end of the shift, Rob apologised that nothing of any substance had happened that day. It had been an unusually quiet one and he wished he could have shown Jenny some real action. He looked forward to working with her again, said he'd enjoyed her company and that it made a refreshing change from the hairy-arsed, sweaty buggers that he usually had to share a car with; and that was just the policewomen.

As Jenny made her way home, she wondered whether she had made a big mistake. She'd allowed herself to be taken in by the loyalty of Steve's friends and she'd believed everything that they and he had told her; about his innocence and good character. It was all so convincing that she'd had no doubt. With the revelation of this new evidence, maybe it was time to face reality and admit that he could actually be guilty.

On the other hand, she'd made some good friends, engendered a sense of purpose and become a bit of a detective in the process. Regardless of Steve, she owed it to herself, her new-found friends and to the memory of Bambi. She must carry on.

In the end the truth would out.

33. The Great Escape

There wasn't a lot to do in prison, and even less when you couldn't get around. Brief though it was, Steve always looked forward to the highlight of the week, where prisoners who behaved themselves were allowed outside to exercise within the confines of the prison yard. He was far from a fitness fanatic, but appreciated a bit of fresh air and the chance to stretch his limbs. Now, three of his limbs were battered and bruised, and the other broken.

In the fourth week of his recovery Steve leant on his crutches at the periphery of the yard and watched his fellow inmates go through the motions. It was a sunny day and a well-built prison officer put the group through their paces. Steve attempted some of the upper-body moves, until it became too painful to continue. He was disconcerted to note that Filbert's thugs were participating enthusiastically, presumably in order to hone their muscles for more thuggery.

A young and fit Jayden vented his frustration in the centre of the yard, using the workout as an opportunity to exorcise the demons of detention. The best years of his life stolen in retribution for his mistakes, it would be some time before he'd be eligible for parole. As the session came to a close Jayden jogged over, the sweat on his head, neck and arms glistening in the midday sun.

'Wh'appen Steve? You're looking better than last time I see you.'

'Yeah, gradually getting mobile again; be back in the library next week, but you'll have to do all the heavy or awkward jobs.'

'Nothing new there then.'

'Had a lot of time to think while I've been laid up and I've decided that, if I can't free my body, I'm going to try to free my mind. See, we're all imprisoned one way or another, whether we're in here or out in the big bad world. I reckon the secret is to ditch all the stuff you can't control; use your imagination to escape.'

'Pardon my cynicism, but that's hippy bullshit,' said Jayden. 'I can read a book and get away for a few hours, but every time I look up from those pages I'm still in this shit-hole. That's the reality, don't matter how good your imagination.'

'But we're gonna be here for a long time,' said Steve, 'we've got to find some way to survive.'

'Yeah, well you find your way and I'll find mine; but mine ain't gonna involve being away with the fairies in some imaginary world.'

When he returned to his cell he tried the same argument on Martin, who seemed equally unimpressed; but then it took a lot to get a reaction from Martin.

'If you see me looking vacant it's probably because I'm meditating,' said Steve.

'Don't make no difference to me,' said Martin. It was probably the longest sentence that Steve had heard him utter during their brief acquaintance.

It was back to childhood for Steve's first journey. Suddenly he was carefree again, nine years old and running through the fields on a summer's day with his best friend Bobby. As was their habit they were racing towards the big tree at the end of the path, straining every sinew in competition. Bobby invariably won, but Steve was getting closer each time, due to a recent growth spurt. His shoes always seemed a size too small, as his feet regularly outgrew the family budget, with frequent reminders from Dad that they weren't made of money.

They passed two girls from their class on the way back and Steve could still recall the feeling that he didn't understand; a tingling sensation that made his heart beat faster and the blood rush to his face. What were these strange, exotic creatures? Were they from another planet? As far as Steve was concerned, they may as well have been a milky way away. Cheryl induced that feeling all the way through secondary school too, her auburn ringlets shimmering in the breeze, but he was always too shy to do anything about it. As the years went by Steve shivered on the side-lines and watched helpless as Cheryl fell willingly into the arms of Vacuous Vincent, the class lothario.

He bumped in to Cheryl in early adulthood and she told how she and Vincent had been through marriage and divorce within the space of three years. Predictably, Vincent had succumbed to one temptation too many. Cheryl was way too good for him anyway. Of course, Steve offered to help her pick up the pieces of her shattered life, but she said no, it was way too soon. He wondered where she was now and hoped she'd had a happier life than he.

A reverberating sneeze rudely interrupted his thoughts, followed by the unedifying sound of Martin emptying the contents of his nose into a tissue.

Steve pressed reset and tried to start again. He'd once had the ability to dream about the way things could have been, the way they should have been; but lately his troubled mind tended to churn over the realities. To escape from here he needed to relearn the skill that enabled him to drift off blissfully into a fantasy world. Easier said than done and it took him a while to block out his surroundings and conjure the right mood.

Eyes closed and deep in thought, he attempted to allow his imagination free reign. A teenager again, he and Cheryl lay together in the sun on a deserted sandy beach. He tried to summon the sound of the crashing waves, feel the heat of the sun and imagine her body against his. As he leant over for the magic of their first kiss, Steve realised that this might work, that he could escape to wherever he wanted to travel in the recesses of his mind; until a loud, rasping fart shattered the tranquillity of his dream. The beautiful Cheryl disappeared as quickly as she'd returned, as he heard Martin shifting in the bunk below and the inescapable odour seeped into his consciousness.

Ah well, it was good while it lasted.

34. A Summer Holiday

The logistical challenge of arranging for numerous, disparate folk to be available and willing at the same time, fell to Sarah. A talented administrator and organiser, though, she took it in her stride and cajoled all for commitment and cash. Hence, the campsite was booked for the two weeks that straddled July and August. Close enough to the centre of their investigation, but far enough away to allay suspicion, Sarah argued that it would be the perfect location. A medium sized family site, they could blend in with all the other holidaymakers, whilst surreptitiously working with James to uncover the truth.

The hardest part had been persuading Alan's wife, Yvonne, to join them, along with their two children, Alfie and Olivia. The fact that they knew no-one in the group was the stumbling block, but a visit from Karen and Jenny convinced her. Karen had immediately hit it off with the kids and they pleaded with their mum till she relented. Yvonne came round, stating that she had no choice with those big expectant eyes staring up at her, and that she could never say no to Alan when he looked at her like that. Jenny suspected that Alan hadn't told her everything about the real purpose of their 'holiday', but said nothing. Alfie and Olivia were great kids and would be good company for George.

All the eager anticipation was dampened however, upon a call from James. He'd been up to the old mansion to replenish Trossard's whisky flask as promised, and was unable to locate him. A thorough search of the grounds later and the old man was finally found. In a homely, ramshackle shack on the side of the hill, with stunning views across the moors, Trossard had drawn his final breath.

James described the peaceful scene – a gentle breeze rustled wild flowers on the hillside, bees and insects buzzed with new life, the sun shone on a wild and untamed landscape. It was probably the way he'd have wanted to go. Jenny wondered if their news of Bambi had hastened his end, but he was an old man and, perhaps, it was his time.

James had taken it upon himself to arrange a dignified service and burial at the local church. A few distant acquaintances had turned up upon James's prompting, those that vaguely remembered

Trossard from the old days, but had never before enquired of his welfare. Apart from one mourner who appeared to be genuinely upset.

'Beatrice was there,' said James, 'Emmeline's sister. Seems that, to her, I'm the harbinger of doom. It wasn't that long ago that I broke the news that her sister was dead, even though she believed she was already; then I had to tell her about Trossard. Never thought that old-timer meant so much to both of those girls, but it transpires that he played a big part in their formative years. Beatrice used to go up there once a week to check on him. She told him he needed proper care, but he wouldn't leave. Said it was the only home he'd ever known and he weren't going nowhere. That explains the groceries in the cupboard; Beatrice did his shopping for him. She was the only one at the funeral to shed a tear, but at least he had someone left that cared.'

'It's a sad tale indeed,' said Jenny. 'Still leaves a lot of questions unanswered though; I'm sure there are more secrets that Trossard took to his grave.'

'Not sure how much more he knew,' said James, 'but he's at peace now. We must find our answers elsewhere.'

∞∞∞∞

With sleep still in their eyes, the convoy took off early. It was to be a long journey and they wanted to get there before the traffic accumulated too much. A chilly morning, but a clear blue sky promised so much to three excitable kids and a rag-tail bunch of adults. Sarah and Trevor led the way; followed by Alan and Yvonne's family saloon; and, bringing up the rear, Jenny, Karen and George. Karen had a natural way with children and kept George amused with games and stories for the duration of the journey, while Jenny concentrated on the road ahead.

Tense tent erections followed, as canvas blew in all directions in a gusty sea-breeze. Only Trevor, and Jenny in her army days, had any experience of putting up a tent, and a few words escaped that weren't for the ears of children. Eventually their habitats for the coming two weeks were assembled to some cynical satisfaction. Trevor shook his effort vigorously to reassure Sarah of its sturdiness. – 'Perfect, that'll survive a typhoon,' he said.

'But will it survive you tripping over the ropes when you return from the pub?' said Sarah.

Despite the prevailing scepticism about whether this was such a good idea, nothing could dampen the anticipant mood of the holidaymakers. Like the Famous Five, their packs weighed down with the perfect picnic of ham and cheese sandwiches, hard-boiled eggs, scrumptious cake, and lashings of ginger beer; their adventure was about to begin.

But what the hell have they been doing so far? It's already Chapter thirty-four!

35. Substitute

'So, I don't suppose you were looking forward to this job,' said Filbert.

Steve shook his head. – 'I assumed that I had no choice.'

'And I would imagine that you don't have a very high opinion of me. You probably think I'm a right bastard.'

'Well, I'm not one to hold a grudge, but what your men did to me was unreasonable and unacceptable. You had me beaten to within an inch of my life, I am still in a lot of pain, and they say I will walk with a limp for the rest of my life. Personally, I prefer a handshake when I'm introduced to someone.'

Filbert smiled – 'Please, take a seat and we can talk about it.'

Steve lowered himself into the chair indicated and sat rigid. In keeping with the surroundings, Filbert's furniture was far comfier than that afforded to he and Martin in their modest cell, but still he felt uncomfortable and awkward. He glanced around him and noted that everything was of a little higher quality; not exactly a penthouse in the sybaritic style of the Ritz, but certainly more luxurious than the austere environs endured by the rest of the inmates. The pillows were plumper, the sheets whiter – he even had a duvet, and the walls were newly painted in a tasteful pale blue. A state-of-the-art digital radio stood next to an iPhone on the bedside cabinet, and a photo of an attractive young lady smiled back at him across the cell.

He averted his eyes and returned them to Filbert. This was the first time he'd seen him up close, their previous encounters in silhouette, conducted in the shadows of his two henchmen or through the blurred eyes of excruciating pain. An imposing man of impressive bulk, Steve wondered why he employed others to strike fear into his victims. Perhaps he just didn't like soiling his hands. Probably in his late fifties, the piercing blue eyes and distinguished blonde hair turning to grey, gave him the appearance of a high-end businessman, or possibly a company director. It certainly wasn't what Steve was expecting.

Jayden was ill, struck down by a bug that had laid him low for the past week, and showing no signs of abating. Filbert had requested a replacement for his English lesson and, by means of the same logic used in Jayden's appointment, Steve had been selected because he worked in the library. He wasn't happy to be here, but here he was and quivering at the prospect of what lay ahead in their hour-long session.

'Please, accept my apology for what happened,' said Filbert, 'it was nothing personal. You were simply in the wrong place at the wrong time and I occasionally need to reassert my position in this prison. You see, in order to run a successful enterprise, a reputation such as mine requires some maintenance and, now and again, I have to remind people who's the boss. And you did refuse to do as I asked.'

Steve said nothing – for some reason, he wasn't ready for Filbert's apology just yet.

'You see, it works,' continued Filbert. 'Most people's stories are told through the eyes of others, and I gather that the word on the landings is that I have a selection of body parts in jars.' His hearty laugh echoed round the cell. 'Can you see any here? No, but it suits my purpose that they believe it, because they remain afraid and compliant.'

'But, what about Van Gogh's ear?' said Steve.

'Ha, yes, that's how the myth began. When he first arrived, he tried to challenge my supremacy and, on our first encounter, came armed with a knife. My men quickly disarmed him and young Gerald decided his head was too symmetrical. He used Van Gogh's own knife to take a little souvenir of our meeting. He wasn't known as Van Gogh back then of course.'

'But hasn't anyone in authority tried to stop you?'

'Once or twice, but then I use a different strategy. You see, most of those who work here are poorly paid in relation to what their job entails. They have families and mortgages etc., just like everyone else, so they welcome a little bonus at the end of the month. Some are even customers of mine, which helps to keep the business ticking over nicely.'

Steve felt sickened; he had an inherent dislike of those who traded in others' addictions and misery. Still Filbert continued; as if he was proud of what he did.

'Those higher up the food chain are simply scared of being found out. None of us are born to this world fully formed and we all make mistakes along the road. These days people are very judgemental and unforgiving, particularly on social media. How many of us can be held up to scrutiny if our past indiscretions were to be inadvertently leaked for all to see. I have friends on the outside who research these things for me; I just have to give them a name and they invariably come back with something worthy of blackmail.'

'Sounds like you have it all figured out,' said Steve.

'I simply use the same methods that put us in here. We are all judged through the eyes of others; whether that be the police that arrest us, the judge and jury that convict us, or our fellow citizens. Our view of ourselves is very different, because only we know our own history. I consider myself lucky in some ways, because I don't give a shit what people think of me. They labelled me a dunce at school and, based on past misdemeanours and my current address, they call me a criminal now. I have no reputation to protect, apart from my image as an evil bastard. Correct me if I'm wrong, but I suspect that you have judged me harshly too.'

'With good reason, I think,' said Steve, 'but you are far from what I imagined. You certainly don't sound as if you need English lessons.'

'Thank you, but I can assure you that I do. I am a perfectly capable speaker, listener and learner; I just have a lot of trouble with the written word. You see, I am severely dyslexic. Diagnosis was somewhat hit and miss when we were younger; it wasn't recognised so much and I was treated as dumb at school, put in the same class as all the other kids with learning disabilities – though they didn't call it that back then; we were simply slow and backward, rapped over the knuckles every time we got it wrong.'

Steve thought back to his own school days and the kids who were perpetually at the bottom of the pile. Filbert was right; there was little differentiation in teaching methods to cater for the various abilities within the class. You either sank or swam and lived with the consequences, usually for the rest of your life; perpetual underachiever or autodidact – no-one there to help.

'You see, the opportunities we get at school and in our environment shapes what we become,' continued Filbert. 'Take your friend Jayden, for instance. He's an intelligent and bright young man, but what chance did he have? There are hundreds of them in here, always told they'd amount to nothing and turning to crime as the only alternative, just to make a few quid.'

'But you're obviously a clever chap,' said Steve. 'Did you never try to find something legit that didn't require reading skills?'

'Yes, but tell me how many legitimate opportunities can you think of? The Careers Officer at school was useless – told him I wanted to work with animals, so he sent me to the abattoir. And imagine how you would function at work if you couldn't read and write. Even if you get past the application form in the first place, the whole world runs on written information once you get the job.'

'That must have been hard and humiliating.'

'It was. Even when I did gain basic employment in a supermarket, I was sacked within weeks. There was a big advert for a new beer; alcohol free, it said. I read it the other way around and helped myself. Somehow, they weren't convinced by my explanation.'

Steve studied Filbert's face and it was evident that he was being facetious.

'If they hadn't fired me, I'd have left anyway,' continued Filbert; 'I was never going to last long in a job like that. I aspired to greater things.'

Steve surveyed the cell and nodded. – 'May I congratulate you on your success.'

For a moment he thought he'd overstepped the mark, for a look of anger flickered across Filbert's face, before it turned to a begrudging smile.

'I suppose I deserved that,' said Filbert. 'I like your way with words and I think we can get along nicely. Listen, I'm not trying to make excuses; I chose the life that put me away and I have to make the best of it. You give me some good English lessons and I could give you plenty of tips on how to survive in this hell-hole.'

'If they involve any of your crazy schemes then I'll decline, thank you.'

'Fair enough; so, where shall we start?'

'What were you reading with Jayden, before he went down with the lurgy?'

Filbert produced a large, colourful book, with a picture of an elephant on the front – Jumbo's Last Stand, plastered across the cover. Jayden had told Steve that Filbert's reading age was in single figures, but he hadn't believed him, until now. Filbert didn't seem embarrassed about it, though; on the contrary, he appeared to be looking forward to his lesson. Perhaps he really didn't care what anyone thought of him; and besides, it was an unwritten understanding that any knowledge of his dyslexia remained within these four walls, on pain of death.

Filbert patted the bed and invited Steve to sit beside him. Steve reflected upon the bizarre sequence of events that had brought him to this point and reluctantly did as he was asked. Once the awkwardness of the situation subsided however, Steve got on with the job for which he'd been trained. This wasn't how he'd envisaged his career progression but, for the first time since he'd been put away, he felt useful.

After a few pages, Steve decided on a strategy. The procedure consisted of Filbert reading a sentence, followed by a review of whether it made sense. That way, Steve was able to encourage Filbert to consider what he'd just said and get him to correct himself in the second reading. It didn't necessarily help him to read the words, rather than sense-check their meaning, thereby equipping him with the skills to understand the gist of story. Steve's theory – that if you could pick out the key words then you could decipher what the writer was trying to say; in this instance, that Jumbo could only fight off the poachers for so long and ultimately couldn't save himself, but he was able to buy time for his mate and calves to escape. It was a heroic, well-written, but sad tale, that Steve enjoyed as much as Filbert appeared to.

'Thank you,' said Filbert at the conclusion of the hour, 'that was a very productive session I feel.' He picked up the picture from the bedside cabinet and held it to his chest. 'The one thing I'd like to do is make my daughter proud. She is the only one whose opinion matters to me. With yours and Jayden's assistance, I know I can learn to read and write. I will prove to her that I am trying to better myself. Now go, and tell no-one what happens here.'

As instructed, Steve remained silent as he was accompanied back to his cell by an inquisitive screw. God alone knew what he imagined went on for an hour in Filbert's den. His expression, which somehow combined a lewd smirk with disgust, said it all. Steve said nothing; like Filbert and most of the inmates, he no longer had any reputation to protect, and besides, it was no-one else's business. Upon return to his modest accommodation, Steve could hear Martin's snores through the steel prison door and they rang out like thunder when it was opened. He sighed and stepped inside once more.

'Sleep well,' smiled the prison officer, as he slammed, locked and bolted the door behind him. Steve would never get used to that sound; the sound of liberty lost, of freedom curtailed, of all hope shattered. He lay awake for hours in contemplation of Filbert's words – "I have friends on the outside who research these things for me; I just have to give them a name and they invariably come back with something worthy of blackmail."

There were people on the outside who Steve would like investigated – the police officer in charge of his case, the acquaintances who traduced his reputation, and the judge who pronounced him guilty without mercy – the bastards that put him in here. He attempted more positive thought – "I'll do all I can to get you out of here," Jenny had promised. Steve wondered how that was going.

36. A Maggot on a Hook

The delightful restaurant had plenty of veggie options for Karen, but fish was the speciality of the house. Jenny and Sarah savoured the delicious sea-bass, simply baked with crushed new potatoes and fresh veg. It was nothing fancy, but they both agreed that lunch tasted a hundred times better when consumed with a sea-view. James apologised to Karen for the unseemly sight of his medium-rare steak dripping with blood, but still pontificated upon its lip-smacking succulence.

In an eatery of obvious quality, recommended by James, they'd convened to discuss the next steps. In their absence James had attempted a little gentle probing of anyone who was around in the old days, to be met with a blanket of silence or declarations of ignorance. They'd been through it all with the police twenty years ago and didn't see any point in raking it all up again. Why was he asking anyway?

As far as the locals were concerned, Emmeline's disappearance was a closed book, consigned to the past and best left there. What he thought were discreet enquiries though, had somehow reached the ears of Beatrice and her husband, John, who were far from pleased with his prying.

'They were almost aggressive,' said James, 'said it was none of my damn business. Suppose I can understand it; they've had to come to terms with the saga of Emmeline once already. Then I come along with the bombshell that she wasn't dead then, but she is now; closely followed by the news of Trossard. I can see why they're none too happy whenever I turn up on their doorstep.'

The conversation turned to Bambi's ex-husband, Richard O'Connell. As usual. Karen had been busy online and had built a pretty good picture of what happened to him after the disappearance of his young wife, and the subsequent ruin of his father-in-law. From Karen's meticulous trawl through the Reports and Accounts of various companies in which he held an interest, it appeared that O'Connell had done OK for himself in the aftermath. His business dealings were complex and clandestine, though undoubtedly lucrative. He held directorships with a few high-end financial services organisations, and had interests in a number of multinational companies. Karen had barely scratched the surface of where he and his money resided, but generally they were both offshore; he on his yacht for half of the year, and his cash spread between various tax-havens. Whether any of it was legal was open to debate, but he had well-paid accountants to deal with all that.

'It's interesting, you know,' said James. 'His father was a property developer who'd grown rich in the boom years. Died young after he'd worked his way up from humble beginnings through the building trade; asbestos poisoning, they reckoned, from his early days on the sites. Richard inherited half the money, invested wisely and grew rich very quickly. Never done a proper day's work in his life, but he resented those born to wealth, like the Foster-Smythes.'

'Did you know him, then?' said Jenny.

'Not really. Used to run into him around town, or at the Foster-Smythes' parties occasionally; always a perfectly charming chap, good-looking too, but you got the impression that ambition was his master. He didn't have much time for the local community; it was always onwards and upwards.'

'You can see how Bambi might have been charmed by this handsome, upwardly mobile young man?' said Sarah. 'She would have been devastated if she found out the truth; that she'd been betrothed by her father for financial gain. No wonder she ran away.'

'The strange thing is that O'Connell left soon after,' said James, 'never to be seen around here again. I've done some similar research to you, Karen, to learn what became of him. Of course, he'd been one of the prime suspects in inquiries that speculated upon all kinds of hypotheses. Had he murdered his wife and hidden the body on the moor; had she run away due to abuse? He pleaded innocence and ignorance to all theories and there was no evidence to link him to any of them.'

'We need to speak with him,' said Jenny. 'Apart from anything else, as Bambi's husband he's her next of kin.'

'Hmm, that could be debatable,' said James; 'according to my research, he married again since then. An unintentional bigamist?'

'It would be interesting to see his reaction though, when we tell him that Emmeline's been very much alive these past twenty years.'

'Is there no way we can get in touch?' said Sarah.

'Possibly,' said James. 'There's a brother, Sean; still local and runs the family business. They never got on, but he may have contact details at least. I'll call him later. You never know, he may agree to talk to us if we bait the hook. We have the knowledge of Emmeline's fate and he must want to know what really became of her.'

Dessert arrived to wide-eyed astonishment. The descriptions on the menu had made no mention of proportions, and the sight of house-brick-sized sticky toffee puddings and apple crumbles, dripping with custard or cream, led to guilty glances all round.

Still, it would be rude not to do it justice.

∞∞∞∞

Upon their return to the campsite, Jenny couldn't help but smile. The kids were engaged in a boisterous game of football, George and Alfie new best friends, and Olivia running rings round both of them. The holiday would do George the world of good.

Trevor had just returned from a fishing trip, rods and nets at his feet as he tried to untangle lines and hooks. He'd been up with the dawn chorus, had nothing but a few nibbles, and wondered whether his gear was up to the job.

'Anyone can stick a maggot on a hook and catch something if you're lucky,' said Trevor. 'Or you can emulate the experts and spend a fortune on all kinds of paraphernalia – flies, floats, fancy rods – guess it depends on whether you aspire to be a Bob Mortimer or a Paul Whitehouse.'

'I take it that means there's nothing for supper, then,' said Sarah.

The picture of relaxation, Alan and Yvonne sat outside their tent with a bottle of beer each. A gentle breeze blew across the site on a beautiful summer's day.

'Has George been any trouble?' said Jenny.

'Good as gold,' said Yvonne. 'It's a pleasure to have him around.'

'How did it go?' said Alan.

Jenny glanced at Yvonne; she didn't know how much of the story she knew.

'Don't worry, I've brought Yvonne up to speed,' said Alan. 'Got a right bollocking for dragging her here under false pretences, but I think she's on our side. Isn't that right, Dear?'

'Yeah, I suppose so. Think it's brilliant what you're doing. If there's anything we can do.'

'Thanks,' said Jenny. 'We have another lead to follow, but it may involve a few more meetings, if we can get access to the right people.'

'Well, George will be fine with us,' said Yvonne. 'You go where you need to.'

'Cheers, it means so much that he's being well looked after.'

'Well, that's what I do for a living, you know,' said Yvonne. 'I'm a childminder. Bit of a busman's holiday, this, but I prefer the company of kids to adults.'

'Hey thanks,' said Alan.

'Yeah, but you're just a big kid anyway,' said Yvonne, as she gave him a hug.

'Those beers look like a good idea,' laughed Jenny. 'Mind if I grab one and join you? I'm determined to relax and enjoy this holiday too.'

It was a relief for Jenny; that Alan and Yvonne were obviously loving parents. She instinctively knew that George would be safe if she had other things to attend to. For the first time in many a year, Jenny felt contented among good company and looked forward to a better future; regardless of what happened in Steve's case.

∞∞∞∞

Surprisingly, Jenny and George slept so well that it took the rattle of pots and pans to awaken them. Trevor took charge of breakfast, seemingly with as much care over ingredients as with one of his famous brews. Each person had two slices of bacon, two sausages, a fried egg, a tomato, half a dozen button-mushrooms, and a slice of fried bread. Karen's veggie option was meticulously prepared in a separate pan and looked equally tempting. The amazing aroma invoked envious glances from passing fellow campers.

It doesn't get much better than this, thought Jenny, as she watched George ravenously devour his breakfast while laughing with his friends. She exchanged a smile with Yvonne and tucked into her own grub, delighted at the alfresco simplicity of it all. Of course, it couldn't last and a call from James to Sarah interrupted the merriment.

Too much noise around the camp-stove, Sarah took the conversation away from the throng of breakfast, warning that she'd counted her sausages and would know if any were missing when she returned. Jenny and the others watched her, deep in discussion, serious face and the occasional nod. They all stared in anticipation as she approached.

'James has come up trumps,' she said. 'He got the number from his brother. Richard O'Connell is in London on business. He's agreed to meet two of us tomorrow afternoon. Didn't want to know at first; said he couldn't recall who the hell James was and that he'd moved on with his life. James told him that he had evidence that could prove his innocence; most people round here still think he murdered Emmeline. Said he didn't give a damn what people think, but James had sufficiently aroused his curiosity. Reluctantly, O'Connell said he had a half-hour window between meetings.'

At last, they had a bite.

37. A State of Mind

An unaccustomed visitor to the library, Van Gogh stood before them with an unsavoury smirk on his face. Steve exchanged a subtle glance with Jayden and enquired how they could help him.

'I want a book, don't I.'

'Well, you've come to the right place, sir,' said Steve. 'We have everything, from the renowned works of Shakespeare, right down to our fellow criminal, Jeffrey Archer. Did you have a particular tome in mind, or would sir like to browse?'

'No good using your fancy words; it don't impress me. I was looking fer something about a couple of ponces that sell themselves to get on with the boss – sound familiar?'

Jayden addressed Van Gogh with distaste – 'Wha ya trying to say, man?'

'Nuthin', but someone must have written books about it. Happens everywhere, don't it?'

Jayden's obvious dislike for Van Gogh was in danger of spilling over to accommodate his inevitable ejection from the library, but Steve encouraged restraint with a subtle shake of the head. He addressed Van Gogh with his best customer service smile. – 'Can you be more specific, sir?'

'Well, word is that both of yous been seen visiting Filbert's cell at night and spending a lot of time there. What's a fella s'posed to think about that?'

'You can think, what you like,' said Steve, 'but I wouldn't let Filbert get wind of your insinuations; not unless you want to lose another ear.'

'He don't scare me. Won't be no surprise if you two grass me up though; he must have you bending over backward.'

Jayden had heard enough. He leapt the counter, twisted Van Gogh's arm behind his back and marched him to the door. – 'I hear you spreading rumours like that, man, and you're dead; understand?'

Van Gogh turned and grinned. – 'It ain't jus me saying it; it's all over the prison. What other explanation can there be?'

Jayden returned with a face like thunder. – 'What are we gonna do now? Can't tell no-one the truth, and they wouldn't believe it anyway. We'll be ridiculed whatever we do.'

'Nothing new for me there, then,' said Steve, 'but I try not to let it get to me these days. Don't suppose we're going to be treated too well by our peers, though.'

'They'll crucify us,' said Jayden, 'and I don't wanna be around when Filbert finds out.'

Which didn't take too long, as the prison grapevine was an ever-efficient instrument of conveyance. Filbert soon made an example of some of the prime suspected rumourmongers, including Van Gogh, who pleaded desperately for the preservation of his remaining lughole. Nevertheless, the story was out there, and Steve and Jayden suffered sniggers and innuendo wherever they went.

The incessant homophobic comments were a nasty taste of the ingrained prejudices of their peers. For Steve, it was a reminder of the abuse he'd suffered at school; but, these days, he had the maturity and verbal dexterity to handle it better. He retorted that his sexuality was none of their damned business; but that he happened to be heterosexual and their suggestions were way wide of the mark.

Jayden however, took it as an affront to his masculinity and was soon threatened with a few weeks' solitary for assault on another prisoner; before Filbert exerted his influence to get him off the hook. Fortunately, Jayden had refrained from lamping a prison officer who'd spread similar rumours among the staff.

As for Filbert, he insisted upon the continuation of his English lessons; said he could sense real progress and that Jayden and Steve were the best teachers he'd ever had. Jayden protested that he had no qualifications and he'd be better off with just Steve, given his previous occupation, but Filbert would countenance no argument; they were both the very men for the job.

Steve felt pressganged. It wasn't that he didn't want to help – he'd actually developed a begrudging respect due to Filbert's dogged determination to overcome his difficulties; but Steve had vowed to keep his head down and do his time without hassle or acrimony. This unsolicited notoriety threatened to hinder any right to appeal his innocence, even if Jenny could come back with new evidence. He was treated with disdain by peers and prison staff alike, and only Jayden knew the truth of the matter.

Their shared exclusion however, did bring them closer together. They'd already formed an unlikely friendship, but Jayden now began to open up about his experiences and feelings; how the lack of a dependable father-figure had influenced his drift into dodgy territory.

'Maybe, if I had someone to say, hey, that ain't right, man; then maybe I wouldn't kill that youth and end up here. But who knows? Perhaps it's just fate and this is where we're meant to be.'

'What about that fella, Simon; the youth centre leader?' said Steve. 'You said he was a good influence on a lot of kids.'

'He was, but in the end he fought just to keep the club open; had no time for nothing but the politics. He was a good man, but they destroyed him like they destroy the rest of us when they close that place down.'

Steve attempted to offer reassurance, stating that there is good in everyone and that many things are beyond our control – children can't decide who sticks around and who goes. Jayden went on tell how he had got in among the bad guys and had to prove himself. – 'All that macho bullshit. You know how it is; they call you weak if you don't follow the crowd.'

Steve considered Jayden's words and drifted back to his own formative years. There was always pressure to demonstrate masculinity, the unwritten rules of transition to manhood. How many girlfriends have you had? Are you still a virgin? Bet you can't get past first base! Peer pressure they call it now; but there was no name for it back then – just endless jibes and mockery. In Steve's head it was as if it happened yesterday, so deep ran the wounds.

'Hey, you OK, man?' said Jayden.

'Yeah, just thinking – about the crowd. By the time you realise that they're all bravado with no substance, it's too late; half your bloody life is over.'

'Ha, especially when you have to spend half your life in this place.'

It's a state of mind, Steve tried to convince himself. You can control access to your sensibilities once you realise that insults from others are really a disguise for their own insecurities. They put you down to make them feel better about themselves. You can survive all this crap by rising above it; so far above it that no-one will ever reach you.

Even those you want to reach out to?

38. This Charming Man

Jenny had argued that it was she who should accompany James to London. After all, it was she who was risking her career for this escapade; she who'd uncovered the evidence in Bambi's room; she who was more impartial to the outcome. The others eventually approved, in deference to Jenny's commitment to the cause of uncovering the truth. Hence, she found herself on another train to the capital. Whatever the conclusion of the case, Jenny was becoming a well-travelled lady.

The high-rise, high-value blocks of Canary Wharf dwarf all who wander among them and Jenny felt overawed and insignificant. James lamented the blatant disregard for the history of the area; the once thriving docks destroyed for these soulless monuments to capitalism. He told Jenny that he'd been here once before, on a visit to the Museum of London Docklands, whilst researching a fascinating family tree consisting of dockers, pirates, aristocrats and villains. In his experience, he said, there was little difference between them, except the fate of birth and opportunity.

They found the venue with half-an-hour to spare. It could have been any one of these well-appointed offices, all modern angles with grey and blue highlights on white. The receptionist invited them to take a seat, and Mr O'Connell would be with them when he'd finished his meeting. As James predicted, he kept them waiting; just to emphasise his importance, he suspected. James hadn't seen him since the scandal hit twenty years ago, and Jenny didn't know what to expect; which all added to the suspense. Eventually, a tall, imposing, handsome man approached and proffered his hand. All high cheek-bones, well-groomed black hair and cologne, the charm-offensive began.

'Richard O'Connell, at your service,' he smiled, with deep brown eye-contact. 'Apologies for keeping you waiting; please come through to the conference room.'

He led the way to a huge room with an oak table that could have accommodated two-dozen people. Tea and coffee urns had been provided and a selection of biscuits laid out; Richard invited them to help themselves. Jenny wondered if it was provided for their benefit or left over from the previous meeting. James referred to the contrast in welcome to their fractious phone conversation the previous day.

'Well, you took me by surprise,' said Richard. 'Had a stressful day and I'd just poured myself a glass of red to help me wind down. Now I've had time to consider your call, I have concluded that you must have important news indeed to come all this way to see me.'

Jenny recounted a condensed version of the story so far, with the occasional interjection from James, while Richard listened intently. A lengthy silence at the end of the tale, before his measured response. – 'No-one has spoken to me about Emmeline for many a year and I have tried to erase the awful memories of what I went through back then. Can you imagine what it's like when your wife disappears without trace; then to be accused of all kinds of abuse and, ultimately, murder, when you are completely innocent. It left a scar that I thought had healed, until you just opened the wound again. This is very sad news.'

'I'm sorry,' said James, 'but we thought you had a right to know what became of her.'

Jenny took the ring from her bag and laid it on the table before him. He stared at it for a moment, before picking it up between finger and thumb and raising it to his eyes. – 'Where did you get this?'

'It was among her effects when I searched her room,' said Jenny. 'She didn't have much, but it was in a jewellery box in the drawer next to her bed.'

'And she'd kept it all these years; thought she would have had it melted down long ago.'

'You knew she was still alive?' said James. 'At the time, you told the police that you had no idea what had become of her.'

'Which was absolutely the truth,' said Richard. Head in hands, he sat quietly in contemplation. Eventually he raised his head and looked from one to the other, as if weighing up their trustworthiness.

'Perhaps it's time the real story was out. I have carried the burden all these years. No-one believed I was innocent back then; even my own family ostracised me. I'd have gone to the priest if I thought he could keep a secret, but he was the biggest damn gossip in town. How do you think everyone knew about young Patrick's unusual tendencies?'

'Yes, I remember that rumour,' laughed James. 'Poor Patrick became something of a recluse as a result. The priest was defrocked soon after, you know.'

'And rightly so,' said Richard. 'A confession must remain between confessor and Father; otherwise, what is its purpose? Who needs that experience, anyway; sitting in that uncomfortable little booth and supposedly talking anonymously through a grill? They drill their doctrines so deep into your skull that there is always a priest in your head, watching your every move and filling you with guilt. Talking of which, what will you do with our conversation this afternoon?'

'We are no priests,' said James, 'we are not bound to secrecy, but we will be discreet until we know the identity of the real culprit.'

'And you will be doing me a great service too, if my name is finally cleared.'

'All we want is to find the truth,' said Jenny.

'Yes, of course; and I guess, with Emmeline's passing, I am released from our unwritten contract.'

Richard hesitated for a moment, before laying bare his sins. – 'It wasn't until six months after, that she got in touch. Said that she ran away because she'd found out about the arrangement between her father and I, and no longer wanted anything to do with me or her parents. I suspected that it was her witch of a sister that told her about the terms and conditions.'

'And what was this arrangement?' said Jenny.

'That the old man would sanction our marriage, as well as introduce me to some influential people. In return I would contribute some hefty sums to maintain his lifestyle and status; in short, to pay for the upkeep of that crumbling mansion. Under normal circumstances that old snob Foster-Smythe wouldn't have passed the time of day with the likes of me, but he was desperate; desperate enough to sell his daughter, because that's what it amounted to. For my part, I wanted it all to work out. Emmeline was a beautiful young lady and I was a young man with good prospects; we could have had a great future together. Unfortunately, she didn't see it that way, and understandably so.'

'So, why didn't you go to the police, after you heard from her?' said James. 'You could have cleared your name and restored your reputation.'

'Because she threatened to expose the whole sorry saga. Then, what would have been my reputation? These days, even a Prime Minister can be up to his ears in lies and corruption and nobody gives a shit. Back then, people still had standards; often hypocritical and double-standards, but standards nonetheless. The scandal would have ruined me.'

'So, she was blackmailing you,' said Jenny.

'I suppose you could put it like that. I genuinely liked Emmeline, you know, and thought she liked me too. We met at one of the balls at the Manor and hit it off from day one. Wasn't till she disappeared that I realised just how much I liked her.'

'What were her terms?' said James.

'Firstly, my promise that I wouldn't come looking for her, or tell anyone where she was. Said she wanted to start anew, would be changing her name and that no-one must know that Emmeline Foster-Smythe still existed. Secondly, she wanted a loan. She'd ran away to London with nothing but the clothes on her back and had been living in squats and squalid bedsits. Needed some cash to tide her over until she could get herself established. To be fair, she paid that loan back with interest the following year, and I heard nothing more; until your call yesterday.'

'And you don't know what she did, in London?' said Jenny.

'I didn't try to find out. I respected her wishes and, in retrospect, our marriage would never have worked. She was a free spirit who wanted to roam the moors with the wild deer and horses; and I was a social-climber, always away on business and making connections.'

'And it seems that things worked out well for you in the end,' said James.

'It was all very unpleasant at the time, but I knew that if I brazened it out, they had nothing on me. In the end she got her freedom and I made my way in the world. People soon forget when money is involved, and I still do business with some of the associates I made through old Foster-Smythe. And he got what he deserved – financial ruin and loss of status; the only things that ever mattered to him.'

'You said you thought it was her sister that revealed the arrangement,' said Jenny.

'Yes, Beatrice was always jealous of Emmeline and she would have enjoyed stirring things up. I have no evidence that she told her, just a hunch; and I don't think even she could have foreseen the outcome.'

'There was also an old copy of Lorna Doone in her room,' said Jenny, 'inscribed from Beatrice. Do you know what relevance that might have?'

'Who knows? That damned book was part of all our lives, whether we liked it or not; we were all forced to read it at school. I'm sure you can testify to that, James. It must have shaped the attitudes of generations of young people from our neck of the woods.'

'That's true,' said James, 'and those attitudes have no place in the twenty-first century. Have you never been back since then?'

'What, to a town where everyone thinks I'm a murderer? No; and good riddance to it. There's a big bad world out there and I'm happy to savour everything it has to offer.'

Richard thanked them for coming to see him and wished them luck in their quest. 'You know, it's quite a relief to finally get all that off my chest,' he said. 'I will raise a glass to Emmeline this evening; she didn't deserve such a fate.'

Back outside and the rush hour was just beginning. Busy people hurried this way and that, dodging each other and the few drops of rain that hung in the humid air. Jenny and James joined the throng and made their way to the Jubilee line. They both wanted out of this claustrophobic place, Jenny keen to get back to George; and James, he hated the city and had no desire to linger any longer than necessary.

Once on the train back to Exeter, Jenny broached the subject of the meeting. – 'What a charming man, and I felt sorry for him; having to keep that secret all these years.'

'Oh, he's charming alright,' said James; 'used to charm the birds out of the trees back then. I guess that's how he's been so successful. Changed a lot, though; not a hint of his father's brogue, and he's obviously used to sophisticated company. But there goes our prime suspect – his story sounded pretty convincing.'

Jenny thought about Steve again and her father's words returned. – "Is this fella really worth it?" It was time to confide in James. – 'I found out something back home, from the officer in charge of the case. He said there was CCTV of Steve near the scene of the crime. Steve hadn't told me that.'

'And you're having second thoughts,' said James, 'thinking he may have done it after all.'

'It's certainly put doubt in my mind. But if you talk to Steve, he's as convincing as Richard O'Connell, and his friends are equally sure he's innocent; I'm more confused than ever and we're no further forward.'

She'd contacted Philip again, Steve's therapist, after being made aware of the CCTV evidence. Once more, he'd played the patient confidentiality card and said he couldn't possibly say whether or not he'd advised Steve to go for a walk. It was however, a well-known strategy for insomnia that, instead of lying awake, you should get up and do something. Philip added that there were places in town where he would think twice about walking in daylight, let alone in the early hours, so he wouldn't have recommended it if Steve, or anyone else, were put in danger.

James stared out of the window in thought as the suburban sprawl sped by; then returned his attention to Jenny. – 'You know, I'm even more determined to get to the bottom of this now,' he said. 'I think our next focus should be on Beatrice. Richard had his suspicions that she drove Emmeline away; which could explain her reluctance to speak to me and her efforts to put me off.'

'You may be right,' said Jenny, 'but I have to prepare myself for the possibility that her disappearance twenty years ago may have nothing to do with her recent murder.'

She fell silent, the hypnotic rhythm of train on track turning her endless speculation to a meaningless mush. At least the train knew where it was going; one inevitable destination. Which was more than could be said for Jenny.

39. Swimming Against the Current

Steve's mood was up and down; one day hopeful and optimistic, the next hopeless and realistic – more in keeping with his desperate surroundings. It had been some time since Jenny's last visit. He hadn't heard from her or his friends since and he was beginning to think he'd been abandoned; and who could blame them?

The powers that be were fully aware of his previous suicidal thoughts, so he had access to the prison psychologist should he require it. However, this time it wasn't he who determined that a consultation might be beneficial; no, that was the prison officer that Steve had given the benefit of his forthright tongue after he'd questioned his unlikely friendship with Jayden.

'Do you think it makes you cool or something,' this officious throwback had said, 'hanging out with the street kids? Bit embarrassing, isn't it? You should stick to your own kind – you have nothing in common with them; apart from the fact you're a criminal.'

Now, Steve's furious tirade about racism and enquiries about the prison officer's education and parentage, saw him seated before another quack who asked whether he needed anger management sessions. His argument, that his response had been reasonable and proportionate given the provocation, had fallen on deaf ears, so here he was again.

Anger? Yes, there had always been plenty in this world that made him furious. Generally, he held it in check; he genuinely liked people and tried to divorce them from their opinions. But occasionally, something would wind him up so much that he couldn't hold back. Of course, the small matter of being cooped up with nothing but his own thoughts for long periods only fuelled any festering negativity.

His only release, the pressure-valve that he used to rely upon, was gone forever – the old grassroots football team that he and Trevor had played for. It was an escape for Steve each weekend; the effort expended in frantic futile sprints and hard tackles, a way to deal with all the pent-up frustration. No matter whether they won or lost, he felt temporarily liberated.

Nowadays, those thoughts had nowhere to go, except round and round in his head. Even if he could muster the energy, he knew his playing days were long over; not to mention the fact that his beating at the hands of Filbert's thugs had left his left leg withered and weak. Yes, those days were well out of reach and he felt like a different person; world-worn, cynical and tired. Steve sighed and resigned himself to the forthcoming ritual, as the psychologist, who insisted on being addressed as Will, rustled the papers before him. – 'So can you tell me, what was the cause of your recent outburst?'

'You could say that I disagreed with your colleague's stance on a certain matter.'

'Not my colleague; I'm completely impartial and you can be open and honest with me. What we discuss here is between the two of us and will go no further.'

'Fair enough,' said Steve. 'If you have a record of what he said, then I think you'll agree that my response was justified.'

Will studied his notes and raised his eyebrows. – 'You called him a racist dickhead and a thick bastard.'

'Yep.'

'And you think that was justified?'

'Yep.'

'Would you like to elaborate on your reasoning?'

'Not really. I know he's in a position of authority in here and has a job to do, but I stand by what I said.'

'And, do you have a problem with people in authority?'

It was a question he'd been asked before and he'd thought about it a lot. His dismay was more with those who blindly followed authority, the crowd and popular opinion. Steve was never one for conformity, but God, he was exhausted with swimming against the current.

'I don't have a problem with authority per se,' said Steve; 'just with people who demand respect based solely on their uniform, badge or rank. Respect must be earned, regardless of status.'

Will nodded – 'That's hard to disagree with. I suspect that this attitude may have got you into trouble in the past.'

'I've had a few moments of conflict, yes. I usually bite my tongue, but they have already taken my liberty; what else can they do to me? I don't see what more I have to lose.'

'Your job in the library, perhaps? It is considered a privilege in here, you know.'

'So, that is to be my punishment.'

'Not necessarily. An apology might go a long way.'

Steve smiled – 'Yeah, why not? There's no dignity in this place anyway. How about this? – I'm sorry, I shouldn't have called you a dickhead; I just listened to what you had to say and it was the first word that came into my head. In future I'll keep my thoughts to myself.'

'Well, I guess that's a start.'

'Is that it; can I go now?'

'We have a half-hour session, be a shame to waste it. Is there anything else on your mind?'

'What, apart from being locked away for a crime I didn't commit? No, let's just say that I will use my time here as a learning experience and look forward to the day that I can take the bastards to court for wrongful arrest.'

Will looked at him askance. – 'And do you think that's realistic?'

'I have no idea, but one must have something to aim for; otherwise, what's the point?

'It wasn't long before you joined us that you were contemplating suicide. Do you still have these thoughts?'

'Sometimes, yes. I can't think of more fertile ground than this for such tendencies; can you?'

'What was the catalyst, before?'

'Oh, you know, going nowhere – on my own and with no purpose. I needed a life-changing event to shake me out of the constant stupor. This wasn't quite what I had in mind and I wouldn't recommend it for everyone, but I now have a reason to live. With a little help from my friends, I will prove them wrong.'

Despite his bravado, the words rang hollow for Steve and that old familiar feeling returned. He was alone; no use dressing things up any differently. Steve had nothing more to say on the subject and said he was sick of thinking about it, let alone talking about it too. Will conceded that Steve's protestations of innocence were as convincing as any he'd heard (and he'd heard plenty), but that ninety-nine per-cent of the time the malefactor was delusional and in denial. Despite his scepticism, Will wished him luck, said he admired his courage, and that he'd put in a good word regarding his position of librarian.

Steve thanked him and stood to leave. He sighed as he considered again the claustrophobic four walls he would have to endure. – 'You know, many years ago I was driving into work one morning. It was before I'd realised my vocation as a teacher and I'd been in this futile, mundane job for five years. I'd just been blown out by yet another woman I fancied and an almost irresistible urge came over me to pass the gates and just keep driving – see where it took me, leave it all to fate and the road. Who knows where I'd be now if I had given in to those instincts?'

40. The One That Got Away

Jenny, Sarah and Karen were worried. It had been two days since the meeting with Richard O'Connell and they hadn't heard from James since. He wasn't answering texts or phone messages which, they agreed based on all their instincts, was out of character. Eager to take the investigation to the next stage, it felt like they could go no further without James's input and approval. Hence, they stood before his door and knocked until their knuckles were sore.

'Can I help you?'

They jumped and turned to see a rotund, middle-aged lady waddle up the garden path towards them.

'We're associates of James,' said Sarah. 'We haven't heard from him for a few days and were a bit concerned. Have you seen him?'

'Dorris is the name; I come in and do a bit of cleaning every so often. Last time I see him was Wednesday week.'

'Do you have a key?' said Jenny. 'Think we should check if he's OK.'

'Yes, I do,' said Dorris, 'but I don't know you from Adam. Not sure I should let you in.'

Jenny flashed her PCSO ID; she knew it might come in handy one day.

'S'pose that's alright, then,' said Dorris. 'Hope we don't find anything too upsetting. He's not been the same since Mistress Anne's passing.'

Jenny grimaced and looked to Sarah and Karen for reassurance, only to notice that they too looked apprehensive as they followed Dorris through the door. They all shouted his name to no reply, checked every room to no avail, and searched for any sign of life. A miaow came from the kitchen and James's cat Sammuel emerged, purred and rubbed against Dorris's legs.

'Now then, Sammy,' said Dorris; 'where's the master, then? I bet you're hungry ain't you.' She opened the cupboard, emptied a tin of cat food into a bowl and watched as the famished feline pounced upon it. – 'There's your answer,' she said, 'proof that Mr Heritage ain't here. He loves that cat and wouldn't see him go hungry.'

'So, where can he be?' said Karen.

'A mystery to me,' said Dorris. 'Ain't like him to take off without letting me know.'

Jenny handed Dorris a slip of paper with her number. – 'Please, give me a call if you hear from him.'

'You being the police,' said Dorris, 'he's not in any trouble, is he?'

'Not at all; he's just been helping us out.'

An all-pervading sea mist enveloped them as they went back outside. Jenny stared out towards the ocean, but could barely see beyond the cliff-edge. – 'Beatrice,' she said, 'that's who James said we should focus on next. Bet he's gone to see her without us. He was adamant that he wanted us below the radar and he wouldn't want to blow our cover.'

'I'm worried; do you think we should report him missing?' said Sarah.

'If we do, they'll want to know what our business is with James,' said Jenny.

'Yes, I know; but if he's in danger…'

'And what can we tell them?' said Jenny. 'We don't know if James has a reason for being away. He's not answerable to us and he may have simply gone to visit family or friends.'

'Something's not right,' said Sarah, 'I can feel it.'

'Time to pay Beatrice a visit, I think,' said Jenny. 'We just need a reason to talk to her without arousing suspicion.'

Sarah clicked her fingers – 'I have it. James told us that she is a renowned local historian, didn't he? Has a website and everything. He said there's not a lot about this neck of the woods that she doesn't know. What if we told her that we're researching for a book on the area?'

As good a ruse as any, they agreed. Jenny called the number on the website and was surprised that Beatrice was able to see her that afternoon. She was passionate about local history and would use any excuse to talk about it. The more books the better and she was happy to help, so long as she was credited and referenced properly.

Sarah and Karen pointed out that James had disappeared and he'd been contemplating a trip to Beatrice's farm. If the two things were connected, then it could be a dangerous place to go. She should take backup.

'OK,' said Jenny, 'perhaps it would be sensible for someone to watch the place, while I go in. I checked it out on the map yesterday;

there's a hillside adjacent to the farm and public footpaths right through it. You could take a picnic and plant yourselves there.'

Sarah and Karen spent the walk back in discussion about what to include in the picnic basket, until Jenny wished that she was coming too.

A beautiful trout, he said it was; and it was this big! An expressive Trevor was keen to expound excitedly upon the proverbial one that got away. – 'Nearly had it. Would have been a record-breaker if I'd been a bit quicker with the landing net.' There was more to this fishing lark than meets the eye, he grumbled. Sarah suggested that he make himself useful for a change and join them for the picnic.

'Wondered when my services would be required,' said Trevor, 'I was beginning to think I was just here for aesthetic reasons.'

'Yes, Dear,' Sarah smiled, 'I only married you because of your uncanny resemblance to Sean Connery. Do you think one so rugged and handsome could pass himself off as a middle-aged rambler on an afternoon stroll?'

'Just try to remain inconspicuous,' said Jenny. 'I'll need you all in place at two thirty, on the hillside overlooking the farmhouse.'

'I can manage inconspicuous,' said Trevor.

41. The Other Side of the Tree

The sun had long since burned away the morning mist and Jenny felt its heat on her shoulders. She'd been told that the track was in bad need of repair, not passable by car, only by tractor. Park at the crossroads and walk the rest of the way, Beatrice had advised. A wiry young lad who worked a nearby field pointed the way when asked – he said nothing, but Jenny could feel his piercing blue eyes in her back as she strolled up the road, flanked by lush green hedgerows. She must have walked for half-a-mile before she realised there was no farm ahead. A check on Google Maps revealed that it was in the opposite direction. Jenny cursed and retraced her steps, eventually finding the concealed farm path. Had that young man deliberately sent her the wrong way, or had he not understood?

As she approached the farm, birds sang in an idyllic setting and she envied the way of life, tending the land and the animals. Of course, she knew that the reality was very different and it meant early mornings and bloody hard work, but the romantic notion of a simple and honest lifestyle prevailed. Suddenly, the tranquillity was punctured by what sounded like a pack of ferocious canines. Jenny froze and awaited her fate, as two enormous Alsatians bounded round the corner. Generally, she wasn't scared of dogs, but had to admit that this pair looked pretty fierce. She tried to remain calm and still, knowing that to run would be futile and provocative.

As Jenny braced herself for the inevitable attack, the piercing whistle didn't come a moment too soon. With an abrupt about-turn, the beasts returned from whence they came, only to re-emerge, tamed and docile, alongside a slight, but tough-looking lady. She held them by the collar and told Jenny not to worry, they were big pussycats really.

Jenny tried to regain her equanimity, but realised she was shaking with fear. She pointed out that lions were big pussycats too and she had no desire to encounter one of those either.

Beatrice laughed – 'Welcome to Moor Farm; you must be Jenny. Did you have any trouble finding us?'

'There was a young man working back there, sent me the wrong way, but I got here in the end.'

'Ah, that'll be our son, Thomas. Apologies, he's just like his father, doesn't like visitors.'

Jenny felt the roughness of Beatrice's skin as she shook her hand; born from years of farm work, no doubt, with little time for moisturiser or manicures. She could see no resemblance to her late sister, Emmeline, and the thought occurred before she could stop it, that perhaps the butler didn't come from such prime stock as Trossard.

'So, you're interested in history,' said Beatrice, as she invited Jenny to take a seat in the garden. A pitcher of iced lemonade had been placed on the table and Beatrice poured two generous glasses. 'And what are your credentials for writing about our area?'

'I have read Lorna Doone – the landscape and the past came to life and inspired me. I wanted to capture the stories of real people and compare them with the romance of the novel. Also, to challenge its attitude to women, contrasted with modern day thinking.'

Beatrice took a swig and nodded sagely. – 'No-one ever comes here without mentioning that book. Legend has it that this is the very place where John Ridd fought Carver Doone, you know.'

Jenny could almost picture it, the two rival giants in a desperate scrap for survival of the strongest. It was inevitable that John would win, the fine upstanding citizen with God on his side, versus the evil villain in league with the devil; otherwise, what would be the moral of the fable?

'Are you sure?' said Jenny, 'I thought they were fictional characters.'

'Who knows? There's a thin line between fact and fiction, and fiction usually has an element of reality for the author; most use personal experiences and observations to flavour their work, no matter how far-fetched.'

'So, you think some of it really happened?'

'Undoubtedly, but there's usually a spin on things to reflect the author's outlook and values, regardless of whether a story is passed off as a novel or historical document. Presumably you want yours to be factual; but how can you ever tell when they're just tales told through generations?'

Jenny nodded. – 'I guess you're right, and stories get altered when they're passed between people.'

'Inevitably, yes. All history is written by folks who only see their side. Take a look at yonder tree and describe it to me.'

Jenny lifted her arm to shield her eyes from the sun. – 'It's a beautiful tree; looks like it's been there for hundreds of years, it's so big; probably home to no end of birds, animals and insects.'

'Yes, very observant and all correct. Now come with me to the other side.'

Jenny took a few welcome gulps of lemonade before following Beatrice across the field, trying to avoid the deep tractor tracks, and the puddles and mud caused by recent storms. They walked beyond the tree for a hundred yards, before turning to gaze upon the majestic oak once more.

'Now what do you see?'

Jenny gasped in shock. Its other face was charred beyond hope, the trunk burnt out, its branches sparse and dying.

'See what I mean,' said Beatrice. 'If you stand here, you get a completely different picture. If anyone lived on this side, they would have another perspective on the tree and its prospects. The lightning struck a few weeks back. Who knows if it will survive? You could come back in ten years and it may have risen from the ashes, or it may be dead and all you'll see is sky. I pray for the former. It was there long before we were born and, with God's will, it will be there long after we're gone. What is a mere human lifetime through the eyes of nature?'

'But you wouldn't know it was so stricken when you look at it from your garden,' said Jenny.

'Exactly, and it's the same with history; you only get one side of the story, usually the side that won. History is nothing but people's stories and one man's history is another man's fiction.'

'So, it's a dilemma, determining fact from fabrication.'

'Always. But that's what makes it so interesting, to unravel the knots and get to the source. If the past is a foreign country, then people should be respectful when they visit. Unfortunately, just as some of our fellow citizens have contempt for other countries, they have disdain for history; ride roughshod over fact, until all that's left is a mish-mash of opinions viewed through a narrow lens. They twist it for their own ends – rape and pillage the past, without a thought for our reputation as historians. And that's just our leaders I'm talking about – not to mention those who blindly follow and believe everything they're told.'

Jenny glanced left towards the hillside and saw three distant dots of figures sprawled between bushes and sheep. She couldn't tell from this far away, but assumed it was Karen, Sarah and Trevor. For an instant, the sun flashed off glass (probably Trevor's binoculars), but Beatrice didn't seem to notice. Jenny felt foolish and guilty for engaging backup, when Beatrice was such an ostensibly pleasant and non-threatening lady. Even her dogs were now happy to be stroked and tickled.

'To be honest,' said Beatrice, as they strolled back to the garden, 'what you are trying to achieve with your book has already been done; by me and many others before. The story of Lorna Doone is well-documented and there are plenty of historical reference books on the area. The information you need already exists if you think you can put a new slant on it; and I'm happy for you to use my stuff for reference, as long as you don't copy it word for word.'

'Thank you,' said Jenny. She rotated slowly, 360 degrees for a panoramic view of the landscape, and took a deep breath of fresh country air. 'What a beautiful place to live. How long have you been here?'

'Married John eighteen years ago. He'd just inherited the farm after his father died. He's as much a part of this landscape as that old tree. When he's not working, he spends his time way up on those rocks, gazing out across the valley. Has this secret place that even I don't know; eats more of his meals on that hillside than at the dining-room table. Reckon if I could capture his thoughts when he's up there, then I could capture the essence of Doone Valley better than anything else that's been written about it, but he won't tell anyone where it is. Ah, here he is now.'

An enormous, muscular man strode towards them, fair hair down to his shoulders and a full beard. He looked like he'd been hewn from the craggy rocks that were scattered randomly on the moor, and could have passed for a fabled giant when stood alongside his diminutive wife.

'Din't know we 'ad compny,' he boomed. The voice seemed to echo through the valley and Jenny noticed that the two Alsatians that had greeted her so fiercely, were now quiet and subservient; not exactly cowering, but certainly respectful.

Beatrice introduced them and John said it was nice to meet her, but his expression was one of distrust, as if he had no tolerance of strangers. John didn't stay to chat – a farmer's work is never done, he said, and young Thomas would need his father's muscle to get the job finished as usual. As he lumbered away, Beatrice seemed to sense what Jenny was thinking and explained – 'He's not the most sociable soul. Only has time for the farm and, if he had his way, we'd never have company.'

Jenny had plenty of unanswered questions (like, what do you know about James's disappearance, for instance), but didn't think it wise to pursue them at this stage for fear of arousing suspicion. She thanked Beatrice for her time and asked if she could call should she need any further help with her research.

'Absolutely; always happy to be of assistance,' said Beatrice, 'I hope you have a pleasant stay in our area.'

Jenny was about to turn to leave, when a notion struck her like a lightning bolt. – 'Hang on – your name is Beatrice Reed, right; which means that your husband's name is John Reed. He's a giant of a man, a farmer, and lives in the midst of Lorna Doone country. He could have stepped straight out of the pages of the book.'

'Ha, yes, you're not the first person to make that observation, of course. We could open up the farm for tourists and sell tickets, but John is a private man with no patience for all that nonsense, as he calls it. And I'm certainly no Lorna – a beauty beyond compare, so legend has it.'

No, you're not, thought Jenny, but I know of someone who was. And what of those initials carved into the louvre screen in Emmeline's old room in the mansion – EFS & JR?

Perhaps, she thought, we've found our JR.

42. Filbert's Influence

A sanctuary amidst a soulless void, the library was Steve's escape. Somehow, he'd kept his job. He suspected Filbert's influence. The prison officer with whom he'd had the altercation had left, citing personal reasons. Once again, he suspected Filbert's influence. Whether his old nemesis simply appreciated Steve's efforts to assist in the improvement of his literacy, or whether in attempt to make amends for his previous ill treatment, relations between them were amicable.

Filbert was now a regular visitor to the library, no longer in an illicit drug scam capacity, but through a genuine interest in reading and a quest to broaden his mind. Both Jayden and Steve considered it their greatest achievement. Invariably accompanied by his thugs, Filbert had also joined and encouraged the weekly recital sessions, in which the two librarians would read excerpts from an eclectic array of fiction and poetry. Soon, the sessions grew, from a few curious attendees to an ostensibly enthusiastic group of listeners. Steve suspected Filbert's influence.

Their audience, a fearsome collection of thieves, murderers and various other reprobates, would have scared the shit out of the most seasoned performers; but the sessions always concluded with polite applause and thanks. Steve suspected Filbert's influence.

Their efforts also stimulated interest from the prison Governor, who revelled in showing-off this new initiative to a selection of local dignitaries; and he no doubt took the credit for it too. He liked to think of himself as progressive, a practitioner of cutting-edge governing. Before long there was talk of expanding the scheme nationally, as part of the curriculum for prison education. Steve didn't think this was within the realm of Filbert's influence.

Inevitably, along with news of Filbert's new found interest, came the assumption that he'd gone soft; an assumption that he worked quickly to quell. As usual, Jayden had his ear to the prison grapevine and brought Steve up to speed. – 'There's a dude on the next landing who now walks same as you. Put the two of you together and you'd be no use in a three-legged race. But rumour has it that Filbert picked on the wrong guy this time.'

'What's so different about this fella, then?' said Steve.

'Mickey's a Category A – top dog at his last place and aspirations to take over here. We're known as Filbert's men, not a position we applied for, but that's where we're at. If there's gonna be a war, I don't wanna be on the front line. We need to keep our heads down and stay on our toes.'

'Could be difficult,' said Steve. 'I'm not a contortionist; especially with this leg.'

'This is serious, man. My man Tyrone's been inside with him before, and this dude don't fuck about. If he wants to challenge Filbert there could be a bloodbath and I'd rather it weren't our blood.'

'So, what do we do? There's not exactly anywhere to hide, is there?'

Jayden frowned – 'Perhaps we have to weigh the odds and pick a winner.'

'And who's your money on?'

'That's the problem – I don't know. They're both evil when they want to be; but one thing I notice about Filbert since you joined the party – he can be loyal when he likes you.'

'He likes you too,' said Steve, 'he told me so.'

'Well, that's good to know,' laughed Jayden. 'Mum always told me to pick my friends carefully. Perhaps I shoulda listened.'

Doesn't matter where you are, thought Steve, there's always someone with aspirations to be top dog. Could be at school, in work, in sport, in politics, or in prison – your ambitious type, typically a man, will angle relentlessly for power, with no concern for those caught in the crossfire. He'd witnessed it so many times and wondered what drove such folk. Did someone once put them down, question their worth – a parent or a teacher perhaps – provoking an endless compulsion to prove themselves? Or did someone once tell them that they were something special – better than others? With an ego the size of a small country, they expect adulation and engender fear.

Then, when you get two people of a similar ilk vying for one position, conflict is inevitable. It was too much to ask that it be civilised, that the spoils be divvied up between them, or that there be a handshake at the conclusion of hostilities. No, Steve expected carnage and Jayden predicted a riot.

Then Mickey came to the library. Jayden saw him first and nudged Steve. They both greeted him nervously and, in harmony, asked how they could help him.

'What's this, some kinda double-act?' said Mickey.

Whether out of curiosity about the library's recent popularity, or to check what was in it for Filbert, Steve wasn't sure why Mickey was here. Either way, given his reputation, he wished he wasn't. A shaven-headed, scary-looking bloke, with an angry scar beneath his left eye, Mickey picked up the nearest book and fanned its pages in Steve's face. A gesture designed to intimidate, it succeeded in making Steve quake in his boots.

'What can we do for you, Mickey?' asked Jayden again, in his politest customer-service voice.

'How do you know my name? We've never met before.'

'You're famous in here already, man. Don't take long for word to get around.'

Mickey smiled, revealing a row of misshapen teeth, with the contrast of a single gold one at the top middle. – 'I'm interested in joining your weekly reading sessions – about time I took my education seriously; and I reckon I could learn a lot from you guys.'

'And do you have a particular area of interest?' said Steve.

'I like fairy stories, especially the Emperor's New Clothes. You know, where the guy thinks he's king of the castle, but really, he's naked and the people laugh at him. But, hey, it's your session – you choose something suitable. Wednesday at five, right? I'll see you there. Might bring a few friends too.'

As Mickey's bulk disappeared through the doorway, Jayden turned to Steve. – 'What you like at refereeing, man?'

'We could read something where they all live happily ever after in peace and harmony – try to diffuse the situation.'

'Yeah, good luck with that. This job was good while it lasted, but there ain't gonna be no library left when them two have finished. See you on the other side, man.'

43. A Staggering Man

This was Jenny's favourite part of the day, when they all convened amidst their tents and relaxed; the day's business done. The kids worn out from an abundance of fresh air and play; all they wanted to do was eat, then cuddle up till their eyes were too tired to stay open. George twitched on her lap, lost in the neverland betwixt adventure and slumber. She smiled at Yvonne and Alan – 'Thank you so much. I've never seen him so happy. He's having a wonderful time.'

'Our pleasure,' said Yvonne. 'You should be very proud – he's a lovely lad.'

'I am,' said Jenny. 'It's been hard for him without his dad, but he never complains.'

The others were growing impatient. They wanted to know about Jenny's encounter with Beatrice, but she insisted that the children were asleep before any revelations. Finally, they were tucked up in their sleeping bags, exhausted as the sun dipped below the horizon – well past their bedtime. Moths banged their heads against any available light source, and bats swooped in and out of the surrounding trees. A humid evening, each sipped their tipple of choice as the discussion began. It was all speculation, of course. Jenny had nothing to go on, apart from a hunch; but she believed that the key to the mystery could lie in the relationship between Emmeline and her sister.

'So, your theory is that they both had the hots for this John Reed,' said Sarah. 'And is he worth fighting over?'

'He's certainly an impressive figure of a man,' said Jenny. 'From our brief encounter, I'd say he has the personality of a tree-stump and just as stubborn roots; but I suppose there's a certain rugged attraction if you're that way inclined.'

'From which I gather that you were impervious to his charms,' said Trevor.

'I was more concerned with trying to figure out where they both fit into the story. I'm convinced they know more than meets the eye, but how can we dig deeper without raising suspicion?'

'Perhaps we could sneak in under the cover of darkness,' said Trevor. 'See if we can locate your friend James in the process.' By this time Trevor had sunk a few beers and was obviously feeling brave.

'I wouldn't recommend it with those dogs around,' said Jenny. 'No, I'll have to gain Beatrice's trust. Think she fell for my author disguise, and she's passionate about her subject, couldn't get a word in once she started talking. You'd like her, Karen, with your shared interest in history.'

It was agreed that Jenny would contact Beatrice again in the morning. In the meantime, Karen suggested a quiz as their evening's entertainment, with each team member compiling five questions on their specialist subject for the others to answer. They all retired to their tents for fifteen minutes to gather their thoughts and conjure some inspiration.

The campsite gradually grew quieter, as other families went through the same ritual to cajole their worn-out offspring to bed. Jenny looked at the sleeping George and smiled – could anything ever surpass the love of a mother for her child? May his dreams forever be happy ones. She quickly cobbled together a few questions for the quiz, unsure whether her fellow campers would know who Jamie Lee Curtis's parents were. Their interests were many and varied.

Sarah emerged first and immediately raised the alarm with a yell to her fellow campers. A man staggered along the campsite's main path, about a hundred yards from their pitch, obviously in some distress. Karen and Sarah rushed to his assistance, with Jenny, Trevor, Alan and Yvonne not far behind. Just as they got to his side, he collapsed, face down and still. Jenny's first-aid training instinctively kicked in and she carefully turned him to the recovery position. In the dusk it was hard to see, until Alan fetched a lantern.

'It's James!' exclaimed Jenny. 'What the hell has happened?'

She checked for breath and pulse and was relieved that both were evident, albeit faint and irregular. Concerned and confused, they all speculated as to how James had got here, and in such a state too. He was barely conscious but, with time and gentle coaxing, he eventually came round and groaned – 'Where am I, what happened?'

Unsteadily and with support, he stood and hobbled to an awaiting camp-chair, grateful for the offer of water. The approaching night had brought with it a cooler clime, so Trevor wrapped a jacket round James's shoulders. As he regained his senses, he realised that his glass contained a clear, tasteless liquid and enquired – 'Don't you have anything stronger than this?'

A bottle of Trevor's finest brew was produced from his cool-box. He poured it expertly into a pint glass and handed it to James. – 'Thank you; don't suppose you have anything to accompany it, do you? I haven't eaten since yesterday.'

The remnants of that evening's feast were retrieved and they patiently watched as James consumed the lot. Thirst quenched and hunger sated, equilibrium and wits partially recovered, he was finally ready to answer their incessant questions. Firstly, he was introduced to the members of the Black Swan Detective Agency that he'd yet to meet. He was pleased to make their acquaintance, he said, before Jenny implored him to spill the beans.

'OK, OK, give me time. I've been imprisoned. I know not where and by whom, but I can guess. I was on my way to Moor Farm to visit Beatrice, when I was jumped from behind. Didn't see my captor, I was blindfolded and dumped in an outhouse somewhere. The door was securely locked, but eventually, I managed to escape by levering some loose panels at the back with a toilet brush.'

'But how did you get here?' said Sarah.

'I thought they might be looking for me, so I kept off the roads. Been hill-walking all my life and I'm still fairly fit, but this was hard. Didn't have a clue where I was to start with but, finally, came across somewhere familiar. Been walking cross country all day, looking over my shoulder. You told me you were staying here and thought it would be safer than returning home. As far as we're aware, nobody knows about your involvement in all this. Someone is obviously spooked by my investigations and is trying to frighten me off. Think they might have succeeded. Can I stay here tonight?'

'Of course,' said Trevor, 'there's a spare room in our tent. Just have to clear out our junk. It's not the height of luxury, but probably more comfortable than an outhouse.'

'Do you have any idea who kidnapped you?' said Jenny.

'Well, it wasn't Beatrice, unless she's grown hairy, muscular arms since we last met. Could be her Herculean husband, John Reed; but I didn't see and, whoever it was, didn't say a word.'

'You can't go back there tomorrow, Jenny,' asserted Sarah. 'If you're not ripped apart by rabid dogs, you could be locked away, never to be seen again.'

'That's a bit melodramatic, isn't it?' said Jenny. 'The dogs are my friends now; and Beatrice was perfectly charming.'

'But there's obviously something dodgy going on,' said Trevor. 'Surely, we have enough to take to the police; to get them to reopen the case – Bambi's murder. That was our mission, wasn't it? Accomplished, I'd say. They could even reopen the case on her original disappearance, based on what you've all discovered.'

'He's right, Jenny,' said Sarah. 'We can't do this by ourselves. It's time to bring in the proper authorities.'

'But...,' said Jenny.

'But you're worried about being in trouble with your boss and colleagues,' said Sarah. 'You've gone behind their backs, questioned their competence and integrity. With good reason, but they may not see it that way.'

'Am I that easy to read? I really wanted us to solve the whole thing and take it to them as a fait-accompli.' Jenny felt dejected and defeated, as if she'd failed Steve and Bambi.

'I know the local Chief Constable,' said James. 'Why don't I have a word with him?'

Jenny sighed and noticed that all eyes were fixed on her. It was only now that she realised how tired she was. The case had been all-consuming and she'd gone through a rainbow of emotions and self-doubt along the way. Maybe it was time to hand over the reins and let Steve sink or swim. She looked from one to the other. – 'And do you all feel this way?'

A series of nods confirmed agreement. – 'It's probably for the best,' said Karen.

'Looks like I'm outnumbered anyway. OK, then. I guess I've been neglecting my duties as a mother too. Poor George probably thinks he's been adopted.'

'Think of all you've achieved,' said Trevor. 'The three of you, along with James, have found out more in these past few months than the police have unearthed in twenty years. They should be grateful.'

Jenny felt a weight lift from her shoulders. Since her initial scepticism turned to determination and full involvement, she'd been immersed in the mystery and quest for the truth. Yes, it had given her a sense of purpose, but also the heavy shackles of responsibility. Maybe the others were right; it was time to share the load.

Once the decision had been made, the mood lightened. The whole group chilled out, enjoyed their surroundings and the general bonhomie. The quiz was resurrected, banter shared, stories told, and laughter echoed round the campsite. They knew they'd all be interviewed by the police on the morrow, but tonight was made for pleasure. The wine flowed freely until all were ready for bed, exhausted; especially James who'd been through such an ordeal.

Sleep – rejuvenation, a time for body and mind to reset; and to awake refreshed, ready to go again.

Until the morning light revealed the chilling message, sprayed in red on Sarah and Trevor's tent – STAY AWAY FROM US!

44. Redundant

Photographs were taken by the police of the message on the tent, the surrounding ground forensically examined, footprints analysed. An excited George quizzed Jenny ceaselessly – why were the police here, had someone been murdered, where was the body? She eventually calmed him down and told him that no-one was dead, it was just a bit of graffiti, and that the police wanted to speak with each of them to try to find out who did it. – 'It wasn't me,' insisted George.

The inevitable interrogation; James was interviewed first, and now it was Jenny's turn to give her perspective on events. She started from the beginning and held nothing back, finally deciding it was time that everything was out in the open. From the evening she'd persuaded Steve not to jump, through their brief liaisons, to the entreaties of Steve's friends to help prove his innocence. Then to her search of Bambi's room and what she'd found there, the trip to see James and the discovery of Bambi's real identity and roots. And finally, Jenny's visit to Beatrice and John's farm, and James's kidnap.

The seasoned cop before her seemed more concerned with whether she had breached any rules or etiquette in relation to her role as a PCSO, than in getting to the crux of the investigation. Jenny assured him that her involvement was as a private citizen and that she hadn't used her position to gain any advantage or evidence – a tenuous argument it could be contended. She would take any consequences that were due, but the pressing concern was to uncover the truth.

'I was involved in the original investigation into Emmeline O'Connell's disappearance,' said Inspector Watts. 'We left no stone unturned and got nowhere, the most frustrating case of my career. I'm as keen as anyone to solve the mystery. OK, let's put aside your potential conflict of interests for now – I'll let your boss deal with that one. I will have to contact him, of course, to advise that our two cases are linked, seeing as you have failed to do so.'

'Fair enough,' said Jenny. 'But this is far bigger than any indiscretions on my part.'

'Indeed, it is. According to you and James Heritage, we have one person – her spouse Richard O'Connell, who definitely knew she was still alive, albeit not till a while after the event. We have her sister, Beatrice, who possibly knew, and we have Beatrice's husband John, who you suspect of being involved in efforts to curtail your recent snooping. That's enough to renew our interest. I have already sent officers to bring in Mr and Mrs Reed for questioning. In the meantime, I would appreciate it if you stop meddling and leave it to the professionals. You are free to go, for now.'

Jenny bit her tongue. She wanted to say that, if it wasn't for our meddling, you'd still be in blissful ignorance, and the whole thing would be eternally consigned to the unsolved cases file. Fuming as she left the station, she joined James in a nearby coffee bar to wait for the others to be grilled and spat out. James took the full force of her tirade about some country bumpkin cop taking the credit for all their hard work.

'From the perspective of a country bumpkin genealogist; so long as justice is done, I don't care who takes the credit.'

'Yes, I'm sorry. Never could get used to being unjustly reprimanded by self-important men in uniform, even in my army days. I blame my dad; he always taught me to stand tall and not take any crap.'

'Quite right too,' said James.

They were soon joined by Sarah and Karen, who were equally indignant about Inspector Watts' condescending nature. A shared feeling of guilt endured, although they'd done nothing wrong, attributed to a cross-examination technique from another age. It seemed that the Black Swan Detective Agency's expertise was neither appreciated, nor required. Nonetheless, all agreed that it would be difficult to take a back seat, now they were so engrossed in the case.

Sarah took the pragmatic approach. – 'Beatrice and John will be questioned, but I doubt we have given the police enough to hold them. They now know we are here and our cover is blown. Regardless of whether we are actively involved or not, we will have to be on our guard. We've opened the can of hornets and they are angry. I know we have a week left of our 'holiday', but should we simply pack our bags and head home?'

'What, and let them win?' said Jenny. 'Anyway, I have met Beatrice, remember; such a welcoming and amiable lady – I can't believe she'd have anything to do with attempts to scare us away.'

'You weren't so sure about her old man, though,' said Karen. 'What do you know of him, James?'

'He's a bit of a recluse; rarely leaves the farm and has no time for the outside world. Our paths have seldom crossed, but let's just say he's not one for small talk. Never had cause to distrust him, though, until now.'

As James raised the teacup to his lips, a little spilled on his white shirt. Jenny handed him a serviette and noticed his shaky hand and watery eye. It seemed that the delayed shock of his recent ordeal, followed by the stress of the police's questions, was beginning to manifest. With a hand on his arm, she reassured that they wouldn't desert him until they knew he was safe.

Sarah made the point that, given James's abduction and the blatant threat emblazoned across Trevor's tent, they were surely entitled to some police protection. En masse they returned to the police station to demand their rights. Inspector Watts was busy, they were told. Probably in conversation with Beatrice or John, thought Jenny.

'I will raise your concerns when he's available,' said the Desk Sergeant, 'but this is a small provincial station – resources are stretched at the best of times and we don't have cops to spare for 24/7 surveillance.'

A detour to allow James to go home, freshen up and pick up a few things. He'd asked if he could continue his stay in Sarah and Trevor's tent for a while, as he felt very nervous on his own. Incessant curiosity greeted them upon their return to the campsite; and not just from the children. The one question they had no answer to, was what happens next?

'We wait for contact from Inspector Watts, I suppose,' said Jenny. 'Now we have involved the proper authorities, as was almost unanimously agreed, we are no longer in control. Redundant. Do you have any spare fishing tackle, Trev?'

Alan and Yvonne suggested that, just for a change, they all behave like regular holidaymakers. – 'You know, chill out, have a good time, play games with the kids, enjoy the sunshine, that kind of thing.'

It was a novel thought, reluctantly embraced; but not such a bad idea as it happened. A welcome distraction, much laughter ensued during a boisterous game of rounders, the participants of varying athletic prowess and ability. Those whose bodies were no longer built for such exertion, stretched and slid to reach a distant base, or to catch an elusive ball. Joints creaked and muscles strained to a soundtrack of oohs and ahs. They'd regret it in the morning, but for now it was a lot of fun.

Jenny laughed as George caught out Trevor; George laughed when Jenny fell over; and, unwisely, Trevor laughed when Sarah was unable to hit the ball. If anyone were watching, they wouldn't be able to distinguish them from your average group of family and friends on holiday.

If anyone were watching, that is!

45. I Wonder

Leave it to the police, they kept telling her; but Jenny felt restless and frustrated. It annoyed her that they'd put in so much effort and were now superfluous to requirements, unable to see things through to their conclusion. Yes, she joined in all the japes and games, and, on a few occasions, forgot herself and had fun for the first time in many a year; but still, Bambi's case nagged at the back of her mind. Had they missed any clues? Had they overlooked any leads? Had they explored all avenues?

A short walk to clear her head, that's what she needed. There was some beautiful countryside around the campsite and she'd yet to explore it. George wanted to come too and Jenny relished the chance to spend the afternoon exploring with her son. It would be their own little adventure. Politely declining Sarah and Karen's offer of company, they made their way to the gap between the trees, the direction that Trevor always took on his fishing trips. The lake was about half-a-mile away on a well-marked path he told her – peaceful and with stunning scenery, at one with nature.

With birdsong and crickets the only sounds, Jenny soon felt the tranquillity of the forest surround them. It wasn't claustrophobic, just comforting, the thick canopy of branches and leaves providing a cool protection from the sun's rays. She loved country walks and vowed to make more time for them with George, even though he'd no doubt protest that he'd rather play with his friends.

We'll be fine, she had reassured everyone, when they expressed concern about a trip into the woods, bearing in mind recent events. That stubborn and independent streak had been with her since infancy and Jenny wasn't about to change.

The snap of a twig behind, she turned to see an empty path. Probably some forest animal in the undergrowth. Jenny and George continued on their way – her ears pricked for any further sounds. Although she told herself that it was nothing, she couldn't overcome the feeling that someone was following. The trees closed in, their branches and leaves no longer a source of comfort, but a hiding-place for all kinds of demons. Fantastically, the things she most dreaded – from childhood, through adolescence, to adulthood – they all hid behind those trees. She tried to hide her unease from the oblivious, carefree child by her side.

Jenny knew her imagination could be a fearful thing and a host of scenarios rampaged through her troubled mind. Most involved men, and she resented the fact that no woman could walk anywhere without fear of attack. Given her army training, she was probably better equipped than most to deal with any eventuality, but that didn't prevent the queasy uneasiness in her stomach.

'Race you,' she challenged George. She quickened her pace and George's little legs kept pace with hers, as he panted with excitement. She stumbled over a tree-root, but managed to regain her balance. Beads of sweat emerged – a mixture of fear and exertion. George was pulling ahead, but Jenny found reserves of energy from somewhere to gain some ground. The lake in sight now, the sun glinting off the ripples, her pulse raced, but her heart beat it to the water's edge and they called it a draw.

With breath heavy, they slumped against a stump, exhausted. An old fisherman on the opposite bank looked up to see who'd disturbed the peace. He nodded, then went back to his angling. Jenny felt comforted that there was someone else around, but couldn't lose the sense that they were being watched. It really was a beautiful scene – a kingfisher skimmed the lake – blink and you'll miss it; dragonflies in translucent blue and green suits dashed in and out of reeds; insects of all shapes and sizes buzzed erratically round the flora; and ducks bobbed comically, the occasional quack punctuating the serenity.

Then Jenny gasped as she saw her – Beatrice, sat nonchalantly on a log, whittling a long stick with a small bone-handled knife. In shock that Beatrice was there, in front of their eyes and seemingly oblivious to their presence, Jenny grabbed George's hand. Nary a glance up from her gnarled stick, except to take in the vista, Beatrice never once looked at Jenny. This couldn't be co-incidence, could it? Perhaps the lake was her favourite whittling location; after all, she would be familiar with the local beauty-spots.

Jenny bit the bullet and approached, a curious George still holding her hand. Inscrutable, Beatrice concentrated on the task in hand, the knife a blur in her dexterous fingers. As they got closer, Jenny could determine an intricate pattern on the wood, as skilful a carving as she'd ever seen. Eventually, Beatrice squinted up,

adjusted her floppy hat to shield her eyes, and calmly spoke –
'Lovely day for it, don't you think?'

'What are you doing here?' said Jenny.

Beatrice smiled – 'Came to see you as it happens. Was going to
talk at the campsite, but saw you leaving just as I arrived. Guessed
where you were heading and took the shortcut here. And, what's
your name, young man?'

'George.'

'How charming. I recall when our Thomas was that age. Happy
times.'

George picked up a rock and lobbed it into the lake. Jenny
apologised to the distant fisherman and explained to her son that he
was disturbing the fish. Beatrice passed George a stick and a blunt
penknife and suggested that he have a go at whitling. Suitably
amused, he sat on a rock with a look of deep concentration and tried
to emulate Beatrice's masterpiece.

'That's better,' she said, 'we can have a private conversation,
keep things between ourselves.'

'And, what makes you think I have anything to say? We've
passed on everything we know to the police.'

Beatrice looked Jenny in the eye, a cold, steely stare. – 'You're
barking up the wrong tree, you know. John and I have nothing to do
with Emmeline's murder.'

'We never accused you, did we? All we wanted was to solve the
mystery, find out who really did it. Surely Emmeline deserves that.
You're her sister; don't you want to know too and bring them to
justice?'

Beatrice gazed over the lake into the distance, her demeanour
unfathomable and thoughtful. Finally, she turned to Jenny and
nodded. – 'OK, the last time you and I met we spoke of history.
Now, I'll tell you of Emmeline's history. Then you'll see that there's
more than one victim in this story.'

She retrieved a bottle of water from her rucksack, took a long
swig, wiped her lips on her sleeve and continued – 'You may or may
not have already worked out that Emmeline and John were once an
item. To him, she was perfect and he worshipped the ground she
walked on. You made the observation that John could have been
lifted from that book; well, the parallels don't end there. What John
Ridd thought of Lorna Doone, John Reed thought of Emmeline
Foster-Smythe, with feelings just as deep and immovable. He'd read

the book too and was taken in by its romanticism and the tale of pure love that could conquer all. Utter bullshit, of course, that we all have to learn one way or another. He had it all mapped out – the farmer's son falls for the lady of higher birth etc. John was devastated when she married Richard O'Connell – inconsolable. Then Emmeline disappeared, eventually presumed dead. Took years for him to function in any capacity again – and only then because his father passed away and he had no choice but to take over the farm – yet another parallel with that damn book. I helped him pick up the pieces, and the rest is history. Eventually he grew to love again, not with the same intensity, but at least in the real world. It's an arrangement that we were both happy with, until you came along to open up old wounds; even deceived your way onto our farm to snoop around.'

Once again, Jenny saw the other side of the tree, the tale from another perspective. With a feeling of guilt and remorse for her clumsy intrusion into Beatrice's life, her mumbled apology seemed inadequate – 'I'm sorry.'

'I've no doubt that you have the best of intentions, but now John and I have to grieve again and be questioned by the police; just like old times. He may look like a giant, but he's such a gentle, innocent soul – doesn't know the evils of the world. He's cocooned on the farm – no desire to venture elsewhere and never been further than the cattle market at South Molton.'

'So, what do you know of James's kidnap and imprisonment; not to mention that message sprayed on the tent? Someone is trying to scare us away.'

'John and I, along with the police, are dealing with that. Our boy, Thomas, is a suspicious and protective lad, doesn't like strangers on the farm. Once the cops have finished with him, I will bring him along to apologise. James is a decent man and doesn't deserve such treatment. Poor man must have been terrified.'

'But, if you have nothing to hide, why does Thomas see us as a threat?'

'He sees everything as a threat to our way of life. John has instilled an inherent distrust of outsiders with his insular lifestyle. I try to broaden his horizons, but he's just like his dad and, like most teenagers, he's confused too, dealing with all kinds of emotions. We probably haven't helped, with our conflicted thoughts on his upbringing. It's the only thing that John and I disagree on. I favour education – learning as a means to improve your mind and prospects. John says that all books do is fill your head with dreams that are unobtainable. He favours physical hard graft and honest simplicity. It wasn't always so. John is a clever man and did well at school, but I suppose our life experiences shape our outlook on such things.'

Jenny felt the same disillusionment as after their meeting with Richard O'Connell. Each time she'd fixed a suspect or suspects in her mind, her theories were dashed by reasonable people and their logical and believable explanations. It seemed that every path was a dead-end.

'So, where do we go from here?' she sighed. 'Is there no link between Emmeline's past and her murder?'

'Perhaps you should look closer to home,' said Beatrice. 'I understand that someone has already been convicted, but you question the verdict. Are you sure they got it wrong? There's also twenty years of her life unaccounted for. Where has she been and what has she been doing in all that time? Has she made any enemies?'

'It's not easy, this detective lark.'

'I admire your perseverance, but not your lack of subtlety. Perhaps more evidence and less jumping to conclusions. We live a quiet life, but it doesn't take much for the veneer to crack when our past comes back to haunt us. Please, allow us to live in peace and repair the damage.'

Jenny nodded. – 'Can I ask one final question? In her room I found an antique copy of 'Lorna Doone' inscribed – "To Emmeline – take a look in the mirror. Who do you see? – From Beatrice xx" – When did you give it to her and what did the message mean?'

Beatrice flinched, before regaining her composure. – 'She still had that after all these years? Emmeline badgered me so many times to tell her what it meant, but I kept her in suspense. Then I never got the chance to. We were teenagers who, shall we say, both had an interest in the same man. I'll admit, I was jealous. I found out that Daddy wasn't her real father – let slip by our darling mother when she was drunk. That's why she and I look so unalike – different fathers. Mummy begged me not to reveal her secret. Think she was more concerned with her own reputation than Emmeline's feelings; but, at the time, I wanted to hurt Emmeline and came up with that cryptic message. Would I have spilled the beans eventually? We'll never know; but I've kept it to myself, till now.'

Jenny wondered whether Beatrice was aware of her own parentage, but decided that it wasn't her place to tell her. This was a family with an intricate web and she felt like an intruder, treading carefully so as not to disturb the sleeping spider. They left Beatrice whittling wistfully away, George proud of his new stick. Barely a sound came from the serenity of the lake, apart from the whoosh of rod as the fisherman cast again.

The walk back through the woods felt more relaxed now that she knew no-one was following; until that crack of a twig raised her hackles once more. This time, Jenny turned and confronted her fears. – 'OK, who's there? You can come out – now!'

A rustle of leaves and a sheepish Trevor emerged from behind a gorse bush. – 'Sorry, I'm not very good at this, am I? Sarah sent me to make sure you were safe. She was worried about you and George heading off on your own, given the possible dangers since you've stirred things up around here.'

'Well thank you, but apart from someone scaring me half to death by creeping around behind us, we're fine. I'd have thought Sarah might have sent someone more fleet-of-foot, rather than a great clodhopping oaf like you.'

'Hey, no need for that. We're only concerned for your wellbeing, that's all.'

Jenny relented a little. – 'Well, since you're here, you can accompany us back to ensure we're not eaten by the big bad wolf. Though I'm not sure how much use you'd be. Ever done any self-defence training?'

'Er, no.'

'Then it's more likely to be me protecting you in the event of any threat. Come on, let's get out of here.'

Surprisingly bereft of dragons, elves, fairies, goblins, trolls or unicorns, their walk back through the forest was uneventful. They emerged to warm greetings and curiosity. While George showed off his new-found carving skills to an unimpressed Olivia and Alfie, Jenny brought the adults up to speed regarding her encounter with Beatrice.

'So, it's another stalemate,' said Karen.

'Perhaps,' said Jenny. 'James – when Emmeline came to see you – do you know if she went home the same day, or did she stick around for a while?'

'I can't remember – think she may have mentioned that she had a room booked that night, but I'm not sure.'

'Then, I wonder,' said Jenny, 'I just wonder!'

46. A View of the Valley

OK, it was a long-shot – a hunch, with little substance to her theory; but Jenny was insistent that she follow it up.

'Not on your own, you don't,' said Sarah. 'We're not having you wandering around the moors without backup. What would we tell young George if anything were to happen to his mum? The police have also warned us to back off and leave it to the professionals. Don't you think it's about time you showed some responsibility?'

Jenny acquiesced, to a degree. – 'I'll take full responsibility for any fallout, but the so-called professionals aren't as good as us. I agree that, perhaps, I shouldn't go alone, but who wants to come? I don't want a big crowd to scare away our quarry.'

'You won't want me, I assume,' said Trevor. 'What was it you called me – a clodhopping oaf, wasn't it?'

'No offence intended,' said Jenny, 'but maybe just us girls again. We'll appear less threatening, and we can use diplomacy rather than the traditional masculine tactic of conflict.'

'That's me told, then,' said Trevor, 'a spare part again.' He flexed his biceps. – 'It seems my brute force and tendency for war is not required. I'll leave a sign on the door – gone fishin'.'

Just like Lorna Doone and John Ridd – Emmeline Foster-Smythe and John Reed would have had their secret meeting place, Jenny argued; a hidden location with a view of the valley below. James too, had hinted that such a place existed. He recalled the climb, in his youth, where he'd happened across a scene so beautiful that he couldn't be sure if he'd dreamt it. Wouldn't like to try it now, though, at his time of life. Jenny pointed out that Emmeline and John were young lovers, with all that entails – a clandestine rendezvous away from adult eyes was a prerequisite.

'You've been reading too many romantic novels,' said Karen. 'Bearing in mind that our darling Bambi buggered off with some flash sod with a fancy car at the earliest opportunity, I see little evidence of young love on her part.'

'It's usually us blokes that get our hearts broken,' said Trevor. 'You can ask Steve about that – he's had plenty of experience.'

Yeah, what about Steve, thought Jenny. She'd become so engrossed in Bambi's case that she sometimes forgot why they were all here in the first place. She wondered how he was doing and whether prison life was breaking him or making him stronger. Jenny suspected the former. He didn't come across as the toughest of characters, but perhaps he had hidden depths.

It was finally agreed that Jenny, Sarah and Karen would go searching that morning and they retired to their tents to prepare. Walking boots and rucksacks, the holiday rambler disguise. No-one would suspect a thing. Jenny took care to don alternative clothes to those she wore on her previous visit to Moor Farm; her hair up in a ponytail and a Fred Perry cap – she even felt like a different person. George noticed too and asked why she was dressed funny. Jenny gave him a big hug and explained that, sometimes, you have to wear the right clothes for the job – 'the same as when you have to wear a uniform for school.'

'Yes, and it looks silly and it's uncomfortable when it's hot,' said George. 'People should be able to wear what they want.'

'But then you wouldn't be able to tell what they are,' said Jenny. 'How would you be able to recognise a policeman, for instance, if you needed help?'

'Not all policemen are good – you said so.'

'When did I say that?'

'I heard you talking to Grandad – you said Rob was too far up himself and wasn't fit to be a detective.'

'You don't miss much, do you? I think you'd make a good detective.'

'What does 'too far up himself' mean, Mummy.'

'It's just an expression – someone who thinks he's clever when he isn't.'

'Like Johnny Mercer at school – I'm going to tell him he's too far up himself when I get back.'

Jenny laughed – 'Sometimes it's better not to say what we think. People can get upset.'

'But Johnny called me a bastard; said I didn't have a dad.'

'And what did you say?'

'I told him my dad was a soldier. It's the truth.'

'Yes, it is. Daddy was a good man, once; but you remember why we had to leave, don't you.'

'Yes, he used to hit you and he said he was going to hit me too if I tried to stop him. We don't have to go back, do we?'

'No, I'll keep you safe,' Jenny whispered in his ear. It was a promise that she knew she couldn't keep forever. Sooner or later George would be exposed to the big bad world. These days there were few places to hide from evil, whether real or imagined. The tentacles of the world-wide web were everywhere, a suffocating invisible presence with more disturbing content and manipulated information than we could possibly make sense of. Jenny no longer knew who the good guys were. Perhaps she never did.

Ten minutes later and George appeared to have forgotten their conversation, as he ran carefree again with Olivia and Alfie. It was a ritual that Jenny was getting used to – thanking Yvonne and Alan for their care of her son and allowing him into their family. It was no trouble at all, they insisted once more.

∞∞∞∞

Rabbits – there were loads of them on the path, as the ramblers rambled their way towards the moorland. Ears pricked and alert to any danger, the wary bunnies disappeared down burrows and into the undergrowth at the slightest sound or movement. Jenny wondered how many vigilant creatures hid within feet of their passing – watching their every move. Was it only the animals that had them under surveillance, or were there human eyes upon them too?

They'd been walking for half-an-hour in a sultry clime, before Karen asked – 'So, where exactly are we going? This is some vast countryside and the term 'needle in a haystack' springs to mind.'

'It's something that Beatrice said, when I went to see her at the farm,' said Jenny, – '"When John's not working, he spends his time way up on those rocks, gazing out across the valley." She said there's a secret place, that even she doesn't know. Don't you see? It's where he would have met Emmeline when they were young lovers, just like in Lorna Doone. It's got to be part of the mystery.'

'So, if it's so secret, what chance do we have of finding it?' said Karen.

'Karen's right,' said Sarah, 'it's a needle in a haystack job. How on Earth do you expect to stumble across it just by wandering around the hillside?'

'Because I've been reading that chapter again, the one where John Ridd first set foot in Doone Valley. There's got to be clues along the way. Thought we could start there.'

Sarah looked up with an expression of horror. – 'You want me to climb up there! I've only got little legs, you know.'

'If we've got to go along with your vague idea, that way looks a bit of a gentler slope,' sighed Karen. 'Might take longer, but it's probably more within our physical capabilities. We know you've done Army assault courses and stuff, but I'm with Sarah on this one. I'm not climbing up there.'

Jenny considered the retort – which is why I wanted to come on my own – but thought better of it. 'OK, there's no rush. We can enjoy the views as we go. It really is a stunning landscape, but imagine what it'll look like from on high.'

They walked on in silence, each careful with their footing on the uneven terrain. As the morning's end loomed it grew hotter still. Sarah commented that mad dogs, Englishmen and us would be the only ones daft enough to be about in this weather. She stopped at regular intervals to take on fluid.

'But you'll run out of water for the journey back if you keep drinking at that rate,' said Jenny.

'What, you mean there's not a pub at the end of this? I need some incentive, you know.'

Jenny smiled – 'We'll find one, once we've completed our mission, I promise. Take a look at how high we've climbed already, not much further to go.'

Twenty minutes later and Jenny turned to gaze upon the expansive splendour of Doone Valley – a lush, deep-green, carved beautifully by nature from the surrounding black wooded hills. Sheep grazed, swallows swooped and hawks hovered, among a veritable feast of flora and fauna. – 'Wow, look at that!'

Karen plonked herself down on a rock and took deep breaths. – 'And very lovely it is too, but there's no-one here. You're shooting in the dark – he could be anywhere.'

'This is too exposed,' said Jenny. 'It'll be somewhere more discreet, hidden from view.' A little stream bubbled lazily through the rocks beside her. 'Over there, we follow the water to its source, see where it leads us.'

Sarah sighed – 'That means higher still, then.'

Jenny spread her arms to take in the vista. – 'Look, even if we discover nothing, you have to admit it's been worth it for that view.'

'Yeah, I guess so,' said Sarah, 'but can I eat my sandwiches now? I'm starving.'

'Not yet,' said Jenny. 'I reckon lunchtime is our most likely window to find him. What better place to take a break when you've spent all morning working in this heat?'

They trudged on, Sarah and Karen's pleas to slow down falling on Jenny's deaf ears – she'd grown accustomed to being pushed to her limits in the Army and thought it did no harm to challenge yourself now and again. Her companions' aching muscles begged to differ. The stream reduced to a trickle between sheer walls of rock that seemed to touch the sky; no other way to go, but at least it was cooler in the shade. On rainier days, Jenny suspected they would be walking through a torrent and the cliff-face would become a waterfall. This must be the way.

Be on your guard, warned Jenny, don't forget why we're here. Karen and Sarah thanked her for the reminder, but asked what she expected them to do about it if someone jumped out and threatened them. 'We stick together,' said Jenny, 'safety in numbers.'

Then, as the rocks ended abruptly, a gasp in unison at a bower of vivid green, interspersed with the most colourful array of wild flowers they had ever seen, all immersed in the bright midday sunshine. We're here, thought Jenny, there can't be another place like this on the planet. So taken in were they with the pure beauty of it all, that they failed to notice they were not alone.

'S'pose ye've came to see me,' roared a voice from the shadows, causing a simultaneous trio of jumps and screams. John Reed emerged and laughed, a colossus in silhouette against the clear blue sky. – 'Been watching thee for last half-hour. Not exactly subtle are ye. There be a much easier track, ye know. Take half the time and half the climb if ye come at it from that way.'

'Now he tells us,' Sarah gathered her senses and wiped the sweat from her brow. 'It's a pleasure to meet you, John Reed.'

John stared back at them impassively. – 'Wish I could return the compliment. Why can't thee leave us be? Police say we free to go, but ye still here digging up old ghosts.'

'Mind if we join you for lunch?' said Jenny. 'It's been a long trek and we need some rest and nourishment.'

John hesitated, as if he weren't sure how to respond. Eventually he remembered his manners. – 'Be my guest; a free country, ain't it? Ye'll have to make do with what ye have. Gave the chef the day off.'

'Can't be many people know about this spot,' said Sarah, 'otherwise, everyone would be here.'

'It's the way I like it. Don't need folk messin' up the place.'

They took care to lay their lunch out carefully on the picnic mat, scared that a gust of wind might blow away a crisp packet or piece of kitchen roll and lead to a severe reprimand.

'You're a lucky man,' said Karen, as she sucked on a pickled onion, 'it's a privilege to spend time in such a beautiful setting.'

'Ye think so? Kind of get used to it as time goes by and forget how special it be. Knowed someone once who looked at home here too. Her beauty put the flowers to shame; but she's long gone. Been a lonely place since then, but it still feels like mine. No-one else ever comes up here.'

'But she came back, didn't she, John,' said Jenny. 'Emmeline.'

John stared into the distance over the valley, with a pensive expression. A barely visible tear fell to the ground. A long silence ensued, before he replied – 'Aye, she did, but I wish she hadn't. The past is best left where it be. Don't do no good to try an' raise the dead.'

'And what did she want?'

'Said she got it all wrong, made a mess of her life; she was sorry and wanted to know if it were too late.'

Jenny spoke quietly, afraid that John might find it all too much to bare his soul. – 'Must have been quite a shock to see her.'

'That be an understatement. Nearly had a heart attack. There be plenty of old tales 'bout spirits wanderin' these valleys. The wind can play tricks through the rocks and you can hear 'em wailing sometimes. Wondered if I were dreamin' again, but she convinced me she was real. I listen to what she had to say, then tell 'er to go back where she come from.'

'You weren't tempted?'

'Course I were; she was still a fine-looking woman; but me an' Beatrice are okay as we are. Y'see I learn a hard lesson twen'y year back. There be beauty on the surface, and there be beauty beneath. It's the beauty beneath that lasts longer and worth more. Beatrice has that, and Emmeline never did. It takes time to know, but it's time well spent.'

'Phew,' said Sarah, 'and have you ever told Beatrice that?'

'No, we ne'er speak of such things, but I'm sure she knows. I'm still here, ain't I?'

'Is Beatrice aware that Emmeline came back?' said Karen.

'Aye – told 'er that night, and I tell 'er why.'

'And was she angry?'

'Aye, course she were, for all kind of reasons; but she din't kill Emmeline, if that's what ye're getting' at. She ain't been away from the farm since then.'

'So, Emmeline just left town when you asked her to,' said Sarah.

'So far as I know. She cry for a bit. Had to stop myself from going back in time and look away so's I didn't weaken. Every bone in my body wanted to hold 'er tight like I used to. Then things went quiet; and when I turned around, she'd gone.'

'That must have been so hard for you,' said Karen.

'Not so hard as it were when she leave me for O'Connell. They say time can heal, but all it does is harden the heart so's ye don't feel anything no more. Now, I got work to do. Can't spend all day chewing the cud. Ye got what ye wanted, heard my story. Ain't nuthin else to tell.' John looked embarrassed, uncomfortable that he'd revealed so much to these strangers. He was obviously itching to remove himself from this situation.

'My water's run out,' said Sarah. 'Is that stream fit to drink?'

'Aye, yesterday's piss woulda washed away by now. Sweetest water ye'll ever taste.'

'Well, that's good to know, thank you,' cringed Sarah.

'Just one more question, John,' said Jenny. 'Do you know of anyone with reason to kill Emmeline?'

'What, apart from me, Beatrice and O'Connell? No; I don't know what she's been doing the past twen'y year or how many other hearts she's broke. Leave the place tidy when ye go.'

And with that, John Reed gathered up his canvas bag and left. They tried to see where he went, but his route was concealed, as if he'd simply disappeared.

Jenny looked at Sarah and Karen with a smug expression. – 'A vague idea, was it?'

'OK, OK,' said Sarah, as she crouched to fill her water bottle. 'You win; but now what do we have, apart from someone else who didn't do it? We're no closer to finding out who did.'

Jenny sighed; her moment of triumph short-lived. – 'Yeah, I guess you're right; but it's all part of the investigation process, isn't it? You rule out all the suspects until you're only left with the culprit.'

'But we're running out of suspects,' said Karen. 'There's no-one left to investigate.'

'So where do we go from here?' said Jenny.

'Well, you promised we'd find a pub at the end of this trek,' said Sarah. 'Don't know about you, but I think we've earned a drink.'

Jenny insisted that they stay to enjoy this beauteous place for a while longer. It wasn't every day that you found somewhere so peaceful and conducive to falling in love, she said. On the other hand, it was a fleeting visit, a fitting metaphor for the transience of true love. It rarely survived exposure to the real world fully intact.

'That's a bit deep, isn't it; not to mention cynical?' said Karen.

'Well, it's a deep subject,' said Jenny. 'Why do you think the greatest philosophers, poets, songwriters, film-makers and authors return to it time and time again? I've never met anyone who's got it sussed; have you?'

'Old Beatrice and John seem to have developed a pragmatic approach,' said Sarah.

'Yeah, nothing like a bit of pragmatism to keep you warm on a winter's night. Come on, let's find that pub!'

47. Mightier Than the Sword?

'You're crazy,' said Jayden. 'What do you mean you want to fight them?'

'We need to show them that bullies can't win.' Steve spread his arms in an arc around the library. – 'Take a look around you. What weapons do we have at our disposal?'

'Nothing that I can see. The prison tend to make sure anything that can be used as a weapon is either screwed down or took away.'

'Well, that's where you're wrong. There are thousands, probably millions of weapons in here.'

'I don't get it.'

'Words, Jayden, words. We'd have no chance in a physical fight, but we can run rings round them when it comes to talking.'

Jayden shook his head. – 'So, what're you gonna do; bore them to death? The odds have come down, but you're still crazy. It'll never work.'

'But if we can get them involved in a philosophical discussion, they won't be taking lumps out of each other, or anyone else. We've had enough sessions with Filbert to know that he might buy into it. Don't know about Mickey, but he won't want to appear stupid in Filbert's presence.'

'Ha, a philosophical discussion with Filbert and Mickey! Now, this I gotta see!'

48. The Apology

On their brief first encounter Jenny hadn't noticed, but young Thomas had something of the build of his old man. Then, he'd been stood in a field with nothing to give perspective; now he sat warily before them, doing his best to avoid eye contact. Yet to fill out to his full height and bulk, it would only be a matter of time before he'd be his father's equal in stature. With the demeanour of a scolded child, however, there seemed no menace in him now.

Thomas had eventually acquiesced to his parents' demand that he must say sorry for his unacceptable behaviour, but he was adamant that he go alone. He was old enough to do things by himself and didn't need anyone to hold his hand anymore.

James was still traumatised by the experience and, initially, was in no mood to re-encounter his kidnapper. Usually such a mild-mannered man, it took a lot to rile James, but everyone agreed that he had good reason for his anger and reluctance to accept the apology. It was Karen that persuaded him to confront Thomas, if only out of curiosity as to his motives. Now, as the two sat facing each other, Jenny had nothing but admiration for James's stoicism. The police had warned Thomas and told him that it would be up to James as to whether he wanted to press charges. James said he was still thinking about it.

Not the most self-assured of young men, Thomas stuttered his confession and regret, until James almost felt sorry for him. All he wanted to know was why. In his hesitation, Thomas appeared embarrassed, as if it were a private affair and nothing he wanted to share. Jenny fetched him one of Trevor's stronger brews in an effort to loosen his tongue and, gradually, he opened up.

'I never heard Ma and Pa argue before you come with news about Aunt Emmeline. Everyone round here knows the tale, about how she disappeared, and everyone thought she was dead. At school they used to taunt me about it, said that Pa did it, that they used to be lovers. Pa was crying after you tell them what happened, and Ma said it were Emmeline he really loved. Pa just walked out and went to his secret place, with Ma shouting after him. T'weren't your fault, you just bring the news, but I was angry. I thought Ma and Pa were gonna split up. Shouldn't have done it, and I'm sorry.'

'And how are your mother and father now?' said Sarah.

'Not the same. Pa never said much anyways, but now he's quiet all the time. Can't tell what he's thinking, and Ma's not talking much either.'

'Must be hard for you,' said Jenny. 'Don't you have any friends you can talk to?'

'Nah, I just work the farm. Pa says it's the best place, and the outside world is cruel and nasty. Please, don't tell him that I told you about all this. He says that family business should stay in the family.'

The apology, such as it was, didn't fully appease James, but it was something he supposed. Sarah thanked Thomas for his honesty; he asked for forgiveness once more and skulked off with tail between his legs, wobbling slightly from the effects of Trevor's brewing skills.

James sighed – 'Well, that was some explanation. Makes you wonder who the victim is here.'

'So, what are you going to do?' said Jenny. 'Will you press charges?'

'How can I, after that? The poor lad needs help, not punishment. It's alright for you lot; you'll be heading home tomorrow. I still have to live round here and I doubt that Beatrice will forgive me if young Thomas ends up with a criminal record.'

Jenny, Sarah and Karen agreed that it would serve no purpose and that the can of hornets would be best left to settle. A hug each for James, with a promise to stay in touch, and they were gone. The end of an eventful summer holiday and the spectre looming of a return to reality.

49. Dread Poets' Society

News had got around and this was the largest and most frightening crowd so far. Apart from each tyrant and their respective entourage of thugs, plenty of others had come along for the show. With impending dread, Steve stood before them and surveyed the array of piercing and threatening eyes. What else was there to do but take a deep breath and quote Gandhi – "Whenever you are confronted with an opponent, conquer him with love."'

The room fell silent as Filbert and Mickey tried to stare each other out. If this were a wild-west saloon – they'd be stood, legs akimbo, trigger-fingers hovered above holsters, ready to draw. A static-electric tension, the slightest movement would have scattered the congregation in all directions; but Steve and Jayden had taken care to lay out the chairs in such a way as to diffuse potential conflict. In other words, they'd kept them as far apart as possible and, as belt and braces, a prison officer sat, arms folded, at the end of each row.

Eventually, Steve's words penetrated the impasse. 'What did you say?' said Mickey.

'"Whenever you are confronted with an opponent, conquer him with love." They're not my words, but I thought they were worthy of discussion. Has anyone studied the words and wisdom of Mahatma Gandhi?'

'Little, skinny Indian fella, wasn't he?' said Filbert.

Mickey grinned. – 'And did it work? Did he conquer his opponents with love?'

'Yes, he did as it happens,' said Steve, amazed that he'd provoked some interaction. 'But a lot of heads were cracked along the way. He preached nonviolence and asked his followers not to retaliate, no matter what the provocation.'

'So, these people just sat there and got their heads cracked cos this guy Gandhi told 'em to,' said Mickey. 'Sound like a bunch of mugs to me.' Mickey's followers nodded in agreement.

'But how else do the physically weak fight the bully? Especially if the bully doesn't carry out the bullying himself and he gets his army to do it for him.' Steve looked at Filbert when he delivered this line. Filbert remained silent and Mickey didn't seem to have an answer either. Was Steve having a pop at them?

'Gandhi's philosophy can be applied to nations, institutions or individuals,' he continued. 'The physically or economically disadvantaged have no chance against the bully; so, what's the point of trying to fight? Ultimately, the bully only stops bullying when he is exposed for what he is – a coward that picks on those who are physically or economically weaker than himself. Eventually, the tide of public opinion will turn against him and he is defeated, without his victims lifting a finger.'

'Survival of the fittest, ain't it?' said Mickey. 'If you're weak you ain't gonna get on in this world.'

'Depends what you mean by weak,' said Steve. 'Everyone has their strengths. I might not beat you in an arm-wrestling competition, but there may be something where I can win. A game of chess, perhaps, or a beauty contest.'

This last comment triggered some laughter at Mickey's expense and Steve wondered if he'd overstepped the mark. Mickey glared at him. – 'And what makes you think you can win any beauty contest?'

'Just a bit of humour, Mickey, to try and lighten the mood in here. I'll leave it to our fellow inmates to decide which of us would win; probably neither of us.'

Filbert had said little so far, but couldn't resist a dig. – 'Let's be honest, Mickey, that's a face only a mother could love. Steve's right, though; physical strength isn't the only kind.'

The hushed atmosphere might have been in anticipation of the seemingly inevitable fight, or it may have been an indication that Steve's words had at least provoked some thought. The prison officers looked on edge, ready to go into riot-control mode if anyone jumped.

Steve glanced at Jayden, who gave him the signal to quit while he was ahead. He took the hint and concluded – 'Now, I'm not saying whether or not I agree with Gandhi, but maybe consider his theories the next time you pick a fight with someone; especially if it's me. You've probably had enough of listening to my monotone, so I'd like to bring on Dylan. He's been coming to our reading sessions for some weeks now, and Dylan's written a poem that he'd like to share with us.'

Thankfully, the culmination of Steve's soliloquy was only met with polite applause, which he couldn't get used to from such an unlikely source as these group of hardened criminals. Given this week's crowd, it seemed even more incongruous; but applaud they did and now it was someone else's turn to entertain the audience.

Dylan was a seasoned activist, moved here after going AWOL from an open prison. Now he was incarcerated once again for twatting a police officer with a hefty, homemade 'Give Peace a Chance' placard at a demo. He'd argued that said police officer had been equally disrespectful towards him, by use of a riot-shield and truncheon, but that he'd got away with it by virtue of the fact that he was wearing a uniform. The judge disagreed – so, here he stood, a brave man about to read poetry to this mob of reprobates. He shuffled centre stage, cleared his throat and began to rant in a timbre and accent reminiscent of Ian Dury:

'A tale to tell of an unsavoury chap,
As popular as a dose of the clap,
A man so low as to fart in church,
Then leave his bride in the lurch,
The congregation cried en masse,
"Shame on him, she's a lovely lass,
It's enough to make a grown man weep,
And they say he left her for a sheep,"
He trod this land and left his mark,
Till they snuffed him out in the dark,
So base and wretched is his story,
But at least he never was a Tory!

As he made his way to the pearly gates,
He saw the spirits of his mates,
Their eyes all turned as he passed a Boeing,
"Where the hell does he think he's going?"
The angels wept and wailed in fear,
"You surely can't let him in here,"
St Peter sighed and did declare,
"Perhaps he doth belong down there,
He really is a vile creature,
But he does have one redeeming feature,
He's been many things in his life story,
But at least he never was a Tory!"

To put another point of view,
None of the above is true,
This much maligned and hated man,
Was the victim of a smear campaign,
Upon its head, you've hit the nail,
It was all made up by the Daily Mail,
Apart from the one fact in their story,
At least he never was a Tory!
Thank you very much.'

Dylan turned and left the floor to a stunned silence. Steve had no idea of the political persuasions of this audience, but he suspected some of them might be to the right of Genghis Khan, and that was just the screws. Nevertheless, Dylan escaped unscathed.

Next, he introduced a reluctant Jayden. Part of the deal was, that if Steve pulled this off, then Jayden would read his poem in order to send them on their way in a tranquil mood. Steve had admired the verse the previous day. – 'Hey, that's really good; you need to share that at the group.'

'No chance – they'll tear me to pieces,' had been his response.

Now, Jayden shook before them, beads of nervous sweat dripping from his brow. – 'This one's called 'Mother.' Hope you enjoy it.' He looked terrified and Steve felt a pang of guilt for putting him through this ordeal; but, after a hesitant start, gradually, Jayden got into his stride:

'You did your best,
Work day'n'night, no rest,
Aim to bring us up good,
In this dirty neighbourhood,
When you on the night shift,
Is the time we drift,
An' find our feet,
'pon the street,
Runnin' with the man,
Make a buck where we can,
But the cops on our case,
Always fix the race,
Now we inside,
An' lose our pride,

Shoulda listen to what you say,
Now there's a price to pay,
An' we atone,
While you alone,
For we leave you to miss,
The child you once kiss,
An' we never get another,
Mother.'

Filbert led the standing ovation. Not only did the words ring true for so many, but it was the way Jayden delivered them – tough and rhythmic, but with a hint of childlike vulnerability. Steve was put in mind of legendary dub poet, Linton Kwesi Johnson, at his rebellious, lyrical peak. The poem hit home and, no matter how hard these guys thought they were, it seemed they all missed their mums. Steve watched in amazement as everyone filed out quietly. Was that a tear in Filbert's eye?

Jayden stared at Steve in disbelief. – 'Did that just happen, man?'

With a high-five and a smile worthy of Jürgen Klopp, Steve was over the moon. He considered it a magnificent achievement to have quelled a potential riot through reasoned debate and poetry.

'Yeah, OK, you smug bastard,' said Jayden. 'I know I said it wouldn't work, but I still think it's a temporary fix. Those two ain't gonna take a challenge lying down. They're still gonna kill each other when they get the chance, or get their Mafias to do it for them.'

'Nah, all we need to do is get you to stand between them and recite one of your poems. They won't be able to see each other through the tears.'

Jayden laughed. – 'Old Dylan did his bit too.'

'I suppose you two are proud of yourselves, then.' Jayden and Steve turned to see the Governor in the doorway.

'We did our best,' said Steve.

The Governor nodded. – 'It was an interesting and courageous strategy to confront a volatile situation. Ever thought about diplomacy for a career?'

'Our careers ain't going nowhere in here,' said Jayden.

'Well, that's where you're wrong. There are opportunities for those that want to take them.'

The governor went on to offer them both the position of Prisoner Representative – the job description, to gather the views of their peers and present them to the Board of Visitors. – 'They are the people who monitor how we run things here. They check that we are treating you all fairly and that conditions are humane. We are looking to improve relationships between the prison management and prisoners and I could do with your help.'

'Prisoner Representatives?' said Jayden. 'Not heard of that before.'

'The roles didn't exist until twenty minutes ago. After your performances this evening, I have just invented them.'

'And the way it will look is that we work for you,' said Jayden. 'People won't talk to us if they think we're on your side.'

'Not if they see real change as a result,' said the Governor. 'I don't see it as taking sides. I want to break down the barriers and get us all talking to each other.'

'Perhaps it's Dylan you need if you want some barriers breaking down,' said Steve. 'Can we think about it?'

'You may. I'll give you to the end of the week; but please give it serious consideration.'

While they stacked the chairs, a sceptical Jayden argued that they'd be seen as part of the establishment. It had always been them and us, and it always would be. Jayden was firmly on the side of us and didn't want anything to do with them. – 'It's OK for you; you're innocent and will get out of here when your friends come good. I'm stuck in here till me time come.'

'Hey, that's not fair,' said Steve; 'I don't know when or if my innocence will be proved. Look, who cares if people think we're working for the clampdown if we can help others; and it won't do our parole chances any harm either.'

'We come from a different place, me and you. I don't trust those bastards. They ain't interested in the likes of me. You take the job if you want, but I'm out.'

Not for the first time, Steve found himself on the horns of a dilemma.

50. On the Shelf

Jenny reached to the back of the shelf and pulled the older stock to the front. She checked the best-before dates, picked new stock from the cage and placed it carefully behind the stock that was nearing the end of its shelf-life. Then she watched, as a customer moved the items at the front aside in order to reach the fresher stock at the back. It was a ritual she was getting used to, an exercise in futility that could have destroyed the soul if she'd cared enough. Jenny nodded good morning to the customer and turned her attention to the next item. The monotony overpowered her, but at least she didn't have to think.

The floor manager permitted her a fifteen-minute break and asked her to work one of the frozen aisles after. Regardless of the weather outside, the frozen aisles numbed her senses even more, a headache-inducing strip-lighted icy hell of pre-packaged crap. Two months, she'd been here now. Down to Earth with a bump after their return from Devon.

The sack had been inevitable, if it could be classified as such from a voluntary role. She'd disrespected her colleagues, questioned their professionalism and competence, broken every code of conduct. How could she expect to carry on as if nothing had happened? Her father had less influence than he thought; he'd been retired too long to know enough people in positions of power. He offered his support, but Jenny could tell that he was disappointed in her.

The Black Swan Detective Agency had disbanded. Jenny had no idea whether or not the guys still went to the quiz nights. She'd deliberately cut herself off and concentrated on finding this job. For her own self-respect, she needed to make a contribution to her parents' costs, and try to eke out some kind of future for her and George. Sarah and Karen had texted, called and messaged, but Jenny's replies had been monosyllabic and brusque. Did she blame them for this situation? No, the decision to get involved was her own; but maybe, subconsciously, she wished she'd never set foot in that pub.

She'd been to see Steve, recounted an abridged version of all they'd discovered, said they'd tried their best but admitted defeat.

Steve seemed remarkably philosophical, thanked her profusely for her efforts on his behalf, and hoped she still believed in him. The despondency in his eyes, however, told a different story. Jenny thought it best not to tell of her fall from grace at the police station and of her new occupation. He had enough guilt to carry around, without her adding to it. Would she come to visit him again? Maybe, but she made no promises. She was depressed enough, without this place bringing her down even further. Jenny had observed the other visitors, hardened to their circumstances. They obviously had enough history, connection and responsibility to return month on month. Perhaps they were married, had kids, loved each other. She'd looked Steve in the eye, felt a strong pang of affection; but was it enough? Goodbye, take care.

Jenny rubbed her hands together in an effort to get some feeling back into her fingers. If she never saw another pack of fish fingers again, it'd be too soon. But it paid the bills and she was earning more now than she ever did as a PCSO.

'Hi Jenny.'

She jumped. This job was conducive to periods of oblivion and it could be a shock when her stupor was interrupted. Jenny turned. – 'Oh, hello Karen; how are you?'

'I'm fine thanks. And you?'

'Oh, you know…'

'What time do you finish?'

'4 O'clock. Why?'

'Can you meet Sarah and I at the Has Bean Café? There's been a few new developments.'

Jenny sighed – 'New developments, or more dead ends?'

'Well, we won't know that unless we follow them up, will we?'

'I'm tired, Karen. Tired of false hope and dreams. There's only so many knock-backs a girl can take.'

'So, what are you gonna do? Is this it – the new Jenny? What happened to all that fizz and spirit?'

'The fizz is in aisle nine, and the spirits are in aisle ten.'

Karen smiled – 'Well, at least it's good to know that the humour's still breathing – just. We'll see you there, then?'

Jenny scrunched a packet of scampi in her fist and, against her better judgement, replied – 'Yeah, sure; why not?'

∞∞∞∞

197

The brown and orange loose-fitting uniform blended into the background as she joined the short queue at the counter. In her previous uniforms, people used to notice her – a media-fuelled public perception that an individual in the army or police is somehow more important than a supermarket employee. Perhaps, one day, thought Jenny, people would come to realise what an essential service this anonymous army of worker-ants provided. After all, a colony can't survive without food. In the meantime, the bored Barista barely looked up as she handed Jenny her cappuccino.

The alluring aroma of coffee revived her senses, as she joined Sarah and Karen at a corner table. She'd never frequented this cosy independent café before, but Karen proclaimed that it was the best in town and it made a statement against all the usual coffee-conglomerate takeovers. A vibrant soul and jazz soundtrack added to its charm and the atmosphere began to rejuvenate that warm feeling that Jenny always had in the company of friends. It had been too long.

'It's great to see you, Jenny,' said Sarah. 'Where have you been hiding?'

Hiding? She hadn't thought about it like that, but that's exactly what she had been doing. Karen was right to ask – is this the new Jenny? – 'It's great to see you both too, but I've been busy, trying to pick up the pieces.'

'Yes, we heard that things didn't go down too well at the station,' said Sarah. 'We're all very sorry. We feel kind of responsible.'

'No, I knew what I was getting into, and the possible consequences. No regrets.'

'What, none?' said Karen.

'Well, maybe a few; mainly the fact that we couldn't solve it. So, what are these new developments, then? Or was that just a trick to tempt me from my hovel?'

'James called,' said Sarah. 'Just to catch up, but he happened to mention that a plan's been submitted to build a golf-course around the valley and to turn the old Foster-Smythe mansion into a hotel.'

'So, what's that got to do with us?'

'I've been digging online a bit,' said Karen. 'The scheme is from a company called On Course Leisure – Managing Director, one Richard O'Connell.'

'I still don't get it. He has links to the area, he's a property developer; what's so unusual?'

Sarah explained that Beatrice had challenged the proposal and questioned the ownership of the mansion. She was happy while it was providing shelter for Trossard but, with his demise, had enquired whether she has any claim on the old place. – 'James thinks she's trying to put the kibosh on the golf course and hotel plan because it will desecrate the area and infringe on their privacy.'

'Didn't O'Connell tell you he would never go back because everyone thought he was a murderer?' said Karen.

Jenny nodded – 'He did; but now that someone else has been convicted, his name is cleared. Or perhaps this is his revenge on his accusers. You said developments, plural; what else do you have?'

Karen showed Jenny her phone. – 'The picture of Bambi that the police released when they were trying to find anyone who knew her – I shared it again on social media. Someone's been in touch and I'm meeting her on Saturday. Could be a chance to find out what she's been up to these past twenty years.'

'Now that *could* be interesting,' said Jenny, as she felt the irresistible pull of the chase once more. She tried to fight against it, but it was no use – her curiosity had been aroused again. – 'But what was it you both said when I suggested that I search for John Reed? "Not on your own, you don't." Saturday's my day off; I'm coming with you.'

Sarah and Karen laughed and reached across the table to grab her hands. – 'Of course you are; welcome back, Jenny.'

When she'd awoke that morning, there was nothing to look forward to but an endless, monotonous drudgery. Now a mystery woman had emerged, potentially with another angle on Bambi. What did she have to lose by listening to what she had to say? What did she have to lose, full stop!?

There was unfinished business to conclude. Jenny had to think of a way forward with her life, but felt that she needed to close this chapter, one way or another, before she could open another.

'Ah, not again,' said Dad. 'Will you never give up?'

Not while there's hope, she thought. There's a road ahead – you either take it or stay in the same place till your time comes. Better to keep moving – that way the reaper won't know where to look.

51. A Recipe for Fireworks

To a degree, Jayden was right. Everyone Steve spoke to was suspicious. He'd been given permission to wander among the prisoners and ask whatever he wanted. 'I don't want any censorship,' the Governor had said; 'well, maybe you can take out some of the choice language, but I want to hear their real views.'

From those willing to speak, the state of the showers and latrines seemed to be the biggest bugbear. The drains were permanently blocked with pubic hairs and God knows what else, leaving the user up to their shins in tepid, scummy water; and there were invariably floaters in the toilets, bequeathed by the previous occupant. They may be the lowest of the low, but felt they had a right to some decent sanitation – more thorough and regular cleaning, and fully functioning bogs. Well, that was the gist of it; the exact words were – 'Martin left a turd in there so big I was gonna stick a flag in it and claim it as a sovereign state!'

Others wanted more educational opportunities in order to make their way in the world when they eventually got out of this hellhole. They tended to be those who attended the weekly library sessions voluntarily, rather than at the behest of Filbert or Mickey, and they were full of praise for the initiative. It won't last though, they predicted, someone would abuse the privilege and screw it up for everyone else.

All of which, Steve was able to convey factually to the Independent Monitoring Board. A self-important-looking collection of volunteers that comprised mainly magistrates and councillors, they thanked Steve for his frankness and promised to look into the issues raised. But that wasn't all they wanted to know. One particularly persistent pesterer pestered Steve to spill the beans on the drug problem in the prison. How widespread was it? Who was responsible? How were they getting the gear?

Much as Steve detested this abhorrent trade in misery, he insisted that the disclosure of such information was not within his remit. – 'That wasn't part of the job description. I was asked to gather views and complaints to improve conditions and relationships, not to grass people up; or have you got me here under false pretences?'

The Governor stepped in and pointedly put the pesterer right. – 'It is my responsibility to deal with such matters. Steve wouldn't survive out there if he were suspected of divulging the culprits, and it is unfair of you to ask him to do so.'

'With all due respect,' said the pesterer, 'if it's your responsibility, then perhaps you should do something about it. From what we've been told it's rampant, and it's someone else that really controls this place.'

Steve sensed conflict. His experience had taught him that whenever someone starts a sentence – "With all due respect…", you know they're about to say something disrespectful. The remainder of the conversation was not for Steve's ears and he was dismissed with thanks from the Governor. He was escorted back to his cell to the sound of raised voices behind him, a fully-fledged argument in progress. Interesting, he thought – the Governor's obviously under pressure to re-assert authority; and then there's the battle for power between Filbert and Mickey. Could be a recipe for fireworks.

∞∞∞

Filbert sat before him with a sheaf of papers on his lap. He tapped the top sheet and smiled. – 'Fascinating reading, this. Once, someone would have read it to me, but now, thanks to your and Jayden's efforts, I can understand most of it myself. You should be proud – you have a real talent for teaching.'

'Thank you,' said Steve; 'it was my profession, you know, before I took this small detour. Is it a good story?'

'That depends on your perspective. It's about a man who's offered the chance to take on new responsibilities. He has to consider who he leaves behind. Does he get into bed with the new gang or stay loyal to his friends? You see, he can't do both – there's a, what do you call it, a conflict of interests.'

'And what happens?'

'Well, so far, he's doing OK. He seems to know where his allegiances lie. But if he were to stray there could be serious consequences. The story is not finished, but I think he'll be fine.'

Steve looked closer – it appeared to be an official document, rather than a fictional tale. – 'So, who wrote it?'

'The Governor's secretary; she's very thorough, records everything word for word.'

'They're the minutes of the meeting, aren't they?'

'Indeed, they are.'

'For Christ's sake, does nothing escape you in here. A man can't even fart without you knowing about it.'

Filbert grinned. – 'Trust me, the alternative would be far worse for everyone. At the moment things are under control and that's down to me. Which brings me to the point – your new position could be to our mutual advantage.'

'No, Filbert, it won't. I took on the job as an independent, unbiased voice for all prisoners, not for your benefit.'

'I could persuade you otherwise; I have my methods.'

Steve bristled as he looked him in the eye, the culmination of Jenny's recent visit still fresh in his mind. He knew it was unlikely that he'd ever see her again and that he was beyond hope. – 'I know all about your methods, Filbert, and they won't work this time. Firstly, I no longer care what happens to me. It seems my innocence can't be proved and my one chance of redemption has gone, probably for good. You can do what you like, it won't make things any worse than they are already. Secondly, I have just decided to resign from the role. Jayden was right, it's them and us, and *they* can't be trusted.'

'Well, what did you expect?'

'I don't expect anything from anyone anymore. Whether criminal or the establishment, you're all the same – only in it for yourselves. And I won't be manipulated by either of you.' Steve realised he was shaking. Had anyone ever spoke to Filbert like this before and lived?

Filbert hesitated, a flash of anger in his eyes followed by a seething silence. He clearly wasn't used to people refusing to do as he asked. Finally, he returned Steve's gaze. – 'Your recent rant about standing up to bullies – you evidently meant every word.'

'I did, and you can do as you please, or more likely, get your henchmen to do it for you. I won't change my mind.'

Steve could almost see the cogs moving in Filbert's thought processes – how could he get out of this without losing face? Eventually, he nodded and conceded – 'Fair enough, I will respect your decision, on one condition. This conversation stays within these four walls – I can't have anyone thinking I'm losing my grip. Agreed?'

'Agreed,' said Steve.

'Now, piss off, before I change my mind.'

'Just one more thing before I go. How about showing off your new reading skills at the next library session. You can choose what you want to read.'

Filbert laughed, an uncommon sound in these parts. – 'Don't push it.'

52. Melody

The intrepid trio had been reduced to a duo for the day, as Sarah had a family event to attend. She hoped they'd manage without her and insisted that Cagney and Lacey report back later. No, tomorrow wouldn't do. Yes, Boss, they'd replied in harmony.

Now, as they surveyed the noisy crowd of cool customers, Jenny and Karen picked out their girl immediately amongst the lunchtime crowd in Vino's – where else but a trendy West End wine bar. Melody had suggested this as the very place they should meet – after all, she'd spent many a happy hour in here with Eleanor Frost, the lady in the picture.

'Eleanor Frost?' Jenny had exclaimed when Karen gave her the details. 'Another bloody pseudonym? How many names does one girl need?'

Melody had told Karen that she'd be wearing a red polka-dot dress, which also made her easy to spot among this exuberant mass of punters. Jenny baulked at the prices as she ordered drinks for them all. Well coiffured, youthful and effortlessly attractive, Melody had the appearance of someone who could afford this extortion. Jenny certainly couldn't on a Supermarket Assistant's wages. She sipped on her glass of red and wrinkled her nose in distaste. It was the cheapest on the menu and tasted as if it would be better suited as a garnish for chips. They made themselves comfortable at the only table left, at the back of the bar away from the throng.

'Thank you for meeting us,' said Karen. 'What can you tell us about Eleanor?'

Melody's suspicious eyes flitted from one to the other. – 'I want to know what your interest is first, before I tell you anything. How do you know her?'

Her use of the present tense indicated that Melody knew not of Eleanor/Emmeline/Emma/Bambi's fate and that this was to be a delicate conversation. Jenny bit the bullet. – 'If you are sure the picture is of the lady you knew as Eleanor, then we knew her as Bambi. We have since found out that she also used the name Emma and that she was christened as Emmeline. I don't know how close you were, but I'm afraid she's no longer with us.'

'What do you mean, no longer with us?'

'She passed away some months ago,' said Jenny. 'We're so sorry to bring you such terrible news.'

Melody's pale complexion turned paler still and she shook with shock. Karen fetched a glass of water from the bar and put her arm around Melody's shoulder as she drank it in delicate sips between sobs. 'W-what happened – how did she die?'

'I'm afraid she was murdered in her room,' said Karen. 'She lived above our local pub.'

'Oh my God, no!' Melody rummaged in her designer bag for a tissue and wiped her eyes. Eventually she recovered enough composure to speak. – 'We worked together, until she disappeared about two years ago. Eleanor helped me to settle in when I first joined and I thought we were friends. Then she didn't turn up for work one morning. I tried to call and, at first, there was no answer. Then the number was unobtainable, as if she didn't want to be contacted.'

'And how did she seem, before she vanished?' said Jenny. 'Was she stressed, worried, scared maybe?'

'No, none of that. We'd been out at the weekend with a few other work colleagues, had a great time and Eleanor was the life and soul. Not a hint that anything was wrong.'

'Can I ask where you both worked?' said Jenny.

'Moorland Events Management; we organise events at the top end of the market – for high profile business and VIPs. I'm still there – in fact, I took over Eleanor's portfolio when she left. She was a natural – had no problem talking to all the big guys. It doesn't come as easy to me, but I get by.'

I'm sure you do, thought Jenny. She could just imagine all those 'important' businessmen drooling over Melody as she goes about her job. It's the same the world over.

'We're trying to put together the pieces,' said Karen, 'to find out who killed her. We have managed to work out where she came from, her early life, and we know something of the recent years; but the bit in-between is missing. Do you know anything else about her?'

Melody took a while to consider the question and shook her head. – 'Now I come to think of it, no. She never spoke of the past, or about her personal life. She was a very private person and I didn't like to pry.'

'Is there nothing that you can think of?' said Jenny. 'This is important – did she tell you where she worked before; about any relationships; family, that kind of thing?'

'No – nothing. I said before that I thought we were friends – now I see that I knew absolutely zilch about her. I'd like to help, but I can't recall her saying anything.'

'Well, you have my details,' said Karen. 'If anything comes to mind, then please contact me, no matter how trivial it seems. And, again, we're so sorry to be the bearers of such bad news.'

∞∞∞∞

As Jenny endured the monotonous rattle of yet another train journey, Karen sat opposite and intently studied her phone. No matter how often Jenny spoke, small-talk seemed off the menu and there was barely a grunt in response to whatever subject she raised. – 'Well, that was a wasted trip,' she ventured.

Karen scrolled up and down her phone again and finally raised her eyes. – 'Not entirely. Been searching Moorlands Events Management and this is very, very interesting. Would you believe that it's a subsidiary of On Course Leisure – O'Connell's company that wants to build the Doone Valley Golf Complex. Now, that can't be coincidence, can it?'

After their clumsy thrashing around in the bunker, were they back on the fairway? Jenny stared at Karen in disbelief. – 'But does that mean that O'Connell employed Emmeline?'

'Well, it's certainly worth investigating, isn't it? Can't wait to tell Sarah about this.'

Jenny agreed that she would indeed be fascinated by this revelation. The Black Swan Detective Agency were back in business.

53. All the World's a Stage

As dads are inclined to do, Dad offered the benefit of his experience, whether it was wanted or not. But this time, Jenny was all ears. She knew her dad was one of the best prior to his retirement, not only due to the fact that he'd told her so, many times, but because he still had a reputation at the station. Anecdotes of his antics and busts were legendary and it had filled her with pride when she heard them. Sadly, she was no longer in a position to follow in his giant footsteps.

Jenny heard the clatter of her mum washing-up in the kitchen. She should really go and help, but Dad was in full-flow at the dining room table. – 'If you want to be a detective, there's one thing you must learn – don't take everyone at face value.'

'But they were all so convincing,' said Jenny. 'How on Earth can you tell the truth from the lies?'

'Anyone can sound convincing; particularly if they know you're coming and have time to practice and perfect their stories.'

'I can't believe they're all such good actors.'

'We're all good actors,' said Dad. 'Everyone pretends and shows a different face to the world. Take you, for instance. You must have been breaking up inside after what you went through with Johnny, but from the outside, you wouldn't have known it. We all put on a brave face, when really, we're falling apart.'

Jenny conceded that she may have played down the impact somewhat.

'Played it down? You were in denial and putting on an act every single day. You put makeup on to hide the bruises and went about your daily business as if everything was normal. That's my point; when you are questioning suspects, you must assume they are all actors. Think logically and put aside your first impressions – who has a reason to kill, who has benefited from the death of the victim, who is capable of murder? When you're looking for your culprit, you must detach yourself from the person you think you see in front of you.'

'OK, logical thinking,' said Jenny. 'Richard O'Connell told us that he'd not seen his wife for twenty years. Now we find out that she was employed by a subsidiary of one of his companies. That makes him the prime suspect again, doesn't it?'

'Possibly, but what was his motive?'

'Well, we know that he's involved in a scheme to convert her ancestral home. Maybe she found out about that and didn't like the idea. We're talking a multi-million-pound project; probably a few influential people involved and he wouldn't want anything to scupper the deal.'

Dad nodded. – 'Good, now you're thinking about different scenarios, instead of being taken in by a seasoned charmer. What about any romantic implications – jealousy, that kind of thing? If O'Connell was lying about losing touch with Emmeline, perhaps they were still romantically attached. He wouldn't have been too happy if he found out about her liaison with John, would he?'

'It's a tangled web, isn't it? Whenever we think we've found some answers, they lead to more questions.'

'But, that's the process of any investigation,' said Dad. 'It's not until you rule out all other options that you can come to the only solution. I'll admit that this is more complicated than most of the cases I worked on, but your approach has to be methodical; otherwise, you'll never solve the mystery. What's your next step?'

'Karen's great at trawling the internet. She's delved deeper into O'Connell's affairs. Apparently, a lady named Eleanor Frost has worked for him in various capacities for some years. So, we know one thing – he was lying when he told us that he'd had no further contact with her.'

'The key is going to be finding out whether that relationship was professional or personal, or a combination of the two. Events Management, you said. Maybe find out what events they've been involved in recently and who attended. I'm willing to bet that one of these soirees involved the launch of this golf-complex project and potential investors.'

'It would be a hell of a lot easier if I had access to police resources and was able to do all this officially,' said Jenny.

'So, are you going to take your new findings to the police?'

'No chance. They've made it perfectly clear that they won't take it seriously. From that condescending bastard in Devon to the Chief at the station, I'm just an inconvenience. No, we're on our own and I think that's the way I like it.'

54. A Day Out with Prose and Cons

The Governor was disappointed, though not surprised. – 'I can see it from your point of view. That wasn't how things were supposed to go and I genuinely wanted to build a better link between the prisoners and those responsible for monitoring our service.'

'A service; is that what you call it?' said Steve. 'I know we're all here to be punished for our various misdemeanours, but some of the conditions are inhumane. If you really want to improve relationships, then perhaps you should invest in some decent plumbing for a start.'

'It's on the list, but we're slaves to ever-diminishing funds. If we hadn't fixed that crumbling wall, then you'd have all been off across the countryside by now. That accounted for most of my maintenance budget this quarter. This is an old building and it's as much as we can do to stop the place falling apart.'

Steve had some sympathy. He'd seen how the lack of funds had insidiously worsened conditions in his old job. It was a massive problem throughout the public sector and those whose responsibility it was to manage costs were under increasing pressure to maintain standards, without the tools to do so.

'I have another proposition for you,' continued the Governor. 'One thing I was able to sell to the Board was your weekly recital sessions. You see, they cost us nothing and they're good for morale; and I have seen first-hand how you and young Jayden inspire a positive attitude. We would like you both to visit another prison and train the prisoners who work in the library to run a similar initiative. If it works, then we might be able to sell it nationwide. What do you say?'

Now, this could be of interest, thought Steve – a chance of respite from the monotony and a brief change of scenery. How could he turn down an offer like that? With a promise to the Governor that he'd give it some serious thought, Steve toddled off to find his partner in crime.

Jayden's eyes lit up. – 'You mean we get out of here for a while – what's not to like? Yes please; or is there a catch?'

'None that I can think of,' said Steve. 'Filbert will probably try to get us involved in some scam to expand his empire nationally, but apart from that, it's a day out. What could possibly go wrong?'

∞∞∞∞

A tree, then another and another. A roe deer skipped away from the roadside and disappeared into the woods; crows and magpies, ripping at roadkill, ascended at the roar of the diesel engine; poppies, cowslip, dog roses, foxglove, gorse – if he were a horticulturist, Steve would have been able to name them, but all he could see was a riot of colour, a stark contrast to the incessant grey concrete of their recent habitat.

The transport vehicle to prison had afforded but a small, tinted window to the outside world, way above eye level, so he'd seen nothing of the landscape around the prison. Then, he'd been a cargo so fragile, it might have broken in transit. This time, the Governor had bestowed upon them an element of trust and they were in a secure prison minibus, accompanied by an uncommunicative escort officer. The countryside emerged in all its glory, a poignant reminder of all he'd missed.

Jayden sat silently beside him, staring through the window as the road dissected the forest. A deeply personal moment, they respected each other's dreams of freedom. Was this such a good idea – a tempting taste of liberty, a fleeting glimpse of nature's fruits before they took away the banquet once more? This isn't for the likes of you!

A subtle shake of the head and Jayden spoke. – 'You know, only time I see country like this was in picture books and on TV. Never got to leave the concrete jungle. A few parks around, but they're mostly populated by gangs and junkies. Rather take my chances with the beasts in that wood than with so called civilisation.'

'You never have school trips or anything like that?' said Steve.

'Ha, they were more concerned with getting us to go to school in the first place; then, once we were inside, they worried about keeping us there. School trips was never on the agenda.'

Steve felt guilty, complaining about his lot when he'd had a relatively privileged time of it. – 'I grew up on the edge of town, nothing but fields as far as the eye could see. All built on now – just a load of characterless new estates. When you're a kid you take it all for granted, never think about what other kids have to go through. Still, we may have come from different places and taken different roads, but we've both ended up at the same destination.'

'In some ways, it must be harder for you,' said Jayden. 'You've had further to fall.'

The minibus trundled on, past fertile farmland and through quaint villages, until they reached a main road. There the traffic grew in number and volume, as they headed towards more built-up conurbations. Peripheral industrial estates littered the ring road, shops and takeaways on the corners of each junction, where traffic lights slowed their progress. Steve didn't care – all these mundanities were like paradise compared to the bookends of their journey.

Two hours later and they reached their destination. With no prior warning they passed an imposing Victorian frontage and turned into a narrow side-road opposite a row of 1930s-built houses. No attempt to dump these guys in a remote location away from civilised folk, this place was in the middle of a reasonable-looking residential area. Steve wondered what the estate agent's blurb would be for the surrounding residences – 'Adjacent to a historical Victorian building in a secure location.'

A young offenders' institution, they'd been told, the site of recent unrest verging on prison mutiny. Placed in 'special measures' after it emerged that inmates were always confined to their cells and only allowed out to shower once a week; Steve and Jayden's visit was just one of many initiatives to improve morale. Unsure what kind of welcome awaited, they entered via the tradesmen's entrance, the guard eyeing them suspiciously, as if they were here to cause further insurrection. Steve wasn't sure if he was developing a deeper paranoia because, it seemed to him, everyone in authority looked at him like that these days.

After begrudgingly permitting them a toilet break after their long journey, a prison officer escorted them to the library and introduced them to their resident counterparts; one of whom, Richard, was a studious-looking young man with a baby-face and glasses. How did he end up in here, wondered Steve, and how does he survive such a cruel environment? His colleague, Raymond, a brick-shithouse of a youth with a disconcerting stare, looked more at home. Steve reprimanded himself for judging these young men he'd only just met by appearances. Surely, if prison had taught him one thing, it was that everyone had hidden depths and unique reasons for their peccadillos and predicaments.

Jayden and Steve presented the concept of their initiative, with emphasis on the increasingly interactive nature of the sessions. – 'Even the roughest roughnecks are taking part,' said Jayden. 'We can't believe it sometimes, what they come out with. There's hidden prose'n'poetry everywhere.'

'I can believe it,' said Richard. 'You wouldn't know it to look at him, but Raymond here has been known to write the odd verse or two. He won't tell anyone though, says it's not good for his image.'

'They'd only take the piss,' said Raymond. 'I mean, look at me; do I look like a poet?'

'That's what we thought,' said Steve, 'but Jayden reduced one of the toughest guys on the block to tears with his piece about his mum. Weren't a dry eye in the house. It's all in the delivery – prose'n'poetry, the new rock'n'roll.'

There followed a discussion on stereotypes, how people were expected to behave in certain ways due to their background, environment and peer pressure. Raymond's fear of ridicule was tempered by Richard's encouragement and insistence that he should give it a go. Raymond retorted that it was alright for Richard, no-one would be surprised if he stood up and read a poem. Richard was offended by this slight on his masculinity and reminded Raymond of the time he'd broken Roy's fingers after he'd had the audacity to call him Dick. Jayden asked whether everyone's name in this damn prison began with the letter R.

A flustered English teacher joined them and apologised for being late. Her previous class had overrun, the traffic was awful, and the security checks here were more onerous every time. She told them she'd been sent by Adult Learning to facilitate this fantastic idea. A woman, thought Steve, not seen one of those for a while. He'd been cooped up with all those sweaty geezers for so long, he'd forgotten how much he enjoyed female company, whether at work or with Karen and Sarah at the old quiz nights. Jenny – he wondered how she was doing and if she ever gave him a thought. He'd given up hope and was sure she'd have moved on by now. After all, she wouldn't have a shortage of suitors.

Caroline, the English teacher, listened intently as Jayden repeated how it all worked and extolled upon the virtues. His enthusiasm was infectious as he confessed that it was the only time that he felt liberated. Another world he could escape to where no-one could touch him – no cops, no judges, no screws. He inflected that last word with so much venom that the nearby prison officer flinched and glared.

It was concluded that a month-long trial-run would commence next week and that Richard would initially lead, supported by Raymond if he could pluck up the courage. Steve presented them with a pre-prepared format and agenda, that they could follow if they wished. – 'But it will evolve, depending on your own ideas and who chooses to contribute,' he told them.

Some sustenance was required before the return journey, not only by Steve and Jayden, but by their escort and driver too. Unsurprisingly, lunch was of similar quality to what they were used to – a lukewarm plate of gristle and gravy, undercooked potatoes and overcooked broccoli, followed by a kind of fruity sludge drowned in lumpy custard.

With full stomachs and reluctance, they were escorted back to the minibus. It had been a bit of a busman's holiday, but the brief change of scenery had been welcome. A quick security check to ensure they hadn't nicked any of the cutlery and they were back on board and back on the road.

It was to be a reverse of their outbound route, once more through the industrial estates and intermittent shops. Steve had developed a slight headache, as he often used to when travelling. He closed his eyes and tried to blot out the throb of the engine and the whiff of diesel fumes. As they ground to a halt at yet another set of traffic lights, he felt a little disorientated and wondered if he was becoming institutionalised. Eventually, the lights turned green and they trundled on. The motion must have made him drop off, because the next he knew a blur of green sped by. They were back in the countryside.

'Welcome back to reality,' said Jayden. 'Sweet dreams?'

'How long have I been asleep?'

'Time is relative. Depends whether you think sleeping is a good use of your day out. Be back before you know it and who knows when we'll escape that shit-hole again.'

'But the only place we've been to is another shit-hole,' said Steve.

'True, but the world has plenty of those. Hey, is it me or are we swerving all over the road?'

The tree didn't swerve. The tree remained static and proved to be an immovable object when they hit it with some force. Jolted and shaken, their seatbelts saved them from being thrown around like ragdolls and serious injury. The driver, however, had fared less well. With bleeding head slumped against the steering-wheel, apparently unconscious, he didn't look too good. The shaken escort swore beneath his breath and called his name, to no avail. He leapt forward and shook him by the shoulder, but no response.

'Shit, I think he's had a heart-attack. Anyone know first aid?'

'I do,' said Steve. First aid training had been a requirement of his old job, although thankfully, he'd never had cause to use it in a real-life situation.

In panic the escort invited him to check out the patient and to be quick about it. Protocol may have required him to handcuff Steve before allowing him to leave the bus, but it seemed he'd forgotten procedure for now. A convoluted process, consisting of double-locks and a combination code, he eventually unlocked the back doors. As requested, Steve rushed to the driver's door, flung it open and checked for a pulse. The escort had already called for an ambulance, but Steve thought it might take some time to get here. He looked around for a sign that said 'The Middle of Nowhere' and concluded that he needed to perform CPR PDQ.

Jayden too, had suddenly found it possible to join them at the scene of the emergency; unhandcuffed, in the open air, on a deserted country road! They'd left the main road a while back and were on the last leg, along the B-roads. His eyes darted this way and that, and Steve could tell what he was thinking.

'Don't just stand there,' said Steve, 'I need your help. You grab his arms, drag him out gently and I'll grab his feet. We've got to lay him flat before I can start the compressions.'

Jayden hesitated, took another longing glance up the road, shook his head, then did as asked. Their escort was useless, probably employed by a private security company on low wages, thought Steve. Inadequately trained for such a situation he looked lost, as he surveyed the horizon for any flashing blue lights to save him from this nightmare. None were forthcoming.

Steve began the chest compressions as trained, but it felt very different to the disembodied plastic torso and head that constituted his only previous experience. He wasn't keen on the mouth-to-mouth option, bearing in mind that his patient sported a full beard, with remnants of that grim prison lunch still in residence. Steve was also concerned about the gash on the driver's head that was bleeding profusely. He suggested that, instead of standing there doing nothing, perhaps the escort might grab the first-aid kit and dress the wound. It was soon established that there was no first-aid kit on board.

'Great,' said Steve. 'What kind of cowboy outfit is this?'

'We passed a garage in that village a few miles back,' said Jayden. 'They'll have one.'

'But I can't go and leave two prisoners here without supervision,' said the increasingly flustered escort.

'Then I'll go,' said Jayden.

'Yeah, right. And we'll never see you again. I wasn't born yesterday, you know.'

'So, what's the alternative,' said Jayden. 'You gonna let the man die?'

The desperation showed on the escort's face, a dilemma way beyond his paygrade evident from his panicked plea – 'And can I trust you to come back?'

'No, but that's a chance you're gonna have to take. Look, I don't know where in hell we are and the cops will be on their way soon; so, I'm not gonna stand much chance if I decide to run, am I? The alternative is I bring back the first-aid kit, help to save this man, and get a tick in the box with the parole board.'

A barely perceptible nod from the escort and Jayden was away, his muscular frame running free between the hedgerows that flanked the country road. Enviously, Steve watched him go as he continued CPR. In an adjacent field, an unkindness of ravens took to the wing, disturbed by the thunder of Jayden's haste. Round a corner and he disappeared from view. Forever?

Nellie the Elephant, the trainer had told them – the ideal song to sing whilst performing chest compressions. Apparently, there were other tunes of a similar tempo that would have performed the same function, but Nellie was the trainer's favourite. Steve resisted the temptation to chant the Dickies' punk version and continued. The physical exertion drained him, but he summoned some reserves of energy from somewhere.

An age it took, and he was about to give up in despair when, miraculously, it worked. Steve's efforts were rewarded by a sudden gasp, followed by a gulp as the driver fought for breath. Steve spoke to him reassuringly – there was no need to panic, he was now going to put him in the recovery position and the ambulance was on its way. Blood dripped through the escort's snot-rag; unhygienic, but the only thing they'd found to stem the flow. Steve removed his shirt and began to rip it up as a replacement for the sodden handkerchief, when a car approached a little too fast and screeched to a halt. Jayden jumped out, a green box in hand.

'Welcome back,' smiled a semi-naked Steve, as he grabbed some antiseptic wipes and a dressing from the first-aid kit. 'That can't have been easy. What did freedom feel like?'

'Good, man. Took all my willpower not to keep on running. Reckon the mechanic thought I was there to rob the joint. He was thankful when all I wanted was this box and gave me a ride back.' Jayden turned to the escort, whose expression of relief was palpable. – 'Hope you're gonna tell them what we did here.'

Ten minutes later and an ambulance arrived, closely followed by the police. Steve thought his and Jayden's heroics could have been recognised and treated with more respect, but no. As soon as the cops were brought up to speed with the situation, they were handcuffed and led to the police car. The escort joined them, while the grateful minibus driver was stretchered to the ambulance. Steve nodded in acknowledgement of his wave of thanks, and prayed he'd be OK.

Adventure over, the final stretch of the journey didn't take long and the prison gates soon loomed.

'Hey, that was some experience,' said Jayden, as they heard the familiar, daunting sound of doors slamming shut. 'Where do you fancy for our next day out?'

55. Murderers Turned Lifesavers

Toast crumbs dropped onto the spread open newspaper on the kitchen table. Jenny allowed herself a wry smile. Perhaps she wasn't such a bad judge of character after all. She took in the headline again, as she sipped her first caffeine shot of the day.

MURDERERS TURNED LIFESAVERS

Beneath this dramatic banner, two men stared back at her, their expressions a mixture of pride and embarrassment.

"Undoubtedly, I owe them my life," said Mr Hussain. "I will be forever grateful."

"A testament to the success of our reform programme," boasted the Governor.

"I made a judgement call," said the escort. "I just felt they could be trusted."

The article went on to give a detailed account of Steve and Jayden's heroism, juxtaposed with some background on their crimes. Given his age at the time of conviction, Jayden came out of the journalist's analysis with more clemency. He was a victim of his environment, never knew his father etc. Steve's case was re-examined with less leniency. The murderer of a defenceless woman, not so worthy of our forgiveness; regardless of the fact that his recent actions had saved a decent man's life.

Mr Hussain's family were unwavering in their praise of his two saviours. His ageing parents were thankful that they still had their loving son, his wife still had her devoted husband, and their children still had a wonderful father. Surely everyone deserved a chance of redemption, they argued, regardless of previous misdemeanours.

Jenny stared at the picture of Steve and Jayden, their smiles hiding the inner turmoil that must surely haunt any prisoner. Overcome by a sensation of affection for Steve, she sobbed into her coffee. Their burgeoning relationship had been brief, never permitted to develop, but his significant impact on her life was ongoing, not to mention overwhelming at times.

She looked-up the reporter who'd written the article. His CV was impressive, with praise from interviewees and peers alike for his balanced and reasoned investigative journalism. I wonder, thought

Jenny, if he might be interested in a follow-up piece. Would publicity help or hinder their efforts to prove Steve's innocence?

Time to reconvene the Black Swan Detective Agency to consult on the matter.

Karen wasn't surprised when she read of Steve's exploits. On the same first-aid course, she had been Steve's partner when practicing the recovery position and they'd indulged in some childish banter about getting his leg over. – 'He wouldn't have thought twice if someone needed help. Bet he was singing Nellie the Elephant too.'

After Karen had explained the significance of said tune, all agreed that Steve was selfless and put others before himself. Alan expressed astonishment that Steve had managed to remember the procedure, given his self-confessed issues with knowledge retention. – 'Unless it's accompanied by a Lennon and McCartney lyric, he's normally forgotten any training by the next day.'

'So, you want to tell this journalist everything we've found,' said Sarah. 'That'll certainly put the cat among the pigeons.'

'But if it raises the profile, they'll have no choice but to re-open the case,' said Jenny. 'They might not take us seriously, but with interest from a national newspaper the spotlight will be on the police again to justify the conviction. And I think there's enough reasonable doubt to get a solicitor to look at it again too.'

'That DNA is their entire case,' said Trevor, 'but there's no denying it was there and Steve has no explanation for it. Unless we can we bring them anything that supersedes that, we've got no chance.'

Jenny looked pensive. – 'That's the main thing that's been bugging me through this whole escapade. Been thinking about it a lot and I have a potential theory that I wanted to run past you. Trevor, you're his best friend. Did Steve once own a black Harrington jacket with a Lambretta logo?'

'Yes, I think he did. Why?'

'Now, this is very important. Did he still own that jacket at the time of the murder?'

'As far as I know. Only recall him wearing it a few times. It was a brief and misguided attempt to spruce up his image, but he put on a fair bit of weight after he gave up football. It looked ridiculous when filled with his increasingly unseemly gut. To be honest, it's probably a number of years since I saw him in it.'

'Did you know that most of Bambi's clothes were second-hand?'

'No, and you wouldn't have thought so,' said Trevor, 'she always looked so immaculate.'

'Yes, and the landlady once asked her how and she replied "charity shops"; said that you couldn't buy designer gear on a barmaid's wages.'

Karen's eyes lit up. – 'So, you're suggesting that Steve took that jacket to a charity shop and Bambi bought it?'

'It's a possibility, don't you think?' said Jenny. 'It would explain why Steve's DNA was all over the place. Don't know why I didn't think of it before.'

'I like it,' said Karen, 'that's got to be the answer. And if we could deliver the killer at the same time, it's problem solved.'

Sarah agreed that it was an angle worthy of investigation, but was still sceptical about involving the press. – 'As soon as the real culprit sees the headlines, they'll be off and we risk losing them for good.'

'But that's when we'll be waiting,' said Jenny, 'watching for that moment of panic when they're flushed out of the woodwork. If we can angle the story to imply that we're onto them, then all we have to do is see who runs.'

'It's too vague,' said Sarah. 'We need a cast-iron suspect; otherwise, we won't know who to watch.'

'I think we have someone who's up to their neck in it,' said Karen. 'I've been busy searching the records and you'll never guess what I've uncovered. No guarantee that they're the murderer, but I know one thing – they've not been straight with us so far.'

Triumphantly, Karen laid a print-out on the table before them. They all huddled to gaze at this momentous sheet of A4. It took a moment for the information to sink in, before simultaneous exclamations.

'You're kidding!' said Alan.

'No way!' said Trevor.

'Well, that explains a lot,' said Sarah.

Jenny smiled – 'So, what do you say; do we have a story for our journalist friend?'

56. Gold Dust

As predicted, Barney Ronson knew a scoop when he saw one. He'd listened intently for the inordinate amount of time that it took Jenny to relay a condensed version of all they'd discovered, enhanced by interjections from Sarah and Karen. Now he pored over Karen's new evidence. The final piece in the jigsaw?

So far, he'd said nothing, as promised at the outset of the meeting. The secret of good journalism is to listen, he'd told them; and any questions could wait till they'd finished. The pad before him contained a series of scrawled notes, a spider diagram that looked as if a spider had stepped in ink, then wandered randomly across the paper.

'Well, what do you think?' said Jenny.

'It's some story,' said Barney, 'but if you want me to write it, we'll have to tread carefully.' He turned to Karen. – 'Are you certain that this information is kosher and she was the same woman?'

'We've told you everything we know,' said Karen. 'It can't be coincidence, can it?'

'I'll admit it's unlikely.' Barney checked his notes again. – 'This lady, Melody, wasn't it? She was convinced that her friend Eleanor Frost was your girl.'

'Absolutely,' said Jenny. 'Went white as a sheet when we had to tell her what became of Bambi. She was genuinely upset.'

'And now you have discovered the name of Richard O'Connell's second wife – Eleanor Frost!'

'Yes,' said Karen. 'They must have planned it all – Emmeline disappears, they wait till the dust settles, she changes her name, then they remarry, start anew somewhere else.'

'But to what end?' said Barney. 'Surely, if they'd stayed put in Devon the inheritance would have been theirs; the mansion and fortune would have been handed down, split between the two sisters.'

'There was no fortune,' said Jenny. 'The mansion was falling down; the only thing left was debt. I reckon O'Connell wanted to get out of any commitments with old Foster-Smythe, and Emmeline felt betrayed by her father, traded in marriage to raise the money he needed. Can't blame them for wanting out.'

'It's a good theory, which may or may not be true,' said Barney, 'but only O'Connell can verify it. We can't go printing stuff like that without further evidence. You've heard of the libel laws, of course, defamation of character, that kind of thing.'

'So, you won't cover it,' said Karen.

'I didn't say that. With your permission, I will write the facts as you have so eloquently imparted them, but I'll leave the conjecture to you and the police. The conclusion will be open-ended and will simply ask the question – Who Killed Bambi?'

'You're not really going to use that for the headline, are you?' said Sarah.

'Inevitably. What else would you suggest?'

'Well, I guess it's to the point,' said Karen. 'We'll have to be prepared for the fallout, though. It will all be out in the open and could put us in more danger once the real murderer gets hold of it. Way beyond what we've experienced so far.'

Barney nodded. – 'Could get interesting, yes. I suspect that all kinds of crap will emerge. I'd suggest that you ask for police protection but, given what you've told me about their engagement thus far, I doubt they'll be too accommodating.'

They all stood and shook Barney's hand, none of them sure whether or not they'd done the right thing. Still, it was too late now. This was gold dust, and they could tell by Barney's expression that he knew it.

'Thank you,' said Jenny. 'All we ask is that you treat the story sensitively.'

'Goes without saying; this isn't the Sun or the Mail, you know.'

Jenny felt disconnected as they made their way home. Things would be way beyond their control once it was in the public domain. She wondered if she should have consulted Steve before feeding him to the wolves, but they wanted to strike while the story of his heroism was still hot. All they could do now was wait for the excrement to hit the fan.

57. See You on the Outside

One of the outcomes of Filbert's English lessons was that he could now read the newspaper by himself, or at least get the gist of it. As Steve entered, Filbert raised his eyes and grinned. – 'Well, you're quite the celebrity, aren't you?'

Filbert always got first dibs on the papers, so Steve's fame hadn't got round the rest of the prison yet. He still had that to look forward to. Filbert pointed to the headline. – 'Who Killed Bambi? Did They Get the Right Man?'

'You know, I've heard all the stories before,' continued Filbert, 'those losers who say they didn't do it; or, if they did, there are all kinds of excuses. But you really are innocent, aren't you?'

'That's what I've been telling everyone all along. Only time anyone listens is when they put it on the front page. I'm not naïve enough to expect justice, though. The way that's written, it's just speculation. No-one's going to change their minds till the real killer is caught. It's enough to make a man bitter and twisted; that's if he weren't bitter and twisted already.'

'Your time will come,' said Filbert. 'Save the anger and bitterness till it's useful. Take the bastards to the cleaners when you have your day in court again.'

Steve fully intended to if he got the chance. They'd stolen his liberty, besmirched his reputation, such as it was, and left him bereft of hope. But he wasn't just angry for himself; an innocent woman had lost her life at the hands of a monster. He wanted justice for Bambi too.

The Governor wanted to see him. He knew not why but suspected it may have something to do with recent events and revelations. The Governor too, had the newspaper on his desk. It seemed that Steve, a generally quiet and reserved man, would have to get used to the unwanted publicity. Invited to sit, he awaited the verdict from the person whose job it was to keep him off the streets, where he was deemed a danger to others.

'I have some good news, Steve. Given your timely intervention when Mr Hussain suffered his heart attack, coupled with the doubt raised about your conviction, it has been decided to move you to an open prison whilst your case is reinvestigated. You'll find conditions there more lenient. However, it is still a prison.'

Steve nodded. – 'That's much appreciated, but what about Jayden? He was there too, equally heroic, if that's what you want to call it. In fact, he proved more than I that he can be trusted; he had the chance to run and still came back. Jayden should share in this privilege.'

'The difference is that he pleaded guilty – there was no uncertainty in his case.'

'Then, no, thank you, I'll stay. We're either treated the same or I'll wait it out here until my conviction is overturned.'

'That may be beyond my control now,' said the Governor. 'I have gone to a lot of trouble to plead your case and the decision has been made in your favour. The prison service is not a hotel chain; you don't get to decide where you reside.'

'You didn't even consider Jayden, did you? Says a lot.'

'Are you implying that there's a racial element to this?'

'I'm implying that there is institutional racism in most of the major institutions in this country, whether subconscious or otherwise. Jayden is essentially a good man who made a horrendous mistake when he was barely out of childhood. He has shown remorse ever since and deserves another chance when his time is done. I'm still guilty until proven innocent, although I thought it was supposed to be the other way around. As such, I remain a prisoner, whether that be here or in a so-called open prison. Until a judge tells me I'm free to go, there is no difference between Jayden and I.'

It was the next day before Steve saw Jayden again, in their usual haunt. As they sorted the returned books, Steve relayed his conversation with the Governor. Jayden told him in no uncertain terms that he was crazy, and to get the hell out of here. – 'I can fight my own battles, man. You've been given a shot at freedom, take it with both hands. Gonna miss your crap jokes, but I'll survive. Five years and I got a chance at parole. I'll see you on the outside.'

Had Steve known that this was to be their final shift together, he'd have given Jayden a farewell man-hug; but it was probably for the best that they were both spared the embarrassment. For on the following morn, he was told to gather his meagre possessions and prepare for transportation. With a wistful look over his shoulder he bade good riddance to that shit-hole. It had been one hell of an experience, with some interesting characters, to say the least; but it was time for the next chapter.

58. Paranoia?

Jenny wasn't surprised when summonsed to the police station, but vowed that she wouldn't be intimidated this time. As far as she was concerned, they'd had no alternative but to follow their hearts and follow up the leads, as and when they emerged. She wasn't prepared to take a rollocking for any of it and had no regrets. She no longer reported to anyone and this gave her all the rights of a private citizen. Jenny was primed and ready for an argument.

It's about time I was taken seriously, she thought, as she climbed the steps to her old place of employment. The Chief Inspector was there to greet her and accompany her to his office. There, sat Rob, with his usual smug expression. Inevitably, he didn't look pleased to see her. Jenny nodded and took the seat next to him.

'It's good to see you again, Jenny,' said the Chief. 'As you can imagine, the recent newspaper reports have raised a number of questions, which we are doing our best to answer. However, I really wish you'd come to us first, before leaking everything to the press. This could really compromise the investigation.'

'There was no investigation,' said Jenny. 'You'd closed the case and relieved me of my duties, remember? If you are going to re-investigate then, unless you are prepared to do it properly this time and allocate the necessary resources, I don't think we have much to say to each other.'

Rob was about to speak, but the Chief held up his hand. – 'You have reason to feel aggrieved. I will admit that we didn't listen to your doubts; but I think that, given the evidence we had, most cops would have made the same assumptions as Rob. If you are agreeable, I would like to employ you in a consultancy capacity. You will work with Rob to bring the case to its conclusion, whatever that may be.'

Rob looked appalled at the idea. Evidently the Chief hadn't discussed this initiative with him beforehand and it was as much of a surprise to him as to Jenny. He began to protest, but the Chief stated that proper justice in this case was more important than Rob's sensibilities. – 'You will treat Jenny with respect, gather and investigate any evidence that she and her accomplices have accrued, and bring your conclusions to me. Jenny must have access to all of the case files, the DNA results, and whatever else she needs. You will work together and, if I hear that you are not co-operating, then it will look bad on your forthcoming review.'

'Yes, Chief,' said Rob, with the indignant look of a scalded child. 'I'm sure we'll make a great team.'

Well, that's a turn up for the books, thought Jenny. I wasn't expecting that. She glanced at Rob with the hint of a smile. Could they really work together? Yes, she would do whatever was necessary; and with access to the case files and DNA – how could she refuse? – 'Can we get started now, Sir?'

'Preferably, yes. The sooner we can sort this out, the sooner I get the press and the Chief Superintendent off my back. That OK with you, Rob?'

'Do I have a choice?'

'None.'

As they retired to the evidence room, Rob seemed to shrink before her eyes. He slumped in a chair and acerbically invited Jenny to show him where he went wrong. A professional relationship, Jenny insisted. She wasn't here to belittle Rob or get him into trouble. It was in both their interests to work quickly and efficiently. Jenny began by bringing Rob up to speed with all they'd discovered. This took a while and, to be fair, Rob listened patiently and took notes, with few interruptions. He wanted to interview O'Connell, that was the first priority, given the fact that he'd lied about his continued relationship with the victim.

Then it was Rob's turn to reveal his methods of deduction. As they re-examined all the evidence – the statements of the Black Swan regulars, landlady and bar staff, Steve's movements on CCTV, his DNA at the scene of the crime, his possible motives and lack of an alibi – Jenny had to admit that Rob had been pretty thorough. He seemed a little placated when she told him so.

The one chink of light in Steve's favour was the presence of another piece of unidentified DNA on the murder weapon, the jacket used to suffocate Bambi. There was no match with anyone else they'd tested locally, or with anyone on the police database. Jenny enquired whether Steve's legal representatives had been aware of this. To which Rob replied that he thought so, yes, but they didn't use it in their case for the defence.

Rob admitted that Jenny's theory, that the jacket once belonged to Steve, before Bambi bought it from a charity shop, was plausible, albeit unprovable. Jenny asked if Steve had been shown the jacket, to which Rob replied that it had been revealed in court, but that Steve was some distance away, under duress and understandably upset. Rob had no objection to Jenny running the theory past Steve. Any evidence gathered from the jacket would be inadmissible, however, if she took it off the premises, so Rob fetched it to enable her to photograph and take the details – make, size, and any stains and holes from wear and tear.

'You know he's been moved, don't you?' said Rob. 'He's in an open prison now. Not somewhere they'd normally put a murderer, but I don't make these decisions.'

'No, I didn't know. I guess they'd only tell his next of kin something like that, even though they don't give a toss. You're still convinced that you got the right man, aren't you?'

'Unless you can prove otherwise, then yes.'

'It's unless *we* can prove otherwise, Rob,' said Jenny. 'The Chief said we're working together, remember?'

'Fair enough. I'm looking forward to it already.'

∞∞∞∞

As she strolled home in contemplation of these unexpected developments, Jenny couldn't wait to tell the others. It meant they were legit, no longer skulking surreptitiously in the shadows, their findings recorded in the official case-files.

Jenny now had Steve's new location and her plan was to visit him to share her theories and expound upon the further adventures of the Black Swan Detective Agency. He'd probably speculate that it would make a good movie and he'd want Brad Pitt playing his part. Yes, Steve, the resemblance is uncanny, she'd tell him.

The fresh air was a welcome respite from the stuffy police station, so she decided to walk the half-hour home. The exercise would do greater good than sitting in a bus or taxi. As she took in the familiar surroundings, nostalgic thoughts of her home town filled her head; this would always be home, but was she happy here? How could it compare with the wild and windy beauty of Exmoor? After just a few short visits, she'd fallen in love with the place and was itching to go back. Could she come up with a reason and claim it on expenses? That's what consultants did, wasn't it?

As dusk began to fall, a fine rain irradiated beneath newly lit streetlamps. Not far now, she quickened her pace as the rain grew more intense. She'd seen the forecast that morning and should have been expecting it, but had forgotten in the excitement of her new found status.

Jenny sensed it before she saw or heard anything. Was it irrational paranoia, or was she being followed? A glance over her shoulder confirmed the latter. He was about a hundred yards away and getting closer. Was it Rob playing silly buggers? She didn't wait to find out as she ran the rest of the way, almost stumbling in her haste. Panting with the exertion, she fumbled the key in the front door and slammed it behind her. She really must make an effort to get fitter.

Her dramatic entrance stirred her father from his usual repose in his favourite armchair. – 'What on Earth is wrong? We've only just got George to bed and you come in with enough noise to wake the dead.'

'I was being followed, I'm sure of it.'

'Are you sure?' said Dad, as he peeked through the curtains. He scanned the street as far as the bay window would allow. 'Can't see anyone. Who do you think it was?'

'No idea; it's dark and I didn't hang around to ask.'

'It's this bloody murder mystery,' said Dad, 'got you jumping at every shadow.' He took another look through the window. – 'Well, whoever it was isn't there now. Probably some poor sod innocently walking home. How did you get on with the Chief?'

Dad laughed after Jenny had recounted the encounter. – 'Ha, bet Rob wasn't too impressed; but the Chief has his head screwed on. He can't lose. If you're right, then he's going to look good for listening and, if you're wrong, then they got it right in the first place. Are you OK now?'

'Yes, I think so. You're probably right; I'm seeing something sinister in every situation. I'm going to bed.'

And that would have been it, forgotten; until Jenny saw the note on the doormat – KEEP DIGGING AND YOU DIG YOUR OWN GRAVE

59. Like a Cop Again

At least Rob was now treating the evidence with the appropriate gravity. If someone was trying to scare Jenny, then she must be on to something. Jenny warned the others to be on their guard, to not go anywhere alone, and to contact her or Rob if they saw anything or anyone suspicious. Dad accompanied her on the school-run, and there was a visible police presence around for much of the time.

A few days later, the DNA results on the scary note came back – unidentified, but chillingly, a match to that on the jacket that had been used to suffocate Bambi! A shiver ran down Jenny's spine when Rob broke the news. He tried to reassure her. – 'Whoever it is, they're getting scared. They thought they'd got away with it when Steve was convicted. Now they've seen the publicity and sussed out the source of the newspaper reports. You should be proud that you've flushed them out of their den.'

'It's alright for you; you haven't got a murderer following you down the street.' Jenny had experienced fear before, but where once she'd been scared to go home, now she was scared to go out.

Rob had been in touch with O'Connell's office to make an appointment, only to learn that he was out of the country, due back tomorrow. – 'He's got to be a suspect,' argued Rob.

'But, if he's been out of the country, then he can't be the author of that articulate note, can he?'

'Perhaps not,' said Rob, 'but he's got questions to answer and he knows a hell of a lot more than he told you and James. I'll sort out the warrant; be a nice surprise for him when he swaggers through Arrivals.'

∞∞∞∞

A hastily convened Zoom call was arranged for that evening, Jenny insistent that all interested parties were included. Given their diverse locations, it was the most practical way to meet quickly and without too much hassle. And besides, it meant that she could stay in the safety of home. Sarah was enlisted to make the arrangements in her usual well-organised manner, including a lengthy call to James to talk him through the mechanics. Once proficient after a practice run, he agreed that it was a damn sight more convenient and efficacious than a carrier pigeon.

James appeared on screen on schedule, fascinated with this technology that could cut across the miles so effortlessly. It was almost as if they were in the same room, he enthused. There had been a further development, he declared, which he thought was pertinent to the case. Beatrice had received an offer to buy the farm – a very generous one that would mean they'd never have to work again.

'I thought she was dead set against the development,' said Sarah.

'She was, but it seems there's been a caprice,' said James. 'Apparently, John's not been too good. The farm was his life; now he's neglecting some of the jobs that have to be done every day. Thomas is taking up the slack as best he can, but they're worried about John. Beatrice thinks that retirement somewhere else might be good for him; says there are too many ghosts around here, for both of them.'

'Not sure John would agree to that,' said Jenny. 'He's as much a part of that landscape as the valley itself. It would be a crime against nature to replace him with a bunch of businessmen in Rupert the Bear trousers and Pringle jumpers.'

'That may be so,' said James, 'but I got the impression that Beatrice, at least, is giving the offer serious consideration.'

'Well, that could all be superseded when we meet O'Connell tomorrow at the airport,' said Jenny. 'We have enough to arrest him for perverting the course of justice twenty years ago, not to mention his more recent deception. Whether he knows anything about Emmeline's murder is something we still need to ascertain.'

'It's *we* again now, is it?' said Karen. 'You're talking like a cop again.'

'Just a consultant,' said Jenny, and proceeded to make everyone fully conversant with recent events.

A stunned silence prevailed, before Karen begged – 'Please, be careful, Jenny. We've grown quite fond of you round here.'

60. From the Ashes of Despair

'You're here for rehabilitation,' Steve was told. 'It has been decreed by the powers that be that you are trustworthy and that you won't abuse the privilege.'

Still, he felt uncomfortable. He wanted his name cleared and apologies for the inconvenience, not this half-way-house; this vague suggestion that they may or may not have got it wrong. He made his position perfectly clear and remained indignant that Jayden hadn't been afforded the same respect. Steve wouldn't accept any favourable treatment and declared that he would do his time as if still fully incarcerated until his case was reheard.

His fellow inmates were there for what society deemed to be lesser crimes, like fraud, tax evasion, embezzlement, and 'minor' sexual offences; not considered too much of a danger to the public. They could wander the grounds with minimal supervision, socialise at leisure – and some even went out into the community to work or volunteer. The prison football team participated in the local league and prisoners were encouraged to get involved in charitable events to demonstrate their willingness to reintegrate.

Strangely, he missed the structure and routine of his recent accommodation, a symptom of institutionalisation more common in seasoned convicts. In short, he'd grown accustomed to his lot and all the dubious reprobates with whom he'd shared the experience. Steve had a word with himself. Had he really grown nostalgic for the likes of Filbert, Van Gogh, and his old laconic cellmate, Martin?

What to do? Did anyone even know he was here, or even care? Was there a prison library? No, if anyone wanted to read, they could order books from Amazon. Would anyone be interested in a poetry group? You could ask, but I doubt it. In short, there was little to get enthusiastic about. Steve's notoriety preceded him and a few people asked him about his journey, but he felt alone – that old, familiar, vacuous sensation.

He found a tree to sit beneath, listened to music – the Beatles of course, but also their influences – Buddy Holly, the Everly Brothers, Little Richard; and those they influenced – Weller, Costello. Petty... the list was endless and provided some comfort. They sang of hope, love and despair – the natural evolution of the human condition. But from the ashes of despair, perhaps a phoenix could rise.

When he got out of here, would things be different? Would he be a new man, a positive force, a conduit for happiness? Or the same cynical old bastard as before, topped up with all the resentment of a man wronged and hurt. Whichever, he would be his own man, no longer defined by the bullies, the unforgiving establishment, or all those purveyors of rejection. Adversity breeds either resilience or hopelessness. It was up to him which; but ironically, in his powerless situation, he knew at last that he had the power to choose.

61. Bigger Than Me

Somewhat aggrieved that she hadn't been part of O'Connell's welcome party at the airport, Jenny was a little rougher than usual when shelving the merchandise. After that threatening note, she'd refused to be confined to quarters and maintained that she'd be safe at work in the busy supermarket, where boxes of cheese straws fell victim to her frustrations. But who cared? They tasted just as good when broken.

Rob had explained that, as a civilian, she couldn't be present at the arrest and interview. He'd update her when it was all over. Rob asserted that, having familiarised himself with all the evidence, he was perfectly capable of giving O'Connell a thorough grilling without her assistance.

Jenny fully expected that O'Connell be confined for at least a day or two while investigations continued, so it came as something of a shock when she turned to see the figure dressed in black at the end of the aisle. Nonchalant and smug, he leaned against the gin promotion and waved. Jenny gasped and looked around her – she was alone among the savouries, apart from a solitary little old lady, oblivious to the unfolding drama. Her instincts said run, but her legs wouldn't move; whether through fear or her inherent stubbornness she knew not. O'Connell smiled as he slowly approached.

'How did you find me?' said Jenny.

'I didn't. I have people who do that for me.'

'And what do you want? I can get you re-arrested, you know, for harassment.'

O'Connell raised his hands in a conciliatory gesture. – 'You have nothing to fear from me. Can we speak?'

There was that charm-offensive again, still evident from the last time they'd met. Jenny barely nodded. – 'I have my lunch-break in ten minutes. Meet me in the café at the end of the store.'

'Coffee?'

'Black, no sugar.'

As he sauntered away, Jenny wondered if she should call Rob. She was sure that he would take a dim view of O'Connell's brazen disregard for protocol, not to mention her own position should she agree to speak to him. However, as always, curiosity got the better of her and she joined him at a corner table. Some of Jenny's colleagues nudged each other and sniggered; their gossip and entertainment sorted for the day. Not only had O'Connell bought the coffee, but there were sandwiches too. He invited Jenny to take her pick.

'Well, this is very nice,' he said. 'Had you down for greater things, though. Take it this job is just a stopgap.'

Jenny felt belittled, but had no intention of showing it. – 'Suits me fine at the moment. So, enough with the small talk. Why are you here?'

'Firstly, to congratulate you and your friends on your powers of deduction; and secondly, to warn you to back off.'

'And, if we don't?'

'This is much bigger than me, you know. Believe me, you don't want to know how high this goes.'

'So, I assume by virtue of the fact that you're walking the streets, you've satisfied the police that you didn't kill your wife.'

'Out of the country at the time; and the same applies to when you received that note. Rock-solid alibies.'

'Very convenient.' Jenny nibbled at a cheese and pickle sandwich. She was starving, but too distracted by the conversation to enjoy it.

'I have proof and witnesses,' said O'Connell. 'That's why they had to let me go.'

'So, if you didn't do it, then the bastard is still out there. We'll just carry on until we get him.'

'Look, you may find her killer and, if your pal at the police station has the nous, I've given him enough hints to do so. What you won't do is find who employed him. You see, in her position in the business, Eleanor had access to all my contacts. She was able to piece together the hierarchies and didn't like what she saw. She threatened to expose the big players in the deal unless I called the whole thing off; and, believe me, there are some powerful men who stand to lose a lot of money if it goes tits up. Then she disappeared. I didn't know where to, till you and James told me.'

'But you do business with these men. Could you not have protected her?'

'Maybe, once, before she ran out on me. You see, we had a big row about some of the people I was getting into bed with; and we're not just talking about Melody here.'

'And it wasn't you who paid for her to be silenced?'

'Absolutely not. You see, despite our disagreements, I still loved her. I married her twice, didn't I?'

Jenny wondered about his definition of love, bearing in mind he'd just confessed to a liaison with Melody. His dubious sincerity galled her and she wasn't about to be taken in by his kiss of the Blarney Stone again. – 'And was it worth it – a life for a poxy golf complex?'

O'Connell shook his head. – 'I couldn't have foreseen this outcome and I'd give anything to have her back. But she was always headstrong and impetuous. We're talking a multi-million deal and she was getting sentimental about the place, the countryside, the wildlife; even that old loser, John Reed; and her witch of a sister, who she never much cared for before.'

'And this multi-million deal is ongoing, I assume.'

'Yes, it's too far down the line now and has its own momentum. I'm just a small cog and have no control over the big decisions. Look, I've given you the murderer and I hope he rots in Hell. That gets your boyfriend off the hook which, I understand, was your mission. If you want my advice, I'd be content with that; unless you want to incur the displeasure of those powerful men. And you've seen how that ends.'

'That sounds like a threat.'

'No, just good advice. That note was a warning. If they wanted you dead, you'd be dead by now. Trust me, you really don't want to piss these guys off any more than you have already.'

62. The Downfall of Weasel Face

Rob brought him in the next day. He allowed Jenny to view him through the one-way glass of the interview room. A wiry, weasel-faced man, who looked every inch the contract killer, bereft of scruples. Jenny trembled as she considered what he'd done to Bambi and what he'd threatened to do to her. A cruel, cowardly man who would have got away with it, had it not been for Steve's friends' loyalty.

A DNA sample had been extracted from this abhorrent specimen, surely just a matter of time before the match was confirmed. Jenny stood in silence as Rob recounted the interview. On the night of the murder, he'd posed as a punter in the Black Swan, before hiding in the toilets at closing time. Once everyone was gone, he'd crept upstairs and impassively honoured his contract. Bambi's life meant nothing to him and he was just doing his job. He'd left through the back door and climbed over the fence to avoid the CCTV.

Rob finally conceded that he'd got it wrong and expressed his respect for the perseverance of Jenny and her gang, as he referred to them. You couldn't call Weasel-Face a professional, as he'd been clumsy enough to leave his chromosomes on the jacket, not to mention on the note he'd dropped through Jenny's door. Rob also stated that they'd found the papers and magazines from which the letters on the note had been cut. No, you couldn't call him professional, but someone had paid him to carry out these callous acts. Yes, there was little doubt he'd done the deed, but he was just a pawn, the fall guy. Rob had mentioned his name, but Jenny had forgotten it already.

And the real instigators would remain free; unless Jenny refused to be cowed and went after them!

"Much bigger than me," O'Connell had said. Jenny wondered who these powerful men were; and did she have the guts to try to expose them? She and her allies had come so far; and O'Connell was right – they'd achieved their mission. Steve would be freed and Weasel-Face would replace him in the prison system. Wasn't that enough?

Jenny fumed at the injustice of it all. Why should they be allowed to get away with murder? Her sense of right and wrong affronted, she confided in Dad.

'Sometimes you have to celebrate what you have achieved and let go of the things you can't,' he said. 'I'm sure Steve wouldn't want you to take any further risks on his behalf.'

Yes, thought Jenny, but if I'd listened when you told me that Steve wasn't worth the hassle, then we wouldn't have achieved anything. She reconvened the Black Swan Detective Agency.

'Powerful men rarely get their hands dirty,' Sarah told Jenny what she already knew. 'They are cushioned by several layers of 'management', their investments filtered through hedge funds, money stashed in all kinds of obscure and dubious places.'

'Bet I could pick up the trail,' said Karen. 'Once we find out who has a vested interest, it's all there if you look hard enough; business relationships hidden in Reports and Accounts, money laundered through offshore banks, politicians in pockets. You just have to join up the dots.'

'What if we give it to Barney at the newspaper,' said Sarah. 'That's his job, isn't it – investigative journalism, holding those bastards to account? He's used to ruffling the feathers of important people.'

And that's what they did, place all the information they'd gathered at Barney's feet, stand back and wait for Barney to do what he did best. Once again, they felt helpless as someone else took over the investigation.

Eventually some news. Barney was to join them in the Black Swan – said he wanted to deliver the verdict at the scene of the crime and at the hub of the investigation. The exclusive was to be in tomorrow's paper and, given their vested interest, Barney said they deserved a preview. Speculation was rife as they awaited his arrival, each with their own theory as to the identity of the man at the top.

'My money's on Colonel Mustard,' said Alan.

'I can think of one powerful person with an interest in golf courses,' said Trevor.

Jenny took in the now familiar surroundings and smiled at her new found friends. They'd travelled so far together, physically and emotionally, and ended up right back where they started, where the adventure began. All eyes were on Barney, as he hesitated, then spoke frankly.

'If you're expecting me put the finger on one particular person, then you may be disappointed. I'm afraid it's really not that simple. My research so far has uncovered a consortium of scoundrels – comprised of high-powered businessmen and minor aristocracy. Then we have a few dodgy politicians to oil the wheels, along with the odd celebrity to give it all a smiley public face. Beneath the surface, there's a labyrinth of contracts, sponsorship deals and endorsements.'

'So, what you're saying is that it's impossible to get to them,' said Jenny.

'I'm saying it's unlikely that we'd have enough to convict one individual. What tomorrow's article will do, is expose all the people involved, reveal the layers of corruption, and put the kibosh on the whole venture. You know how it works – there will be a scandal for a while, before the public move on to the next sensational story and forget about it.'

'So, who's involved,' said Sarah; 'anyone we know?'

Barney laid out a meticulous hierarchy document on the table before them. James would like to see this, thought Jenny; it looks just like a family tree. They all pored over it and exclaimed at some eminent names. Jenny pointed at one near the top – 'Never did like him!'

'Or him,' said Sarah.

Karen retrieved a crumpled piece of paper from her back pocket, unfolded it and placed it next to Barney's. It was almost identical.

Barney smiled. – 'Very impressive; so, you didn't need me after all.'

'Thanks, but I haven't got a newspaper in which to publish it,' said Karen. 'I'd pretty much reached the same conclusion – it's a minefield and we'd be crushed by the best attorneys that money can buy if we went after any one of them.'

'And these men will carry on regardless,' fumed Jenny, 'oblivious to the plights of Bambi and Steve, and anyone else caught in the crossfire. Why do you bother, Barney?'

'Because they'd be far worse without any checks and balances. Imagine what the bastards would get up to if no-one asked any questions.'

Jenny tried to be philosophical. OK, maybe they wouldn't catch the big fish, but they'd sure raise a stink, ruin some reputations, and inconvenience a few powerful players. It proved that, if the small fish swam together, they could baffle the sharks, if only temporarily. She knew they'd be back in a different guise, protected by their cronies in high-places as they conceived their next crooked scheme.

She thought about all they'd achieved – Steve's impending freedom, and justice finally realised. The beautiful landscape, where Bambi roamed as a child under the protection of her anonymous father, would remain untouched. And the wild deer could run free, without fear of golf balls.

It had been some escapade and Jenny had learnt a lot – about detective work, resilience and perseverance; but more importantly, about friendship, loyalty and love. But she still wasn't quite satisfied. There must be a way to get to the real culprit.

63. What Next?

Steve felt dizzy and disorientated upon his release. After the relative solitude of prison, it was sensory overload, where all his wits were being attacked at once. The modern world offered few avenues of escape, urban life a barrage of traffic noise, music, smells, neon lights and people, people and more people!

Jenny gently attempted to calm him down and help him recover from the traumas of the past year. She'd invested so much into this quiet, self-effacing man, and it wasn't in her nature to walk away and let him sink or swim. Gradually, they tried to pick up where they left off and rekindle their fledgeling relationship, Jenny adamant that he take things slowly, as if recuperating from a major operation.

'Well, Filbert's men did try to rearrange some of my organs,' said Steve. 'Gonna take a while to get over that.'

'But it's your head that needs fixing too,' said Jenny, 'after what you've been through.'

'Ah, that's been broken for years,' laughed Steve. 'It'll take a lot of patience to unravel all the spaghetti in there.'

An emotional reunion with the quiz team ensued, as Steve expressed his eternal gratitude for all they'd done. Never one for public displays of affection, or even private ones come to that, Steve hugged everyone and didn't care when uncontrollable tears flowed down his face. Trevor laughed and said steady on he couldn't breathe; Sarah cried in empathy with Steve's uncharacteristic outburst of emotion; Alan clapped him on the shoulder and said welcome back old chap; and Karen couldn't stop smiling. Jenny kept her eyes on Steve as if she didn't want to let him out her sight. After all, he wasn't safe on his own!

Ruby, the landlady, even included a special Beatles round just for him; ten nailed-on bonus points, but they still didn't beat the Swots. Steve took in the bonhomie and atmosphere of his local as he savoured a pint of his favourite brew, and he vowed never again to take any of this stuff for granted.

He met Jenny's father again, and her mother for the first time. Jenny blushed as he told them what an amazing daughter they had. He was introduced to George, who asked him if he was really a loser like Grandad said. Grandad admitted that he may have been a little hasty in his judgement and apologised.

'Oh, I've been called far worse things,' smiled Steve.

To Jenny's surprise her feelings for Steve ran deeper than anticipated and, against her better judgement, the thought entered her head that this relationship could actually work. After a few months Jenny suggested a break, get away for a week. She knew the very place, she enthused.

Of course, Steve fell in love with it too – the wildness, fresh air and stunning landscapes. On their second day though, he wasn't quite so keen on the early alarm in order to catch the sunrise. Jenny thought that it would do them both good.

'The last time I saw a sunrise was on my way home after a night out,' said Steve, as arm-in-arm, they braved the cold of dawn. Once awake, however, he got into the spirit of things as the rising sun took a sip of the morning dew. Refreshed, it warmed the souls of the two unassuming figures below. Of all the multitudes it could have chosen to shine on, it was as if it had reserved a special ray for them. Despite all past travails – Jenny's heart-breaking plunge into reality and Steve's many head-in-the-clouds futile pursuits – perhaps, in this idyllic place, they could both dare to dream again. They sat on a hillside and took in the amazing view. Jenny gasped, nudged Steve and pointed beyond a nearby thicket, where a graceful deer sipped contentedly from a stream. Eventually, it sensed their presence and stared at them for a few moments. Then, with a barely perceptible nod of the head, it turned and ran.

'Hey, you don't think that was…?' said Steve.

A shiver ran down Jenny's spine. – 'Definitely not,' she said.

Steve took a deep breath of cool morning air and took Jenny's hands in his. – 'Why don't we move here?' He immediately apologised and admitted that it wasn't like him to be so impetuous.

Jenny stared at him in shock and told him there was nothing wrong with a bit of impetuosity, but he could have warned her. She savoured the stunning vista once more, the mottled sky in subtle shades of pastel pink and blue, and considered this surprise proposal. Was it such a bad idea? Ever the realist, she immediately addressed more practical matters. – 'But what would we do? How would we earn a living?'

Steve hesitated; he'd been considering an unorthodox idea for a while and was concerned that Jenny might think him crazy. She probably already did, he thought, so what the hell. – 'You know I've been thinking about what I've done with my life up to now and it amounts to not a lot. My time in prison has given me a new perspective and I want to do something to help people; to make some kind of difference. I have the beginnings of an idea, but I can't do it on my own.'

'Sounds intriguing; go on.'

'OK, here goes – it's about giving kids a better chance. Look at young Jayden, for instance. His whole life was determined by where he grew up and the negative influences around him. I'm not saying it was inevitable that he did what he did and ended up inside, but his environment made it all the more likely.'

'So, what do you want to do? People have been trying to change that shit for years and it's still the same the world over.'

'Yes, I know, but I'm thinking relatively small-scale. I'm not looking to change the world, just to give some kids the chance to experience a different outlook. For most of the young people I met in there, all they'd known was inner-city life and poverty. They never got the chance to walk in the countryside, to see hills and forests, wildlife and farm animals.'

'And what are you suggesting; that we invite them all over to our place?'

'In a way, yes. It depends on how big our place is. I'm due compensation for wrongful arrest and imprisonment, and my solicitor tells me that it could be a substantial amount. I could sell my house and I reckon I can get some charities involved, inner city councils etc.; it's a case of making the right connections.' Steve looked Jenny in the eye, her face contorted in contemplation at the magnitude of his plan. – 'What do you think?'

Jenny shook her head. – 'Nothing, at the moment; you've only just dropped this enormous bombshell, and I had no idea you were even thinking about such an ambitious plan.'

'But I wanted to get the concept right in my head before I raised it with you.'

'My first thought is that we have no experience of running anything like that; no knowledge of youth work, no social care qualifications; and then there's the catering – these kids will have to eat, you know, and if they're anything like George, they'll have big appetites.'

'So, we can learn; and maybe we bring in a couple of other people to manage the bits we can't do. Think I may know of someone with the experience. It's just a question of finding him.'

'You've given this a lot of thought, haven't you?'

Steve looked pensive. – 'Wasn't much else to do, was there?'

'Wow, this is a bit different from the man who was ready to jump of a bridge a year ago. Whatever happened to that desperate fool?'

'I've met a few inspirational people since then; some old friends, who put their own interests aside to save my sorry arse; Jayden, who knows he's done wrong but is trying to turn his life around in the harshest of places; even Filbert showed he had a human side in the end; and then there's you – the amazing woman who saved my life, not just on that bridge but in so many other ways too. I owe you everything.'

Jenny smiled and put her head on his shoulder, as they took in the spectacular view. – 'Don't get too big-headed, but I guess you're worth it.'

'I guess you're worth it,' repeated Steve, 'that's the nicest thing anyone's ever said to me.'

'OK, so let's assume for a minute that I'm daft enough to go along with this absurd idea. How big a place are we going to need and how many kids are you looking to accommodate?'

'Well, I suppose the size of it will depend on a number of factors – how much money we have for a start; where else we can get support from, financial and practical; can we get local people and businesses onside? It's not just about giving them somewhere to stay, they'll need stuff to do too – horse riding, climbing, canoeing, that kind of thing.'

A deep, deep breath and Jenny concurred with Steve's own instincts regarding his sanity. – 'You're crazy, but I'll think about it.'

It couldn't really work, could it?

∞∞∞∞∞

On Jenny's insistence, there were a few people that Steve had to meet while they were there. First was James, the man who'd contributed so much to the investigation; who hadn't dismissed their fanciful quest, and instead, had become a great friend. Steve shook his hand firmly and voiced his sincere appreciation. James, a complete stranger, had dedicated so much time, effort and expertise on Steve's behalf and he'd be forever in his debt. Steve asked James to join them for lunch, where they spoke of Bambi's tragic journey. Yes, Steve had been through quite an ordeal, but she was the real victim in this saga.

Next, they visited Beatrice, where Steve offered his condolences and apologised for his part in raking-up so many painful revelations. Beatrice was philosophical and said that these things can fester beneath the surface for years. – 'They are always there, scratching away at your soul. At least when they're out in the open, you can deal with them.'

'And, how's John?' said Jenny.

'Even more remote than usual. He's withdrawn into himself and rarely speaks. He wasn't the most conversational of men before. Now he's practically mute.'

'What about Thomas?'

'Growing up fast. That little indiscretion taught him that we all have to take responsibility for our actions. He'll be fine, but he's still worried about his dad.'

'Well, if there's anything we can do,' said Jenny.

Beatrice raised her eyebrows, so Jenny decided to change the subject. She broached the topic of her and Steve possibly moving to the area and Steve's somewhat vague ideas for their future vocation. Surprisingly, Beatrice didn't baulk at the prospect of them becoming neighbours, or ridicule Steve's pie-in-the-sky notions. – 'Interesting. You know, one unexpected development is that, apparently, I have inherited the old Manor. It should rightly have been split between Emmeline and I, but as I'm the only one left… Haven't got a clue what I'm supposed to do with it, but your little venture could put it to good use.'

Steve's excitement was palpable, but Jenny was horrified. She introduced a note of realism. – 'You haven't seen the place. It's practically derelict. It would cost a fortune to make it habitable again.'

'Still, wouldn't do any harm to take a look,' said Steve.

64. Ghosts

The next day and James drove them there, Steve relishing the ride in that luxurious old Jaguar. Jenny recollected her last visit. She'd only been once before, but now she knew so much about its history and inhabitants, it somehow felt familiar. The vintage car ground to a halt once more on the gravel courtyard. She recalled how they'd speculated whether the old mansion was haunted and, with Trossard's passing, thought it even more likely now. With a feeling of déjà vu, she stared up at its imposing façade. Why were they here? It was completely impractical and would be way beyond their, admittedly indeterminate, budget.

Steve, however, saw only the possibilities as they entered. He stood in awe in the hallway and took in its immensity. – 'Wow, imagine what we could do with this. How many rooms does it have?'

'Too many,' said Jenny. 'You can't seriously be thinking about it. Where in hell would we get the money from?' But Steve wasn't listening. He was off up the ornate staircase before Jenny could utter another word of protest.

Jenny shook her head and turned to James. – 'Can you talk some sense into him?'

James laughed. – 'They say aim for the stars; you may fall short but, if you never try, you'll always wonder whether you could have got there. Alternatively, you could stay grounded. I'm sure he'll reach the logical conclusion once the figures are laid in front of him.'

'But how much would it cost?'

'I have no idea, but you could ask your friend O'Connell. He was going to turn this place into a hotel, wasn't he? He'll have done the maths, and be in possession of the plans.'

'Ha, I doubt that O'Connell would want to speak to me,' said Jenny. 'We've just discredited him in the eyes of his high-powered associates and completely knackered his business venture. He'll slam the door in my face.'

Steve returned; almost bursting with excitement. Jenny had never seen him so animated. – 'It's perfect,' he said. 'What do you reckon?'

'I reckon you should open your eyes. You're dreaming, Steve. I mean, just look at the state of it.'

'But…'

'But, no,' said Jenny.

'And that's your final word?'

'I'm just being realistic. What's got into you? There's no way you'd have conceived such an elaborate plan before prison. It's changed you, Steve.'

'Well, you can't go through that experience without some kind of transformation. And if I can persuade all those hard men to attend poetry recitals, I can do anything.'

'OK, it seems I'm gonna have to prove it's not viable before you'll listen.' Jenny looked to James for support, but he simply spectated with an expression of amused impartiality. Still, he had planted the seeds of an idea in her conflicted mind.

65. Simon

It didn't take Steve long to find him. He'd enquired at a few homeless shelters near Jayden's old neighbourhood, before happening upon one run by an amiable, long-haired chap named Dave. Steve handed him a scrap of paper with his phone number and asked him to give it to Simon if he saw him. 'Just tell him that I want to pass on Jayden's respects,' said Steve.

Dave nodded. – 'He drops in from time to time. I always ask if he needs a bed for the night, but he always turns it down. Says there are too many nutters in here, too many junkies and people with mental health problems. He's right too; they're souls that need professional help and care, but society had deemed them expendable. Simon says he feels safer in his sleeping bag in a back-alley, than in this place that's meant to provide shelter for guys like him. We try to make it safe, but things can get a bit volatile round here at times.'

'And how's he doing?' said Steve.

'It's a hard life, man. Looks at least a decade older than his real age. Known him for some years and you can see toll of the streets in the lines on his face and his hunched posture. I worry about him; don't know how many more winters he can survive, but he just takes his food parcel and goes on his way again.'

The next day and Steve's phone rang. He hoped it was Simon and not another of those incessant scam calls he'd had recently. – 'Hello.'

'Dave says you want to speak with me. Who is this?'

'Is that Simon? We have a mutual acquaintance; a young man named Jayden.'

'Last I hear, Jayden was in prison. How do you know him?'

'My name's Steve, I was in prison with him.'

'And why should I want to speak with a jailbird. You must have done someting bad to be there in the first place.'

'No, I was innocent. I've just been released on appeal.'

'And what's your business with me?'

'Jayden talked about you a lot; he made me promise to try to find you. Listen, can I buy you a coffee somewhere? It's better than talking on the phone.'

Simon hesitated until Steve wondered if he was still there. Eventually he spoke – 'OK, where do you want to meet?'

'Your choice, I'll come to where you are.'

'There's a place called Café From Crisis, on Commercial Street, near Spitalfields Market. It's one of the few places that don't kick out people like me. Do you know it?'

'No, but I'll find my way there. Can you give me an hour?'

'Yeah, sure man; I got nothing better to do.'

As he approached, Steve saw him staring apprehensively out of the window. At least he assumed it was Simon – be a bit embarrassing if it wasn't. He wandered over and proffered his hand. – 'Hi, Simon I presume. My name's Steve. It's an honour to meet you.'

'Ha, an honour, is it? I heard everyting now.'

'What can I get you?' said Steve.

'Any kinda coffee do me.'

'How about some lunch?'

'Yeah, why not? Surprise me.'

Steve returned shortly with two large mugs of coffee. – 'Burgers on the way.'

Simon nodded thanks, warmed his hands on his mug and took a suspicious sip. He explained that this was a cool joint and though he didn't have any cash for coffee, they'd let him sit and wait for the guy who was going to buy it for him. The place had been set up to give opportunities to the homeless and had empathy for people in his position who just came in for shelter. – 'So, what this all about, man. You in the habit of pickin' up vagabonds off the street?'

'Jayden and I became friends while I was inside. Don't think I'd have survived without him. He told me about all the good things you used to do for the kids. Said you was the only one who cared.'

'Not the only one. There were a few of us run the youth centre. Lot of kids came through that old place. They come from poverty, abuse, all kinda ting. They could escape there for a few hours. It destroyed a lot of lives when they close it down. Mine too.'

'He remembers it fondly,' said Steve. 'You made a big impression.'

Simon shook his head sadly. – 'Jayden was a good kid; always had a book under his arm when he first come, but gradually they wear him down, told him that reading wasn't cool. Once they have you under their spell it's hard to get away and I see so many kids go that way. Only route to escape that shit is sport. Some yout are good at football, boxing, or other ting, but they have to be the best to make it. Then they get tempted by an easier way. If you come from nothing and suddenly you see a few quid just taking a package from one place to another, it turn your head; then they got you and they won't let go. I try, but, in the end, it was all a waste of time.'

'No, it wasn't wasted; Jayden still talks about you and he remembers everything you taught him.'

'Well, I suppose that's someting. I tell him the only good way out of here is education – keep reading those books and one day someone might give you a chance. But the odds are against where we come from.'

'He runs the library, in prison.'

'Ha, ha, well I guess that's an achievement of sorts,' said Simon, as he took a hungry chunk out of his burger. 'Thanks, man, this taste good.'

'My pleasure.' Steve let him savour it for a bit, before dropping the bombshell. – 'Look, I'm not just here for Jayden. I may have a job opportunity for you if you're interested.'

Simon stopped mid-chew in astonishment. Was this some kind of joke, he asked? He listened in silence, as Steve enthusiastically proceeded to set out his sketchy business plan, leaving no lack of detail unturned. At the conclusion, he looked at Simon expectantly. – 'Well, what do you think?'

Mastication and conversation don't mix, so Simon finished his lunch first, deep in thought before his considered response. – 'I reckon you're mad. What mek ya think the yout be happy in the countryside? And if they are, they still have to come back here after. And what experience you got with inner-city kids?'

'Nowhere near as much as you. Used to teach in a college, before the shit hit the fan, so I'm used to supporting young people. But if you're asking if I'm streetwise, you only have to look at me to get your answer. Which is why I'm asking for your help.'

'You know, the Salvation Army come round sometime. Try to preach they know the way. Their intention is good, but they a long way from reality. And they nearly always white; just like you.'

'Ha, I'm not offering salvation,' said Steve, 'just a chance to get away and a safe environment. There's not a lot I can do about the fact that I'm white.'

'You say you an Jayden become friends in prison. How did that happen?'

'I really don't know. Only thing we have in common is a love of reading. Jayden helped me out when I was lost. I knew nothing about how to survive in there. He showed me the ropes and warned me who to avoid, although that bit didn't work out so well. Didn't seem to matter to him that I was white. Look, this mad idea of mine may or may not get off the ground but, if it does, I want good people on my side. Jayden said that you were one of the best, and that's good enough for me.'

An involuntary tear formed in Simon's eye. – 'Means a lot that someone remember my work. I used to make a difference and have pride in what I did. Ain't had that feeling for a long time.'

'Yeah, me too,' said Steve. 'How about we try to get that feeling back. At least think about it. There's a ticket to Devon waiting if you want to take a look at the possible location. We have someone else to see in London. Let me give you a call later and you can give me your answer then.'

'Ha, you don't wanna see me CV first?'

'Jayden's your walking, talking CV,' Steve smiled. 'Like I said, it's an honour to meet you.'

Simon shook his head in incredulity as Steve walked away, pausing to wave as he passed the window. Simon waved back and tucked into his dessert.

'Everything OK, sir?' said the waiter.

'Not sure, man. Tell me someting – is this a dream or reality?'

'It's the only reality I know. If this was a dream, I'd be somewhere else.'

'Yeah, me too. And it's been too long since I had a dream!'

66. Charitable Nature

'And you're sure he's expecting us?' said Steve.

Jenny nervously squeezed the soft upholstery on the arm of a luxurious reception-chair. – 'Well, he's expecting someone, but not us exactly.'

'What do you mean, not us exactly?'

Sarah had set it all up in her usual efficient manner. All she'd told O'Connell however, was that she had a potential investor on her books that wanted to open a hotel in the area. She'd been told by one of her contacts in high places that a recent venture had fallen through. This could be his opportunity to resurrect his interest in the property and to ensure that all of his hard work didn't go to waste.

'Well, he's expecting someone with a viable business proposition,' said Jenny. 'I suspect that he might call security as soon as we walk through that door.'

Jenny's instincts weren't far wide of the mark, for they got a – 'What the hell are you doing here; haven't you done enough damage already?'

It was a fair appraisal of the situation. O'Connell was now persona-non-grata among his high-powered associates, seen as the source of the leak that led to the collapse of the project, along with the now very public disgrace of a number of dubious individuals.

The MP for Cringeworthy South was particularly unhappy; for Jenny and Rob had followed up the leads in Barney's article. A seasoned politician, it transpired that he'd been apoplectic when told of Eleanor's ultimatum. The instruction to his trusty assistant to 'make it go away' had been interpreted, rightly or wrongly, as license to hire a contract killer. Of course, Cringeworthy South's esteemed representative was able to escape prosecution by stating categorically – "that's not what I meant." His trusty assistant, however, fared less well and had been invited to join Weasel-Face in prison. The good citizens of Cringeworthy South were now looking forward to an impending by-election.

Steve had shaken his head when told of this astounding development. – 'And just when you think they can't sink any lower...'

O'Connell was practically ruined, with little prospect of gaining any more of the profitable contracts to which he'd become accustomed. Hence, he was mindful to throw them both out immediately, until Jenny used her natural charm to persuade him to hear them out. They had five minutes, he asserted. He was a busy man with better things to do. As Jenny introduced him to Steve, O'Connell looked him up and down with barely disguised contempt and questioned why she'd gone to so much trouble.

It was Steve's turn to present his plan, a prospect that filled him with dread and further doubt with each sentence uttered. His humiliation was complete at the conclusion. Predictably, O'Connell laughed and enquired whether Steve was serious. He thanked them for the entertainment and suggested that they bugger off and don't come back. No, he wouldn't talk figures. They couldn't afford to replace the front door, never mind the rest of it.

Steve suspected that this was part of Jenny's plan to put him off the idea, although he noticed that she flinched each time O'Connell landed a punch. There was nothing more to say. If he wanted to go through with his irrational concept, he'd have to do it without O'Connell's plans or Jenny's support. O'Connell wished them good day and asked his secretary to show them out. Jenny apologised, but said she needed to use the bathroom before they left, leaving Steve in O'Connell's company and prolonging both of their agonies. This was no time for small-talk.

After what seemed like an age, Jenny returned. They made their way outside in silence. Eventually, Jenny spoke. – 'I'm so sorry. That was uncalled for. He didn't have to treat us like that.'

'Well, what did you expect; a welcome party?' said Steve.

'So, what happens now? Do we try to find somewhere else; somewhere more realistic?'

'Not necessarily. You see, while you were powdering your nose, I persuaded him to change his mind; appealed to his charitable nature and suggested that it would be good for his and his company's image if they were to get involved in the project. After all, he needs something to resurrect his good name, doesn't he?'

'You're joking! I was only gone for ten minutes. How on Earth did you manage that? He hasn't got a charitable nature, has he?'

'Just a logical argument that demonstrated the benefits,' said Steve, 'financial and reputational.'

Which wasn't strictly true. O'Connell's response had been – 'I don't mind giving to charity; after all it is tax-deductible. But I already have accountants to look after my charitable donations.'

No, it wasn't his better nature that made him acquiesce. What had tipped the scale in their favour and caused O'Connell to quake in his boots was Steve's casual mention of an associate from prison; a chap named Filbert!!

67. A Wonderful Life?

The Manor was set up as a Charitable Trust, with Beatrice, James, Trevor and Sarah as trustees. During the renovation, Jenny and Steve pooled their meagre resources and rented a little place in Lynton. Jenny registered George at the local school and, after a period of adjustment, he made new friends and loved living by the seaside.

Inspector Watts at the police station wasn't quite so condescending this time. Jenny was welcome to work there as a PCSO, until the venture got off the ground. With Sarah's help, and publicity courtesy of Barney, Steve concentrated on the business side, gaining the backing of councils, charities, churches and celebrities. After a year of hard graft, not least by O'Connell's men, they were ready to go.

Simon and Karen handled invitations for their first batch of guests, a rag-tag bunch of characters who ranged from 'why are we here?' to 'hey, this is cool'. Jenny and Steve watched from the periphery as Simon held court in the courtyard, every inch the learned old sage that Jayden had described.

Jenny smiled and hugged Steve tightly. – 'Just consider the differences you've made by not jumping off that bridge. Simon would still be sleeping rough in some back-alley; Jayden has a job to look forward to if he wants one when he gets out, and he's had his sentence reduced because of your representations. Not to mention that the train-driver can sleep at night, and so can I. And check out the looks on those kids' faces. Simon has them spellbound. None of this would have happened if you weren't around.'

'And none of this would have happened if my guardian angel wasn't there,' said Steve. 'I suppose you're going to tell me it's a wonderful life.'

'No, life can be pretty crap at times, but you can do some wonderful things within it.'

'Yeah, and this is just the beginning…'

68. Disclaimers and Acknowledgements

Firstly, well done for making it to the end – you have remarkable staying-power and endurance!

A few things to say about what you've just read:

On my clumsy attempts to tackle the minefield of mental health: Well, we all have it, don't we; and sometimes things get too much. You may have noticed some parallels to a certain 1940s classic Christmas movie. The denouement here is the same – one of hope over adversity. I have no sage advice, apart from, please, reach out if you ever feel that down. In the words of Steve's guardian angel, Jenny – 'Please, don't ever let it come to that. There are always people who can help.'

On the legend of Lorna Doone: In my impressionable youth I was enchanted by the story, or more to the point, by Emily Richard, who played Lorna in the 1976 TV series. This prompted me to read the novel, which I have revisited recently in the interests of research for this book. Struck by the contrast in attitudes compared to what is considered acceptable in the modern-day, I thought it was a fitting metaphor for the struggle to drag us blokes into the 21st century.

In October 2021, I based myself in Lynton for a week in an attempt to capture the essence of the area. I would like to thank Lesley and Steve at the Woodlands Guesthouse for their hospitality and amazing breakfasts. Also, for the use of the dining room to write for a large proportion of the week, when it was tipping it down outside. And to the guys at the Crown for beer and sustenance to oil the cogs of creativity in such a genial atmosphere. I have taken the liberty of using both of your establishments for inspiration; hope you don't mind!

Parts of Doone Valley are now looked after by the National Trust, so, thankfully, it's unlikely to be turned into a golf complex!

On the prison scenes: Fortuitously, I have avoided incarceration so far, although some might say I should be locked-up for crimes against literature! For those that will tell me it's not really like that inside, I offer the defence that this is a work of fiction that probably owes more to episodes of Porridge than reality. I did consider robbing a bank or something to make it more authentic, but thought that was going too far in pursuit of my art (is that what you call it?).

On the cultural references: Many of which will make more sense to those of us of a certain age! For the younger reader, there's a treasure trove in there if you have the inclination and patience to unravel it. Of Steve's favourite band, The Beatles; their timeless words are as familiar as bible parables. Oops, didn't John Lennon once get into a lot of trouble for saying something similar!?

On the humour: Although this book broaches some serious topics, I am strong believer in the old adage – if you don't laugh, you'd cry. Some of the more dubious elements of my humour have been left on the cutting-room floor and, hopefully, what's left is not too inappropriate! I believe that humour is a powerful weapon against some of the shit that goes down in this world. I hope that bits of it made you laugh, to counteract the more serious stuff.

Thanks: They say don't judge a book by its cover, but I am happy for you to do so on this occasion. Whodunnit? Many thanks to Dave Roberts for a cover design that screams blue murder!

My previous efforts haven't gone far beyond friends, family and work colleagues. If you have read any of my other books, thank you so much and I hope you enjoyed this one too. There are a few people who not only enjoy my stuff, but go out of their way to recommend it to others – a special cheers to Dan Jones, Sherrilyn Bateman and Jeremy Hay. Thanks also to Kris Needs for the review of Skinny Ted in Shindig magazine, and to Attila the Stockbroker for your endorsement.

To Gina Blaxill from Cornerstones for the report and consultation on plot, characterisation and editing. The Black Swan Detective Agency has been much improved as a result of your recommendations and encouragement. Thanks, as always, to the team at New Generation Publishing for getting it out there.

To Alan Porter (the inspiration for Philip's Tottenham tie). I enjoy our chats over coffee about writing and publishing, not to mention all that reminiscing!

And finally, to my family for putting up with this unhealthy obsession, once again!

Tony